# StoneDust

# Books by Justin Scott

## Mysteries

HardScape *(A Ben Abbott Novel)*
Many Happy Returns *(MWA Edgar Nominee Best First Novel)*
Treasure for Treasure
The Widow of Desire

## Thrillers

The Shipkiller
The Turning
Normandie Triangle
A Pride of Royals
Rampage
The Nine Dragons
The Empty Eye of the Sea *(Published in England)*
Treasure Island

# StoneDust

A Ben Abbott Novel

# Justin Scott

VIKING

VIKING
Published by the Penguin Group
Penguin Books USA Inc., 375 Hudson Street,
New York, New York 10014, U.S.A.
Penguin Books Ltd, 27 Wrights Lane,
London W8 5TZ, England
Penguin Books Australia Ltd, Ringwood,
Victoria, Australia
Penguin Books Canada Ltd, 10 Alcorn Avenue,
Toronto, Ontario, Canada M4V 3B2
Penguin Books (N.Z.) Ltd, 182–190 Wairau Road,
Auckland 10, New Zealand

Penguin Books Ltd, Registered Offices:
Harmondsworth, Middlesex, England

First published in 1995 by Viking Penguin,
a division of Penguin Books USA Inc.

10  9  8  7  6  5  4  3  2  1

PUBLISHER'S NOTE
This is a work of fiction. Names, characters, places, and incidents either are the
product of the author's imagination or are used fictitiously, and any resemblance
to actual persons, living or dead, events, or locales is entirely coincidental.

LIBRARY OF CONGRESS CATALOGING IN PUBLICATION DATA
Scott, Justin.
  StoneDust: a Ben Abbott novel/by Justin Scott.
    p.  cm.
  ISBN 0-670-85213-9
  1. Private investigators—Connecticut—Fiction.  I. Title.
PS3569.C644W43  1995
813'.54—dc20      94–20139

This book is printed on acid-free paper.

Printed in the United States of America
Set in Minion
Designed by Virginia Norey

# For My Daughter

Laura Patrick

# StoneDust

Stone dust makes a livelier bed for a flagstone terrace than does concrete. It's more forgiving: There's nothing rigid for ice to crack; and on barefoot days it lets the cold ground swallow the heat of the sun. You'd best be sure of your mason, though. Wide joints inspire weeds.

# 1

---

The Fisks' weekend party, a sleepover for select couples, was the talk of the town, even after we found Reg Hopkins's body in the covered bridge.

My friend Scooter MacKay—who mourned Reg no less than I—applauded Newbury's gossips, said they displayed a healthy preference for the antics of the living. I told Scooter he could afford such generosity because he lived an orderly life.

Rumors had started when Zweig Plumbing installed a Jacuzzi-for-eight under a mirror in the Fisks' new party room. Reports from their cleaning woman that Duane and Michelle had laid a carpet as soft as a mattress fleshed out voyeurs' dreams. "Facts" were netted by the Fish Line, Newbury's keep-in-touch telephone network for senior citizens: Several couples, all close friends of the Fisks, had arranged to send the kids to Grandma's Saturday night.

Sounded good to me. Though I suspected a night somewhat more innocent than the gossips hoped. The Bowlands, the Barretts, the Carters, and the Fisks were solid couples. While too young to be pillars of the community, it was fair to say they were pillars-in-waiting.

The wives were wonderful women, each special in her way: Georgia Bowland, a stylish honey blonde, new in town, with a witty outsider's take on the world; Susan Barrett, the group's great beauty, a seasoned nurse, yet so ethereal she seemed to float; Sherry Carter, supple as a gazelle and Newbury's premiere flirt; Michelle Fisk, a feisty businesswoman, sexily round.

Their husbands were hardworking good guys—not exactly orgy material, except maybe handsome Ted Barrett, whom women did go silly for—good friends and friends of mine. (I assumed I'd have been invited too, had I a spouse to contribute to the proceedings.)

When word about the party got around, Duane and Michelle Fisk were besieged by people trolling for invitations under the guise of asking whether they themselves were free Saturday night for dinner? For drinks? A barbecue? A beer? I even overheard Steve La France at the Liquor Locker inquire whether Duane could stop by with his Sawzall to enlarge a hole in his deck that was strangling his maple; to hear Steve tell it, the tree was firewood unless Duane saved it Saturday night.

I was surprised they didn't postpone. Most people would have issued rainchecks, but Michelle was bold, a real counterpuncher. She countered with a two-stage party—similar to the two-tier stock offerings I'd helped float back in my Wall Street days, where the insiders got dividends and the commoners bought promises. We commoners were invited at six for a cookout on the lawn. Six to nine, Michelle said in her cheerily firm way. The insiders stayed late, quietly drifting indoors around nine-thirty while Michelle and Duane eased stragglers into their cars and waved them down the drive.

On the morning after, the Fisk follies were topic one at the General Store. I retreated—preferring my Sunday *New York Times* with a quiet Bloody Mary in the Yankee Drover's cellar bar—and had just ventured a tentative "hello" to First Selectman Vicky McLachlan outside, when Trooper Moody's steel-gray state police cruiser came briskly up Main Street. His siren whooped a "don't even think about it" warning at a pickup truck about to pull away from the General

Store and another of the "let's exert some discipline here" variety at a family of bicyclists wobbling out of their driveway.

"Where is *he* going?" asked Vicky.

Ordinarily Newbury's resident state trooper directed traffic as the churches clustered around the flagpole on the corners of Main and Church Hill let out eleven-o'clock services. But Trooper Moody growled through the intersection. His hopped-up Fury continued up Main, gleaming darkly in the shade of elms and maples arched overhead, past bright Colonial houses smothered in pink azalea, and stately mansions on broad, green lawns. At the edge of town, it dug its tires in and roared north.

Vicky peered anxiously after him. She was facing a stiff primary challenge from Steve La France of the Liquor Locker—an antitax troglodyte with an angry citizenry on his side—so any breach of the peace made her nervous.

She and I had had an on-and-off sort of thing born of friendship, occasional loneliness, some memorable heat in the dark, and delusions on Vicky's part. She tended to ignore certain flaws in my character, till I found some method I later regretted of reminding her.

The latest incident was fairly recent, which was why I had greeted her tentatively. Vicky's problem was that she didn't hold grudges, so she said, "Good morning, Ben," with a warm smile and another worried look after Oliver Moody.

An active mass of curly chestnut hair framed Vicky's fine features, a crown that made a petite woman look bigger than she was and drew cameras on the campaign trail like a black hole drinking stars. Until Steve's challenge, no one had doubted she'd be governor of Connecticut before she was forty. Now no one was more aware than she that the New England landscape was littered with public servants who had failed to springboard out of their small towns when they were young.

"Where is Ollie going?" she asked again.

"Probably just an accident."

She was wearing dark sunglasses, not her style at all.

"What's with the shades?"

"Headache— Come on, Ben, we better help."

At the flagpole, Episcopalians, Congregationalists, and Catholics were blundering around with tight smiles. Vicky plunged into the automobile traffic, sorting cars with emphatic gestures and a two-finger whistle. I walked old Mrs. Adams and her sister from Poughkeepsie across the street, then lent an arm to Scooter MacKay's grandfather, up from the MacKays' winter place in North Carolina.

I next offered my arm to my great-aunt Constance Abbott, who was waiting to cross to her Federal mansion. Connie, who admitted to ninety, was ramrod straight, with a magnificent head of thick white hair. She wore a half-veil Lily Daché hat this morning and a pale blue suit she'd bought at B. Altman for a welcome-home Lucky Lindy tea dance.

My chinos and tieless shirt received a look that could freeze gasoline. And I, a witheringly formal reproach in the tones of a diplomat informing a pesky warlord that he deserved the cruise missiles headed his way.

"I missed you in church, Benjamin Abbott."

About the only slack she cut me was that she used neither my middle name (Constantine, it being the custom of the Abbotts to bond newborns to their wealthiest relative), nor my ordinal (III).

"I'm sorry, Connie. I was showing a house."

She softened, slightly: Industry ran a close second to Godliness and Honesty in her book. "To early-rising infidels?"

"They had an eleven-thirty tennis date. Help you cross? Trooper Moody's off preserving the peace."

Connie shooed me aside with her silver-headed walking stick. "Incidentally, Ben: Would you please inform Pinkerton Chevalley that I am not at all happy with the repairs on my car? It's developed a rattle."

Her car was a thirty-year-old Lincoln. Pink, who ran the Chevalley Enterprises garage, was my wrong-side-of-the-tracks cousin. My mother was the only one in the large and disorderly Chevalley clan for whom Connie had affection.

Traffic stopped dead as she strode onto Main Street. It stayed stopped while Connie paused in the middle of the busy intersection to greet the First Selectman with a spirited, "Good morning, Victoria," and to shake her hand—a grande dame seal of approval artfully calculated to garner Vicky a hundred votes in the primary.

The traffic jam of the week dispersed in minutes.

"Bloody Mary?"

Vicky was still gazing worriedly up Main Street. "I wonder where Ollie went."

"Come on, we'll check it out."

I dropped my paper on the Yankee Drover's porch. Then I led Vicky up the street to my house, a white Georgian with black shutters, my "Benjamin Abbott Realty" shingle out front, and a red barn at the end of the driveway.

To Vicky's puzzlement, instead of going into the house, I took her past the barn and squeezed through the privet hedge. She squeezed after me, grinning like a kid stealing apples, and whispered, "Where are we going?" We emerged in the back yard of Scooter MacKay, publisher, editor, and ace reporter of the *Newbury Clarion*.

Scooter's barn was white. Inside it smelled of dry rot, pine mulch, and gasoline. Spider-webbed windows cast daylight on a shiny green Range Rover. Beside the luxury wagon crouched a fourteen-thousand-dollar Kubota lawn tractor better suited to mowing estates than Scooter's in-town yard.

I indicated a pile of mulch bags Vicky could sit on and mounted the Kubota. Bracketed to the tractor's instrument panel was a Bearcat radio scanner.

"*What* are you doing?"

"Now you know how Scooter never misses a moving-violation story." Scooter kept scanners running twenty-four hours a day in his car, office, and bedroom.

Programmed to troll police, emergency, and tow-truck frequencies, they'll do so forever, hour after hour, scanning, scanning, scanning, as patient and hopeful as a clutch of teenagers waiting for something to happen in the Grand Union parking lot.

We listened awhile.

Vicky was looking particularly accessible in a summer dress and smelled delicious. She paced, ran into spider webs, and retreated hastily to my side. I offered a comfortable lap, which she refused.

Every now and then the scanner locked on to a signal. The volunteer ambulance responded to a homeowner-electric hedgetrimmer confrontation; and Pinkerton Chevalley was conducting a heated discussion with his tow-truck driver, who'd managed to get lost on Morris Mountain. Otherwise the CB waves were Sunday morning quiet.

Pink, a large man with a temper, started losing it.

"If I were that driver," I told Vicky, "I'd find my way to the Bridgeport Ferry and send the truck back UPS."

"Why isn't Ollie reporting in?"

In truth, I doubted we'd hear Ollie. Trooper Moody was a loner. He ruled his sixty square miles of Newbury turf by sowing terror in the hearts of any who might even consider breaking the law and was unlikely to radio the Plainfield State Police barracks for backup against anything short of Serbian artillery. But suddenly the Bearcat fixed onto a state police frequency.

"What are all those numbers?" Vicky asked.

"Code, so snoopy citizens like you and me can't eavesdrop."

"It must be important. He wouldn't bother for a traffic accident."

Just then I caught a phrase from the dispatcher that made me lean closer to the scanner: *"Hold on, Trooper. I'm patching you in to Sergeant Boyce's home phone. . . ."*

"Marian Boyce," I explained. "She—"

"I know who Marian Boyce is," Vicky reminded me icily. My occasional dinners with Marian were not the high point in Vicky's week.

"She made sergeant. Major Case Squad. Maybe Ollie found a dead body."

"Don't even say that."

"Relax, it's not your fault."

The scanner locked in on Marian's strong, resonant voice. She sounded damned proud of her promotion, as well she should. The state police were never generous with rank; young sergeants were rising stars. *"Sergeant Boyce. What's up, Trooper Moody?"*

More numbers. I thought I heard a "Four-four," which was trooper code for "Untimely Death," but the signal was breaking up and I was not sure. Suddenly the trooper and the Major Case sergeant got down to the kind of stuff you can't put in numbers.

*"Okay,"* said Ollie. *"What you do is you drive north on Main, past the flagpole, and continue out Route Seven four miles, left on Crabtree, follow Crabtree along the river, till it turns to dirt. Stay on the dirt eight miles, bearing left at the forks. Just before the Indian reservation you'll hit a covered bridge. Give me a holler if you get lost, only remember you gotta get up out of those swamps before I'll copy your radio. . . . No, it's not on the reservation, we're okay. . . . No, the bridge is ours."*

"Lucky you," I told Vicky. "Or they'd have to call the *Federales*."

Marian said, *"According to my map, I could drive there through Frenchtown. Or cut across further up Seven."*

Ollie wasn't that bright, but he'd had twenty years' experience maintaining his independence from the barracks in the county seat. While not insubordinate, his answer conveyed clearly that the only thing he disliked more than a superior officer from Plainfield was a female superior officer from anywhere. *"Yes, ma'am, you could, but you'll get lost."*

Marian said she would call the medical examiner.

Vicky was gnawing her lip. As Newbury's first selectman, she had inherited all the misery of the Republican prosperity that had gutted the local economy, and the Reagan-Bush tax reforms that had made a shambles of state and local finance. All she could promise frightened voters was cost control and honest, hard-working Vicky McLachlan stability; while anything that went wrong, from a Main Street break-in to a brawl at the high school, lent credence to the grim generalizations that her challenger dispensed across his busy counter.

"Want me to drive you out there for a look?"

"Can't, Ben. It's not my place."

"Want me to check it out for you?"

"That's really kind. You know I'm worried." She stood up on her tiptoes and kissed my mouth.

I wasn't in love with Vicky—I had a long history of directing that overwhelming emotion at women disinclined or unable to recipro- cate and was currently pursuing one who was fashioning macramé from my heartstrings—but Vicky was one of the sweetest kissers I had ever known. I was just about to suggest Bloody Marys upstairs next door in my four-poster, when the barn door slid open and Scooter MacKay burst in like a Saint Bernard in a hurry. He was a big guy with a booming voice.

"What are you two— Oh— What's the matter, Ben, no hay in your hayloft?"

"We were just listening to your radio scanner," the first selectman informed the newspaper publisher.

"Sure. Eleanor and I used to come out here and do the same thing. . . . Before the kids."

"Shut up, Scooter."

"Have fun." He backed the Range Rover out and raced down his drive.

"You think there's really hay up there?" I asked.

"Ben, he heard it too. He thinks it's important. Could you please . . ."

She was really distracted—bed was the furthest thing from her mind—so I said I couldn't think of anything that would give me greater pleasure and ran back through the hedge into my barn, fired up the Olds, and headed north.

My Olds—my father's sedate old Oldsmobile, his very last car— had come with a standard engine better suited to powering a Bra- zilian sawmill than an American automobile. When I inherited the sedan, my cousin Renny—the best of the Chevalley boys—had in payment for a loan installed a lovingly bored and stroked Cadillac V-6. With Pirelli tires and beefed-up shocks and struts, the car, as Renny used to say, hauled freight. (Pink said that if General Motors had built 'em like that back in '85, the Japanese would have stuck to Walkmans.)

I sped north on an empty Route 7, secure in the knowledge that the only cop in twenty miles was babysitting a crime scene in the deep woods.

It was glorious late June. Apple, shad, and native dogwood had faded, but the mountain laurel was bleeding pink and hemlock forests hung heavy with pale green new growth. The only disappointment on the drive was a minor one, a slight shimmy in the low hundreds when, on a short straight, I rocketed past Scooter's Range Rover.

Once Crabtree turned to dirt, it was a full twenty minutes before the covered bridge hove into view around a bend. Ollie's cruiser blocked the road. Ollie stood behind it, facing me. His flashers were off. He didn't even bother raising a hand. He just stood there—mirrored sunglasses and full gray uniform, six-foot-five plus hat, arms folded like anvils across his chest—the message clear as an electric roadwork sign: STOP. TURN AROUND. GET LOST.

I couldn't see much past him and his car, but it looked like someone had parked a dark Chevy S10 Blazer in the shadows of the one-lane bridge and left the driver's door open. The bridge itself, which spanned a fair-sized brook, running low this dry spring, was about fifty feet long with a shingled roof and barn-siding walls. A couple of square holes were cut between the timbers as unglassed windows, and in the light spill from one I saw an arm hanging white out the open door of the Blazer.

# 2

As I drew within point-blank range of the cannon holstered at his waist, Trooper Moody said, "Get lost."

Like many country troopers, Oliver Moody had grown up a younger son on a struggling farm. When big-brother Bob inherited the disaster, Ollie joined the Army, where he had enjoyed a couple of hitches in a famously sadistic MP unit. Discharged, he brought his talents to the state police and took up residence in a little saltbox Newbury provided next door to Town Hall. In his eyes I would always be the spoiled kid from the big house on Main Street.

In fact, there were several houses on Main Street bigger than mine, and I was never spoiled. My parents had neither the means nor the temperament, but if they had, Aunt Connie would have put a stop to *that*, thank you very much. I had run a little wild, however, and Trooper Moody had taken it as a turf challenge to tame me, which had, over the years, caused near equal suffering on both sides.

The fact that Ollie owed me a big favor, if not his life, didn't make him love me any more.

I said, "I'm going over to the reservation." Thanks to some service my great-grandfather had performed, the Housatonic tribe turned to the Abbotts for their rare real estate dealings.

"Crime scene," said Ollie. "Bridge is blocked."

"So I'll leave my car and walk."

"Ben, get the hell out of here before I punch you in the mouth."

Given the absence of witnesses in the woods and our long, unpleasant history, Ollie would have enjoyed doing that very much. While I, a hundred pounds lighter and a lot shorter, would, in the long run, have suffered more than he.

I took a step left, and before he moved to block my view I saw that the white object hanging from the Blazer's door was definitely a man's hand. Then, with a jolt, I noticed the plastic WindVent installed on the window.

"Is that Reg Hopkins's Blazer?"

I sidestepped again and finally got a glimpse of the vanity license plate.

"E-FLU-NT? Looks like Reg to me. Somebody steal his car?"

Suddenly jousting with Ollie wasn't fun anymore.

Reg and I went back to marbles and Little League. More recently, our businesses had meshed on the occasions that Benjamin Abbott Realty steered new homeowners toward Reg Hopkins Septic—steering I did with an easy conscience, as Reg was a straight shooter in a service that bred hustlers. I hadn't seen much of him since Janey left him, and now I wondered, too late, what I should have done to help.

Ollie heard Scooter MacKay rumbling up the dirt road and transformed, grudgingly, from vicious bully to peace officer: "Get in your car and drive away or you're under arrest for obstructing an investigation."

Couldn't argue with that. Didn't feel like it, if that was Reg's hand.

I turned around and walked to my car, at an angle that produced a view of the right side of Reg's Blazer. I thought I saw a scrape—a long scratch that ran from tail light to front bumper.

The Range Rover skidded around the bend like a pig on tiptoe. Scooter jumped out with his camera, glowering at my ten-year-old sedan, which had left his latest extravagance in the dust. "What happened?"

I told him that there seemed to be a dead man in Reg Hopkins's

Blazer. His face dropped and he suddenly looked like a big dog that had been kicked for no reason.

"Reg?"

"His car."

"Jesus. What happened to him?"

"I don't know. Except he's dead. Ollie ran me off."

"Can't be Reg." He headed toward the bridge.

I stopped him. "Do me a favor? Give me a wave if it's him."

Ordinarily Scooter would have made a lame joke about journalistic ethics and I'd have countered with a lamer retort. Instead we held eyes a moment, until Scooter muttered, "We're too young for this."

We'd all played baseball together, in Old Man Hawley's side yard, ridden bikes and hung out. We'd drifted a little apart, of course, when Scooter and I were enrolled in Newbury Prep as day students and Reg entered the public high school. Eventually he'd married a newcomer, which took him further from our sphere. But business, the Lions, and the Rotary had brought us back, and I felt the same numbing astonishment Scooter did that a kid from our childhood could actually die.

I got in the car and turned it around slowly while Scooter interviewed Ollie.

I watched in the mirror until he boomed, "Reg Hopkins?"

Then I eased past the Range Rover. Around the next bend I came within a foot of a head-on collision with a beige unmarked state police car. A siren whooped and lights flashed. I made a show of backing off the road, leaving so little room that she had to inch past.

"Hi, Marian."

A very annoyed, very attractive brunette with all-business eyes I once called an arresting shade of gray lowered her window. "Ben, what are you doing here?"

"Fleeing," I said, and when she didn't smile, I added, "Trooper Moody chased me."

Marian Boyce was a terrific woman who deserved three good men: a decent stepfather for her little boy; an energetic lover; and someone to hold her coat while she fought her way up the ranks of the state police.

"Lobster night next week?" I asked.

"So you can pump me about the body in the bridge?"

"Did I pump you last time we had dinner?"

"I'm off lobster."

"How about a picnic?"

She drummed the steering wheel with her big fingers and gave me an uncharacteristically shy smile. "I'm sort of seeing someone."

"Congratulations. Bring him along."

"Yeah, right. . . . Listen, call me next week if you still feel like it."

I stopped at the junction of Crabtree and Route 7 to wait for Scooter. The Newbury Volunteer Ambulance came along, slowly and without running lights, trailed by Dr. Steve Greenan's old diesel Mercedes. Steve doubled as an assistant medical examiner. I ducked down, too shaken to talk. Finally Scooter pulled alongside. He'd been crying.

"Steve thinks maybe some kind of convulsion."

I almost felt relief. I'd been afraid he'd killed himself.

"From what?" I asked.

Scooter dried his eyes on his sleeve. "Maybe drugs . . ."

"Oh for crissake."

"Yeah." Scooter found a sudden interest in the Range Rover's instrument panel. I inspected my steering wheel, wishing I had stuck a little closer to Reg during what was by all accounts a particularly sad and destructive divorce.

Scooter said, "We asked him to dinner last month. He cancelled last minute."

I said, "Yeah, we had coffee a couple weeks ago." Actually, more like a month.

Back in Newbury I found Vicky at the Drover, sitting with a sullen crowd watching the Red Sox get pounded by the last-place Milwaukee Brewers. I ordered a Bloody Mary and hid in a booth. Vicky hurried over. I told her the little I knew.

"Oh, Ben. I'm sorry. He was a sweet guy. . . ." There was nothing more she could say. She hadn't grown up in Newbury, so the connection wasn't deep. In fact, she and Reg had gone head to head on land-use battles. Battles Vicky had won.

We sat silently awhile. Vicky worried her lip. I said, "Relax. It's a damned shame. But it's got nothing to do with the election." I patted her hand and made the kind of joke you can only make with friends: "Reg wouldn't have voted for you anyhow."

And there it would have ended, for me at least, if Janey Hopkins hadn't showed up at my office the day after the funeral.

# 3

Abbotts from Stratford cut the first deal with the Indians in this neck of the woods and bought what is now the central borough of Newbury for a dozen broadcloth coats, some ruffled shirts, seven guns, and forty pounds of lead. We were farmers and merchants and ministers.

Aunt Connie's branch of the family were more adventurous: Led by the piratical Constantine Abbott, they flourished in the China trade and plowed their profits into canals, whaleships, and railroads; but my people stuck close to Newbury.

Around 1900 Great-grandfather Benjamin—a minister with doubts—observed the farmers fleeing to the cities at the same time that wealthy city people were seeking bucolic retreats. He opened a real estate agency. His son led the town to write zoning regulations and *his* son, my father, got himself elected first selectman to enforce them. They never got rich out of it, but their legacy was Newbury's pristine Main Street, a historic medley of Colonial houses and Federal mansions, unblemished by Seven-Elevens, gas stations, or McDonalds.

Hidden down Church Hill are the Grand Union, a liquor store, biker bar, and similar amenities. But on Main Street the only visible commerce is the Newbury Savings Bank, where a flash advertising concept is a fresh coat of white paint; the Newbury General Store, so quaint that last year when I had it on the market I had to discourage a guy who wanted to truck it to Florida; the Yankee Drover, a white clapboard inn as respectable looking as the churches with which it shares the flagpole corner; and, of course, my "Benjamin Abbott Realty" shingle, and a few of my competitors.

The morning after Reg's funeral, Janey drove past all of them and knocked on my door.

"I have to talk to you about Reg."

"I'm real sorry, Janey." I offered her a chair beside my desk and whisked the current issue of the weekly *Clarion* off the coffee table. As Scooter MacKay couldn't very well publish the rumors that Fisks and friends were screwing each other's brains out Saturday night, Reg's death was page one in the *Clarion*, if not in the General Store.

Photos of the covered bridge, Reg's Blazer, the Newbury ambulance working morgue duty, and Doctor Steve puttering around the death scene illustrated interviews with Oliver Moody and Sergeant Marian Boyce.

Scooter had composed a somber editorial, likening the death of a friend to an interrupted dream. The only laugh in the entire paper that week was a murky story about a ginmill brawl up north, where a logger who'd been refused service had chainsawed the bar in half.

Janey Hopkins declined my offer of coffee and watched impatiently while I settled down. She was an athletic, solidly built woman whose face had gotten a bit gaunt under stress. She wore her brown hair short and loose, but her eyes betrayed her, narrow with anxious concentration. When she and Reg were riding high, she'd been a leader of the young golf-and-business pack.

Reg Hopkins had built himself and Janey a make-believe "English cottage," circa Black Death era, with an authentic roof he had learned to thatch himself. My competitor Fred Gleason was handling the sell-off.

So I groaned inwardly, figuring she'd come to discuss their other property. The main parcel was a partially developed scar on a hillside off Mount Pleasant Road. The plan had been to carve a beautiful old orchard into twelve four-acre lots. In partnership with the party-givers Duane and Michelle Fisk, who owned Newbury Pre-cast Concrete and supplied Reg's tanks and galleys, they had bulled through a zoning variance and blasted a road up the hill, just in time for the real estate collapse.

I had liked nothing about the deal. They had snookered old Mrs. Fosdick into selling it indecently cheap. Then they had weaseled out of proper retaining walls by heaping trap rock on a too-steep slope, so that the entry to the subdivision looked like the front door of a gravel pit. All I could say in their favor was that the Hopkinses and the Fisks weren't the only couples who had talked the banks into backing skeezy developments of land better left alone.

"He was clean," she said.

"Beg pardon?"

"My lawyer just called. Greg Riggs in Plainfield?"

I nodded noncommittally. Greg Riggs, Esquire—a comer at the county seat, destined for an early judgeship—was handling Janey's divorce in a full-service manner, if gossip could be believed.

"Greg says the coroner is reporting a heroin overdose as cause of death."

I didn't want to hear that. "The *Clarion* said it was a convulsion."

Janey Hopkins was one of those people who spoke loudly and slowly to make a point. "The medical examiner will report that a heroin overdose caused his convulsion."

"I see."

The cops called it a "hotload"—a lethal high-grade heroin clumsily cut by crack dealers pushing a new product in a saturated market. Inhaled, to avoid AIDS-infected needles, it had already killed a hundred people in Connecticut. Like Reg, most of the victims were middle-class and white.

I looked out my window at the elms that cradled Main Street from the sky. It was too sad and dreary to picture Reg cruising the Blazer through some littered Bridgeport neighborhood, scoring, driving home to the thatched cottage he was about to lose to snort it up for a lonely evening's recreation. Hit like a sledgehammer. Euphoria. A stab of terror. Oblivion.

"No, you don't see, Ben. I'm telling you, Reg was clean. He hadn't done coke or had a drink in months. And he certainly didn't do heroin."

I was curious how she knew that a man she had left six months before, and was in the process of separating from his house and his kids, hadn't backslid.

Janey said, "Ben, we got the kids, we got the business. We talked. A couple of times a week, on the phone. I know what he was going through. I would have known if he was doing it again."

"But from what you say it sounds like he was."

"Ben. Are you listening to me? He joined AA, for God's sake."

I had heard. "Why are you telling me this?"

"I want you to ask around and find out what really happened."

"What do you mean, 'what really happened'? Ask what?"

She said, "Hey, I'll pay you. You're going broke here." This last was accompanied by a derisive glance around my office.

A mite shabby, though clean and neat as a pin, it occupied a sunroom porch my father had winterized when he took over the business. The weeping cherry outside had long ago blocked the sun, so it smelled a little musty—in a cozy way that fit the floral-printed customers' couch, Dad's curlicued oak desk, the yellowing aerial photographs, and the handout maps and pamphlet histories of Newbury stacked hospitably on the coffee table.

"Why me?"

"Because you know everybody in town."

"Plenty of people know everybody in town."

"But you're trained. You know how to ask. Reg said you were in Naval Intelligence. Weren't you?"

"If there is such a thing."

"An investigator."

"Half-assed."

"And he was always raving about how much you learned in jail."

I frowned at the grieving widow, intending to shut her up. But she kept talking, plowing up the present, exposing a past most people had the courtesy to discuss behind my back.

"Reg used to say, 'Ben learned stuff in prison the rest of us can't even guess.' "

By the time my turn came to sell pieces of the prettiest town in New England to country-home hunters, I had ventured much farther afield than my father and grandfathers. Yanked out of Newbury Prep in my junior year, I boarded at Stonybrook Military in preparation for Annapolis Naval Academy. Commissioned, I saw that part of the world you see from naval vessels and garrison towns, served out my obligation, and landed on Wall Street for the 'Eighties money boom. There I flourished—every bit the under-aged, overpaid insider—until a righteous United States attorney and a humorless Securities and Exchange Commission convinced a federal judge she'd be doing society a favor by sending me to Leavenworth Penitentiary. Three years. Or until I testified against my friends. Whichever came first.

I survived the three years and came home, to the relief of Aunt Connie and my mother and the delight of our neighbors, who finally had a big one up on the Abbotts. My father died the day I got out. Connie swung her considerable influence to speed up relief from civil disability so I could get my license, just in time for northwest Connecticut's longest real estate slump since the Erie Canal put our wheat farms out of business.

So instead of growling "Ben learned stuff he'd rather forget," I slid open my desk drawer and stole a glance at the recent entries in my checkbook. Nothing there I hadn't feared, and no happy surprises, either.

Business had been picking up, as some people, at least, began making money on Wall Street, and I'd had a pretty good half year. But I still had to pay off the grim years that preceded it and catch up with all the put off expenses—like a roof on the house, a furnace and a paint job. The good news was that I'd finally paid my arrears tax bill at Town Hall.

Janey kept pushing. "You helped that woman who shot her boyfriend."

"She didn't shoot her boyfriend."

"She was new in town. Reg was your friend forever."

"I felt affection for her." In truth, I would row to the Arctic for Rita Long, but that was none of Janey's business. Nor was it her business why I was sure Rita hadn't shot her boyfriend. And it was certainly not her business, nor anyone else's, exactly what had happened to the murderer. Suffice it to say, Rita was not in jail.

It appeared, however, that Janey had made an avid study of *my* business: "Who'd you feel affection for on Scudder Mountain?" she demanded. "Reg said you were in that up to your eyeballs."

"I was only trying to swing a land deal."

"That's not the way I heard it— And how 'bout when you tracked down old Mr. Butler?"

Trooper Moody couldn't find the old gent, so the Butlers had come to me, fearing that forgetful Granddad had wandered off. He had, into the arms of a New Milford waitress, who had every intention of keeping him.

It was mildly informative seeing my life through someone else's window, but I'd seen enough. So before Janey could remind me about the time I rescued the Meeting House cat from a maple tree, I asked, somewhat harshly, "Why do you care?"

"Reg Hopkins was not the kind of man to kill himself."

"I hear you're living with your lawyer."

"So what? I have a legal separation. I can live with who I want."

"So what do you care?"

"Our children have a right to know their father wasn't a suicide."

"Nobody's calling it suicide. It was an accident."

"Great. They'll be relieved to know Daddy was only a drug addict."

"Okay. I see your point, but I don't—"

"He never was—until things got bad—maybe a toot on Saturday night. You know."

Like anyone else with an hour to spare for "Sixty Minutes," I knew that *somebody* had to be snorting up the container shiploads of cocaine and heroin landing daily on America's shores. But if such tonnage never left the confines of city ghettos, wouldn't ghetto dwellers need snowplows to cross the street? The numbers suggested that even in the clean, lean, alive and alert 'Nineties, even upright citizens in bastions of reality exemption like Newbury, Connecticut, might enjoy a Saturday-night toot that had not escaped from a state-licensed bottle.

So yes, Janey, "I know."

"So will you do it?"

"Janey. If I start asking around, first thing I'm going to find is what you're *not* telling me. So I ask you again, save me time and you money: Why do you care?"

"Me and the kids are the beneficiaries of his life insurance."

"They won't pay on an OD?"

She nodded.

"What about your lawyer? He must have an investigator he can recommend."

"Greg doesn't want me to do this. He says forget about the insurance and let's just get on with living."

For a minute or two, I watched the cars swish by on Main Street. Her fella sounded remarkably ungreedy.

"How much money are we talking about?"

"Enough to pay off the mortgage and keep us going a couple of years."

"How much?"

"Eight hundred thousand— Ben. Don't get all righteous on me. The house is mortgaged up the wazoo. I don't have a way of making a living. Until I get one, that insurance money makes me and the kids independent."

"You mean you won't need the lawyer?"

"I mean I won't need him for the money. If I want to make a life with him, fine, but not because I have to. You can understand that, can't you?"

I could. Sort of. I guess in every couple there's always one person you like a little more. Reg and I had played together. Janey's parents had moved up from Bridgeport when she was a sophomore, right before I left for Stonybrook. I hardly knew her.

Adding up the nasty crack about my being broke, the reminder I'd served time, and the rape of the hillside on Mount Pleasant, I stood up to show her the door. And would have, if she hadn't started crying.

# 4

I said, "Excuse me, I'll make some coffee," and went out to the kitchen. I brewed a pot, slowly, and when I carried it and cups, sugar, cream, spoons, and Sweet 'n' Low back on a silver tray, I banged into some chairs in the dining room to give her some warning and thudded heavily across the living room, through the foyer, and into my office.

Janey looked refreshed.

I said, after we'd poured and stirred, "Tell me again: What's the main reason you're sure Reg was clean?"

She looked me straight in the eye. "The main reason? I just know, and I'll pay to prove it. Can't you buy into that, Ben?"

I could; on that she had my sympathy, because when my cousin Renny was killed, everyone said he was a smuggler. I knew he wasn't—just knew it. I told her, "I charge New York rates."

Janey said, "I hear twenty-five an hour is the going rate for private investigators in Connecticut. I'll go thirty-five so you'll concentrate."

"Seventy-five."

"But this is local."

Our negotiation was no contest. Janey had learned business tactics managing Hopkins Septic, while I'd been taught by M&A specialists who regarded their mothers as bargaining chips.

"Naval Intelligence and jail weren't local. Call me when you make up your mind."

"All right," said Janey. "Seventy-five."

"Terrific." I offered my hand. We shook, and I took a clean notepad from my desk.

"Who are his friends these days?"

"Same as always," said Janey. "I moved to Plainfield; he got the friends."

I refrained from reminding her she'd gotten the house and the kids. "Was he dating anybody?"

A look of profound distaste twisted her mouth like a dried leaf. "No one I knew."

I raised an inquiring brow, wondering why she seemed to care so much. She said, "Why don't you go talk to his AA sponsor? He'll tell you Reg was clean."

I told her I just might do that. She didn't know the sponsor's name—hardly surprising, as the second *A* stands for "Anonymous."

"You know how they stick together," she said with a trace of bitterness.

She gave me a check for a retainer. A hundred and fifty bucks. Two hours. She seemed surprised I didn't want more. But I figured that two hours was plenty of time to locate someone who'd seen Reg bombed on Saturday night.

I might even find somebody he'd shared his dope with, as he was a generous guy.

It wouldn't be right to inquire about Reg's sponsor from any AA friend who had confided in me. But thanks to a revealing slip of the tongue at a recent Planning and Zoning Commission hearing, I knew a source I could legitimately tap.

A woman new to town, who was applying for a variance to site a swimming pool too close to her neighbor, had requested that the commissioners stand up and introduce themselves.

Rick Bowland was the first to rise. His mustache was trimmer than a midshipman's salute, but he smoothed it anyway and straightened his necktie. "I'm Rick Bowland. I'm new in town too. I moved to Newbury two years ago this July with my wife, Georgia. We live on Mine Ore Road and I commute to IBM headquarters at Southbury."

Ted Barrett kept it short. "Theodore Barrett. I teach shop at the high school." But as his laser-blue eyes and dazzling smile embraced her, the swimming pool lady's knees appeared to go weak.

I glanced at Susan, Ted's platinum-blond goddess of a wife, who was sitting beside me in the audience. Her smile was serene: Ted was Susan's and Susan was Ted's, and woe to anyone who tried to get between them.

Then came the slip. Eddie Singleton stood up and said, "I'm Eddie and I'm an alcohol— Oh."

Poor Eddie went red to his hairline. There was some embarrassed laughter, and a number of people found that the ceiling required their attention. At last Eddie shrugged, and, recovering nicely with a smile, said, "I'm also Edward Singleton, who owns the Smoke Shop on Church Hill Road."

So I walked down Church Hill to the Smoke Shop—a combination tobacconist and magazine stand—and browsed the racks until a high-school dropout paid for *Car & Driver* and left us alone. I brought my own *Car & Driver* to the cash register, but before Eddie could say hello, a UPS driver came in with a delivery and bought a Connecticut lottery ticket. Then, as he was going out, in burst eighty-year-old Al Bell. Al saw me and whooped, "Say there, Ben, how about that Fisk party?"

"Sounded like fun."

"I heard they had a stripper jump out of a cake. And she ran off into the swamp. Ben, single guy like you, should have wangled an invite." Al winked.

He'd been Newbury's most prominent Lothario in his day, so I leered back to honor past glories. "The way I heard it, you had to bring a spouse."

"No, I hear there was a crasher, stayed late and joined in the festivities. Figured maybe that was you."

"No such luck, Al."

He bought some pipe tobacco and now he gave Eddie a wink as he asked me—as he always asked me, with a significant glance in the direction of Town Hall—"How you making out with the government?"

I answered this reference to First Selectman Vicky McLachlan as I always did: "Just friends."

Al roared off in his Jeep and finally Eddie and I were alone. I said, "Sometimes I think Al assigns me his fantasies."

"Whatever keeps him going, right?"

"Eddie, I wonder if I could ask you a sort of personal favor."

"Like what?"

"Could you possibly ask Reg's AA sponsor to give me a ring?"

Eddie stopped smiling, though his open face remained friendly, if a little puzzled. "Why?" he asked.

"Between us?"

I usually bought my newspapers at the General Store, and I don't smoke, but I did stop in for magazines. And, of course, we saw each other monthly at the P&Z meetings.

"Sure."

"Apparently the Plainfield medical examiner is going to report that Reg died of a heroin overdose."

"*What?*"

"I know. Same feeling I had. Some kind of super-potent load. Probably never knew what hit him."

"Jesus."

"Anyway, Janey can't buy that Reg fell off the wagon. Any wagon. Booze, dope, she says he was totally clean. She doesn't know who Reg's sponsor was. She asked me to check it out with him."

"What for? She dumped him six months ago."

Eddie's expression made it clear whose side he was on, so I saw no profit in explaining about the life insurance. "I think it has to do with their kids. She wants to be able to tell 'em Dad wasn't a drunk."

"He was a recovering drunk," Eddie said bluntly. Like most of the AA people I knew, he had a gentle manner and it was hard to tell whether I was annoying him or whether he was just trying to get the facts straight.

I said, "That's what I thought. And that's what Janey thinks. But she doesn't know his sponsor. . . . Since I heard you at the meeting last month, I thought I could ask you."

"Jesus, that was weird," said Eddie. "I've been thinking about it ever since, and you know, I think some part of me just wanted to come out of the closet. . . . Listen, I'll give him a ring. You going to be in your office?"

I walked home, went through my bills, culled a few I could put off, and renewed a couple of house ads in the *New York Times*. Then I wrote a new one for the Richardson place, a lovely old estate that was going to earn me a wonderful commission one of these days.

I was out in the kitchen heating the rest of the coffee in the microwave, which I use exclusively for warming coffee and taking the chill off refrigerated red wine—information I make a point of sharing with aggressive oenophiles—when I heard Joe Pitkin's house-painting van clatter into the driveway, aluminum ladders banging like a train wreck. Joe swung down, carrying his lunchpail, and I opened the kitchen door as he knocked.

"I was just thinking about you. Wondering if I could get away with painting just the front of the house."

"Or bulldoze it," said Joe.

This was a once-a-month or so spontaneous visit. While he emptied his lunchpail on the table, I made myself a peanut butter and banana sandwich, poured my coffee, and gave him a cup for his.

"Eddie told me you were asking about Reg."

"*You?*"

I was surprised. Painter Joe—who I recommended to new homeowners as the best housepainter in Newbury—was an especially upright citizen: daddy of four, Little League coach, deacon at the Frenchtown Methodist Church. Then I recalled that AA meetings were held in that church basement, with the parking lot privately around back. I wondered if he was the good Samaritan who had founded the chapter. I had seen him at the funeral and he had looked pretty broken up. Now Joe sat there placidly munching on a liverwurst sandwich.

I said, "Thanks for coming. I'll keep this quiet, of course. I'll tell Janey what you say, but I won't name you."

"What do you want to know?"

"Janey doesn't want to believe that Reg died snorting heroin."

Joe gave me a look and stopped chewing.

"She heard from her Plainfield lawyer that's going to be the medical examiner's finding."

"I'm sorry to hear that."

"Well, according to Janey, he used to—recreationally—when he was still drinking."

Joe Pitkin put down his sandwich. "I'd be very sad if Reg Hopkins was snorting heroin or drinking alcohol."

It seemed to me that someone who served as a sponsor for Alcoholics Anonymous had probably seen plenty of what old-fashioned Christians like my Aunt Connie would call backsliding. "Sad or surprised?"

"Anybody can relapse."

"And Reg hadn't been in the program very long, had he?"

"Reg was coming up to his first anniversary."

"I thought he only joined up after Janey left him."

"Almost a year."

"So the divorce had nothing to do with it."

"Probably the other way around," said Joe.

"You mean because Reg stopped drinking and Janey didn't?"

"Been known to happen. Maybe when he got sober he figured out what he wanted was different than what she wanted. But you could talk circles all day trying to make things simple when they aren't." He pulled a bandanna from his overalls and wiped his mouth, then waited patiently while I thought of something smart to ask.

"When'd you see him last?"

"Saturday after work. The day he died, I stopped by on my way home. He was doing paperwork. Said he'd be at the Sunday meeting."

For the first time since he'd carried his lunch into my kitchen, Joe Pitkin seemed unsure. It wasn't his expression. It was the way his hands got quite suddenly busy, wrapping up the second half of his sandwich, popping it into the lunchpail, drawing out a Granny Smith apple. He weighed it in his palm like the pitcher he had been, debating a knuckleball versus his slider—a slider that had broken the heart of many a strong boy, myself included.

"Isn't there a Saturday evening meeting?" They were listed in the *Clarion*.

"He wasn't going."

"How often did he usually go?"

"Almost every day. Which is the one thing that surprises me a little. Most people who relapse have stopped going to meetings."

"Did it bother you he wasn't going Saturday night?"

Joe smiled and took my eye with his. "You can't hold a man's hand twenty-four hours a day. Sometimes just being available is the best you can do."

"Joe, were you worried?"

"No," he said quickly.

"Did you ask him to reconsider?"

"I invited him home for supper. Reg said he had to work late, but he promised he'd get a bite at the diner."

"Promised?"

"You can get in trouble when you get too hungry. Low blood sugar. It's something to look out for. Reg knew that. He promised he'd take a break at six."

"And that was the last you saw him?"

"I drove over to Lori Match's to give her an estimate. Couple of bedrooms. Indoor work I can do on a rainy day. Lori's not in any rush. She doesn't need them until leaf season."

I nodded. Lori Match owned Matchbox, a tourist home on Church Hill Road.

Joe said, "On my way home I saw Reg's Blazer at the diner."

A silent orange ERROR light started blinking in the back of my brain. I wish I could report that my years on Wall Street had tuned my ear to falsehood, but in fact, the lie lay in hometown geography.

Janey Hopkins had claimed that the AA crowd stuck together; Joe had suggested why she sounded bitter, but now he was holding something back. I marked time while I debated what to do.

"Six o'clock?"

"Five after."

"Just like he promised."

"Like he promised. . . . What are you going to tell Janey?"

"Not much. I'll tell her I talked to his sponsor and his sponsor was surprised and saw him stone-cold sober at five o'clock. But I've got to find somebody who saw him sober at ten o'clock. And midnight."

"Maybe that medical examiner is screwy. Or the lawyer heard wrong."

I made my decision as we shook hands at the door.

"Joe, the Church Hill Diner is not exactly on your way home from Lori Match's, is it?"

"What do you mean?"

"You'd go up the hill around the flagpole. The diner's down toward Frenchtown."

Joe ducked his head and gave the floor a rueful smile. "Yeah. Right. I was praying hard I'd see him there, and I thanked the Lord when I did."

"I'll bet."

"You know, the only thing worse than getting ripped off by a friend is suspecting a friend."

"Can I ask you something, Joe?"

"Shoot."

"Did you swing past the diner because—I mean, *why'd* you suspect him? Did something happen at Reg's office?"

"I don't follow."

"You said you were relieved to see him there. Were you surprised? Like maybe you didn't trust him?"

Joe crossed his big arms and hugged his lunchpail to his chest. "Maybe I didn't."

"Because of something he said?"

"No."

"Something that passed between you?"

"No."

"What?"

"Just a funny feeling. . . ."

"What feeling?"

"Who knows? . . . Like he was leaving something out."

"Like what?"

"He wasn't telling me something."

"Something he wanted to hide?"

"Yeah. . . . I thought he was hiding something."

"Drinking?"

"What else?"

"How about heroin?"

"Janey had it right, Ben. Booze. Dope. Just different seats on the *Titanic*."

"So you were worried?"

"Until I saw him at the diner. Then I knew he was okay."

"Not hiding anything?"

"He was there. Just like he promised."

When Ed Hawley, the short-order cook, saw me enter the Church Hill Diner, he quick-popped a Certs into his mouth. The lunch rush had just ended and he invited me to join him in a booth where he sat down for the first time since he had started breakfast at six. He was a weathered-looking guy with burn-speckled hands and a walrus mustache. His eyes were weary, his nose rosy as mulled cherries. The Certs had taken effect by the time I carried my coffee to the booth, and Ed's breath smelled like a mint julep in horse country.

I had nothing against a couple of shots of bourbon after a long shift. But Ed had had his problems with booze, which he apparently regretted telling me.

"So how you doing?"

"Long day. You get a little older, it's the standing that kills you. How *you* doing, Mr. Abbott?"

"I don't know, Ed. Lost a friend last week. Kind of knocked a hole in things."

"Mr. Hopkins?"

"Yeah. We grew up together. You know, played ball." Ed was from elsewhere. He'd drifted into Newbury around the time I got out of prison and had for several years lived in the woods, until I found him a rental with front money requirements he could afford.

Ed said, "Good man. He came in every day after his wife left him. Couple of times I gave him a hand working at his house. You know, he thatched his own roof."

"Only thatched roof in the county. . . . Were you working on Saturday night?"

" 'Til seven."

"Did you see him?"

"The day he died? Sure. He had breakfast and then he came back for supper."

"How was he at supper?"

Ed Hawley thought about that. "A little keyed up."

"Nervous?"

"No, uh, hopeful. Turned on? Like he was looking forward to the evening. He was wearing a necktie. And a blazer. He was dressed up, going out."

"Did he say where?"

"No, he wasn't very talky that night. Just ate real quick and left."

"See which way he went?"

"Well, he was parked in front and just drove off, didn't turn around, so I guess he was heading toward Frenchtown."

To go home, Reg would have turned around and gone the other way.

"Didn't really eat supper, you know."

"No?"

"Just a BLT and coffee. He'd usually eat a lot more than that for supper. Pot roast or the haddock special. A real meal. But Saturday was just a sandwich."

"You said, 'keyed up,' Ed. Was he drinking?"

"No. No. Absolutely not. He always drinks coffee or diet Coke."

"But had he maybe had one before he came in?"

"Didn't smell it," Ed said, and he looked at me and looked away as we both realized that with a couple under his belt, Ed wouldn't know if he was downwind of Jack Daniels's distillery.

I stood outside the diner and looked down Church Hill Road. There was the video rental in the old railroad station, and Buzz's Getty, and beyond that a long stretch of empty road to Frenchtown. The Cedar Hill Feed Store would have been closed by six, as would the Town Line Dry Cleaners.

I hit Buzz's first. Like most of the local businessmen, I kept an account there. I filled the Olds with Super; as it ages, it seems happier burning the expensive stuff. Buzz opened the book when I went in to sign.

"Did you see Reg Saturday night?"

"Night he died? No. I took off early."

"Who was on?"

"Pete Stock."

"Is he around?"

"In jail."

"*Pete?*"

"Over in Plainfield."

"Why?"

"You hear how they chainsawed the Hitching Post?"

"That was *Pete?*"

"No. But when everybody ran, he couldn't get his truck started. Next day the troopers impounded it. And when Pete tried to get it back, they arrested him, thinking he knows who did it."

"They can't do that."

"Tim Hall's trying to get him out."

"When was this?"

"Same night Reg died."

"He's been sitting in jail since *Sunday?*"

"No, no, no. Took him 'til yesterday to screw up his courage. Freddy Butler drove him over to the barracks and the troopers just locked him up."

The pump bell rang. Buzz looked out, saw old Mildred Gill's Dodge, and went out to pump for her. I flipped pages in the gas book, back to the Saturday before last, and found the final entry, where Reg Hopkins had signed for 12.4 gallons of regular.

He was dressed for a date and gassed up to go anywhere. On the other hand, he might have been all dressed up with nowhere to go, a state of affairs I occasionally found myself in on a Newbury Saturday night.

So I stopped at the Rail Road Video.

A gigantic turquoise Harley-Davidson gleamed outside, which meant the clerk was Brian Chevalley, another cousin of mine, who doted on his bike and once rode it all the way to Bridgeport. He was perched behind the cash register, long-haired, earringed, and snaggle-toothed, reading *TV Guide.*

"Hey, Ben."

"Brian. How you doing?"

Brian waved the *TV Guide* in answer. "When they get a load of what's on television tonight, they're going to knock the door down. You know, I think the people who make TV shows own video stores— Hey, we got that *Strictly Ballroom* you was asking for."

"I'll take it. . . . Listen," I asked as he boxed the rental, "Saturday before last—the night Reg died—were you on?"

"Sure. I'm always Saturdays."

"Reg come in that night?"

"Nope."

Now I headed uphill.

No matter how bad Reg might have wanted a drink, I doubted

he'd have gone into the White Birch Inn wearing a necktie. The last guy to try it had exited through a closed window. But I went into the biker joint anyway and asked Wide Greg. Wide Greg said definitely, no, Reg had not been in his joint in years.

Franco, proprietor of my own local, the Yankee Drover Inn, which stands a convenient two-hundred-foot stumble from my house, hadn't seen him either.

He hadn't hit the Newbury Package Store for booze or wine, said red-haired Ramona. Over at the Grand Union, the busy manager told me he didn't think Reg had bought beer, though he couldn't be sure, considering the volume of his store traffic.

Sherry Carter came loping out of the produce department, lean and alluring in tight stretchies and a remarkably short polo shirt.

"Feel," she said, extending a shiny avocado. "What do you think?"

I was thinking what a treat she must have been in the Fisk Jacuzzi. I couldn't resist saying, "Heck of a party at Duane and Michelle's."

"You left early."

"Did it go on?"

"And on— Is this too hard?"

I told her it felt too hard to me.

"But I want it tonight." She stroked it with her long fingers, and we exchanged secret smiles, based on the briefest of mutual gropes at a beer-drinking picnic last summer.

"That's not going to make it any softer— Say hi to Bill."


When I drove a mile out to the Liquor Locker and asked troglodyte candidate Steve La France, the answer was the same: Reg hadn't come in in months, Steve assured me—and several voters stocking up on Bud.

I declined his offer of an "I BELIEVE IN STEVE" bumper sticker. Handsomely printed in red, white, and blue, it projected a jaunty "new broom" image that spelled more trouble for Vicky McLachlan.

I suspected the professional hand of Georgia Bowland. Georgia had quit a hot public-relations career to become Rick's IBM wife and childbearer. Bored stiff and drinking a mite, she'd fallen in with the golf-and-business crowd. Whatever else had gone down in the Fisk Jacuzzi, it looked like Michelle and Sherry had recruited Georgia to advise the candidate whom their husbands trusted to take a bulldozer to Newbury's zoning laws.

Steve grinned at his audience. "We understand, Ben. You got better reason than most to support the incumbent."

"Heard you enrolled Steve Junior in Newbury Prep."

"Well, my wife is considering it. He has special needs."

"Excellent school," I told the fellows with the six-packs. "I went there. Of course, back then it wasn't so expensive. I guess everyone'll send their kids to Newbury Prep if we don't pass a school budget —what's tuition up to now, Steve? Sixteen, seventeen thousand a year?"

Steve muttered something about an eroded tax base. I started out the door. Then I got a wonderful, sneaky idea—the sort of killer idea that would have appealed to patient guys, like Machiavelli, Sun-Tzu, and the inventor of the time bomb. "Hey, instead of private school, why not shut down the public school—temporarily—'til we balance the budget?"

Steve's customers smiled. Fond memories of snow days. "Hell, you'd win the kids' vote, Steve."

"Interesting thought," said Steve. "Weird, but interesting. Just might steal that from you, Ben."

"In that case, I *will* have a bumper sticker."

I slapped it on a truck with Texas plates.

Early that evening, I hit paydirt. Sort of.

Recalling from somewhere that recovering alcoholics often have a sweet tooth, I stopped at Dr. Mead's Ice Cream Drive In. The parking lot was crammed with Little Leaguers, coaches and parents lining up for postgame malts and sundaes.

I got on line and, when things quieted down, bought a low-fat yogurt and asked Doc Mead himself if Reg had been by Saturday night. "The night he died." I dropped my change in a tip cup marked: "For the kids' college."

Mead scratched his shiny bald head.

"Yeah. I was probably the last friend to see him alive."

"What time?"

"Eleven. I was closing, but I pulled him a soft pistachio. Thank God. Can you imagine turning a customer away the night he dies?"

"How'd he seem?"

"Down. Ordered a double in a cup with a cover. Then he ordered a cone and ate that while we talked a second. Inhaled it and split."

"Wha'd you talk about?"

"Nothing, really. Weather. Late night. Glad he'd caught me open, said goodnight, and split."

"Was he drinking?"

"I don't think so. Didn't smell it. He looked fine, just down."

"Which way did he go?"

"Why, Ben?"

"Curious. Which way?"

"I really don't remember. I was mopping the floor when he pulled out."

"Toward Frenchtown?" I don't know why I asked. He could have ended up in that bridge from either direction.

"No. He headed up toward the flagpole."

Pondering the five hours between a BLT and ice cream, I went to the Town Hall movie theater to take one last shot with Cindy Butler, the tax assessor's clerk who doubled as a ticket taker. The last of the seven-o'clock crowd were hurrying in. Coming attractions were blaring in the dark. I waited in the lobby until Cindy had shut the doors.

"Did you see Reg Saturday night?"

Her eyes got big. "What Saturday? The night he died?"

"Yes."

"No."

"Are you sure?"

*"One Hundred and One Dalmatians?* —Besides, I'd remember, Ben. If I'd seen him *that* night . . . Maybe he went to the Fisks' cookout."

Maybe I was too dumb to live.

# 5

I had my excuses: For one, blazer and necktie weren't exactly cook-out dress code; for another, I'd been at the cookout and I hadn't seen him. Though I had left early, hoping to get a call from Rita Long, who I had thought might have come up from New York for the weekend.

Still, I should have thought about it on my own.

Reg Hopkins and Duane Fisk had been best friends since kinder-garten. They'd built their businesses side by side, pooled their profits and made a bunch of fast money together, back in flush times when new houses and mini-malls were sprouting like jewelweed in July. Their summer deep-sea fishing trip had been an annual rite—boys only, no wives and kiddies. Same as their Montana elk hunt, from which they would return, usually elkless, with half-grown beards their women would make them shave.

I went home, denuded my fledgling basil crop to make a pesto, and, when dinner hour was over, telephoned the Fisks. Michelle answered.

"Hi, it's Ben with a belated thank you. Great cookout."

"Oh, I'm glad. When you left early I thought maybe you hated it."

Were she a WASP, people would have called Michelle perky; being

Italian, she was more like fiery. She was round, chubby sometimes, with a knockout face, short black hair, and eyes that seemed to crackle. The thought of her frolicking in the Jacuzzi-for-eight was intriguing, though I suspected that even up to her chin in swirling water and houseguests, she'd be talking a blue streak. She loved to talk. This evening, however, she sounded subdued.

"No, it was great," I rattled on. "I was wiped and I had clients coming up from the city real early Sunday, so I figured I'd better crash."

"Were they worth getting up early?"

"They loved the town."

"Do they want to build, by any chance? You know, we've still got that ten acres on Morris Mountain."

"They say they want old—you know, authentic Colonial—but then, they don't want to be near the road and they want views and big bathrooms and lots of glass."

Michelle laughed. "Don't forget our ten acres."

"Top of my list. They're coming back next weekend, and I'll just happen to swing by Morris Mountain."

"Tell them we'll give them a break on the footings and the septic."

I let silence build a moment. Then I said, "Speaking of which . . ."

"What?"

"Reg."

"Poor Reg. God, poor Duane, he's just destroyed."

I'd seen Duane at the funeral, a thirty-five-year-old guy looking middle-aged with grief.

"Who do you think is going to move in on Reg's business? I doubt Janey's going to run it."

"She's looking for a buyer."

"Lots of luck. Without Reg, what is it but some used machines and a bunch of upkeep?"

"I don't know, Ben. Duane's been talking to Tony Canning."

"Oh, come on. I wouldn't recommend Tony to build an outhouse."

Michelle laughed. I asked, "Why don't you guys buy it?"

"Like you said, Ben: Without Reg, what is Hopkins Septic except some old machines?"

"Good will."

"We'd still have to get someone to manage it," Michelle said firmly, and it was pretty clear that she and Duane had kicked the idea around and found it wanting. She sounded a little cool all of a sudden, so I switched back to party talk.

"Was that lamb marinade a dark secret? I noticed Duane hardly used the dome at all and it was still moist." They had grilled a butterfly lamb vegetarians would have killed for.

"You like that? Soy, sherry, and olive oil. Grate in a big ginger root and crush a bunch of garlic."

"How long?"

"Five, six hours. You can use the low-salt soy so you don't get Chinese eyes."

"Terrific . . . Hey, Michelle, you're not doing a mother-in-law recipe on me, are you?"

"Huh?"

"Leaving out one major ingredient?"

"Ben, I wouldn't do that to you. . . . Probably." She laughed.

"Thanks. And thanks for the party. You know, I didn't see him that night."

"Who?"

"Reg. Did he get there after I left?"

"No. We didn't invite him."

"Oh, I just figured . . ."

"Reg was a different guy since he stopped drinking. We tried, but he just couldn't relate. Just between you and me, it got really uncomfortable. One time we did the lamb he got all bent out of shape because of the sherry. Jeez, Ben, the alcohol cooks off. But he wouldn't touch it."

"But you still did business."

"It was hard. Sure, Duane and Reg went way back, but, you know—hey, people change. What are you going to do? Right?"

"So you didn't see him the night he died?"

"No. Like I told you. He wasn't invited. Listen, Ben, thanks for calling. You take care now."

"Thanks for the marinade."

"Don't forget Morris Mountain."

I hung up, put my feet on the desk, and imagined what it felt like not to have invited your best friend to your party the night he overdosed.

What could I report to Janey Hopkins? Reg Hopkins had been cold sober at five in his office. He had left the diner shortly after six, apparently sober, gassed up the Blazer, disappeared for nearly five hours, and surfaced for ice cream, again apparently sober, only to disappear until they found him in the bridge.

I guess Janey had gotten her money's worth. I'd certainly touched a lot of bases. But five missing hours was a long time. Not to mention the hours between ice cream and dawn.

The next day I got smarter.

I drove down to Frenchtown, to Chevalley Enterprises—a seven-bay garage my cousin Renny had created and which was now run by his widow, Betty, and his big brother Pinkerton. Pink had been a hell of a dirt-track racer in his day, but like most Chevalley men —Renny being the notable exception—he was long on aggression, short on patience, and utterly devoid of managerial skills. The outfit was lumbering along regardless. Betty Butler Chevalley was learning fast how to operate the office, and Pink, while no manager in the conventional sense, managed to terrorize his mechanics into turning in a reasonable day's work.

Mainly because they were the only show in town, they had hung on to the state police towing contract for the area, which was why I was visiting. I located Pink by his shouting.

*"Which one of you guys took my screwdriver?"*

Six mechanics buried their faces in car innards. A seventh scuttled off to the parts room, and two men took a Buick for a test drive.

"It's a Philips. It's marked 'P.C.': Pink Chevalley. My screw-driver—"

"Hey, Pink? Got a minute?"

"Got all day with no goddamned tools. Turn your back and some son of a bitch is using your best screwdriver to open oil cans. What's up, Ben?"

"Come on, I'll buy you a cup of coffee."

There was free coffee in the Chevalley waiting room, a very comfortable space with good chairs and newspapers and coffee and donuts.

"May I buy you a donut too?"

Betty Chevalley, redheaded, plump, and harried, called from the computer, "He's already eaten twelve today."

Pink snatched up his thirteenth and lumbered outdoors, where he was happier. I followed. "Listen, you towed Reg's Blazer?"

"Towed into Plainfield. Battery was dead. Lights on all night." Pink laughed.

"What's funny?"

"Ollie Moody tried to dump us. Hires this Exxon asshole from down Route Seven. Guy couldn't respond to his first call. Truck wouldn't start and he had four flat tires. Can you imagine that?"

Knowing the Chevalleys—a far-flung family, clannish and not entirely civilized—I had little trouble imagining their competitor's problems.

"Did you notice how much gas was in the Blazer?"

"Battery was dead."

"Yeah, right. Did the needle swing up or down?"

"He had them high-tech idiot lights. No juice, no computer, no idiot lights."

Smarter, but not smarter enough.

Pink looked anxious to get back to his yelling.

"Did it bounce?" I asked.

"Did what bounce?"

"The Blazer, when you towed it."

"Of course it bounced. It's a Blazer."

"Did it bounce like with a full tank or with an empty tank?"

"Huh?"

"Reg told me he had to keep the tank full, otherwise it would bang his head on the roof."

"Oh, yeah. Yeah. I know what you mean."

"Full or empty?"

Pink thought back. "I had to pick it up myself 'cause that high-school kid I had driving Sundays got lost in the flatbed. . . . You know, I'd guess nearer empty than full. Came around a bend and the rear wheels busted loose."

"She bounced?"

"Sliding like a snake. Guy coming the other way must have swallowed his teeth. Dumb Blazer. Half the town's riding around in a goddamned empty truck. Of course the goddamned things bounce. I told Reg a hundred times, chuck a few sandbags in back. No big deal for a man who digs septics, right? He kept putting it off, puttin' it off. Now look what happens."

"I don't think the bouncing killed him, Pink."

"No, but I'm the guy doing the towing, and the 'sucker's sliding over the road. I gotta go to work before them bastards steal the rest of my tools."

"By the way, the Olds got a little shimmy in the front end."

"How fast?"

"One-ten."

Pink looked grave. "That should not happen. Bring her in."

"I was hoping it was something inexpensive, like balancing the wheels?"

"Could be."

"Pink, how much gas does the Blazer hold?"

"Twenty gallons."

"How many miles they get to a gallon?"

"Twenty if the wind's behind you."

"So half a tank of gas, ten gallons, two hundred miles."

"Ask Betty, she'll figure it out on the computer."

He thundered back into the garage, and I went and told Betty that Aunt Connie was a little upset about something they had done to her Lincoln. Betty said she'd take care of it.

I drove home to my office, wondering how Reg had racked up two or three hundred miles in less than five hours. One thing was for sure: He hadn't done it bar-hopping around Newbury. Nor had he burned more than a gallon driving to the covered bridge. But he could have run up to Hartford to buy heroin. Or over to Waterbury. Or down to Bridgeport, Stamford, or Norwalk—the old Long Island Sound cities that boasted busy ghettos. He could have driven to New York, for that matter, or maybe even Boston. Or he could have just driven lonely circles, hour after hour on the country roads.

I remembered something I'd meant to ask Pink. I telephoned. Betty paged him and he picked up the phone, bellowing over the shriek of airguns.

"Hey, Pink. Did you see the scratch down the side of Reg's Blazer?"

"What are you, an insurance adjuster?"

"Did you see the scratch? Did he hit the bridge?"

"Naw. Looked to me like some son of a bitch ran a church key along it."

Can-opener scratches on a shiny car had been known to happen on ghetto streets.

I typed up some notes on the eight or nine conversations and calculated I'd spent another hour with Pink. I didn't feel right charging Janey for another hour, however; nor, despite all the talk, did I have much to tell her.

As it was, she called me, sounding very tense, and came by my office. I said, "I don't know what to tell you. But so far, I haven't found anyone who saw him high. That's about it."

"Look at this."

She handed me a sheet of typing paper rolled up in a rubber band. I slipped it off and spread it out; someone had chopped up magazines to cut out a word here and a letter there and then pasted them down in the following order: "HAVEN'T THEY SUFFERED ENOUGH DAMAGE ALREADY?"

"Who's suffered enough damage already?" I asked.

Janey's face was tight, with twin red dots flaring at her cheek-bones. "This was inside." She unrolled a photograph of her children. Mark and Jason, I recalled. Or Gabriel or something like that. Two cute little guys—miniature versions of Reg with Janey's ambitious mouth—waiting for their schoolbus.

# 6

My first thought was a weird one: Janey could have taken this; cut up some magazines and faked the threat. It was the anger in her face. You'd expect a mother to be afraid, terrified, but she looked ready to kill someone. Also, the kids were smiling, right at the camera, like they would for someone they knew.

On reflection, the thought made no sense. For one thing, she had no motive. For another, when I put myself deeper in her shoes, I understood the anger. I was a sort of semi-surrogate father to my little neighbor Alison Mealy, and if someone ever threatened her I'd feast on his lungs.

"You should take this directly to Oliver Moody."

"What's he going to do? Give it a speeding ticket? Besides, I live in Plainfield."

"Then take it to the Plainfield barracks."

"And have a bunch of state cops lunking around the yard?"

"Have your friend Greg show it to the state's attorney. If they were my kids I'd take it as a serious threat."

"You don't get it, do you?"

"Get what, Janey?" I really had a lot of trouble liking her. It was chemical. I just plain didn't like her. She seemed to feel the same about me.

"You scared somebody asking questions. They're trying to warn me off."

"Oh, for crissake, Janey. I asked a bunch of people if they saw Reg bombed."

"Did they?"

"No," I admitted.

She glowered. "What did I tell you?"

I said, "He looks clean from five-thirty to eleven Saturday night. I haven't found anybody yet who saw him after eleven, drunk or sober."

"Did he go to Duane and Michelle's party?"

"Wasn't invited. Did Greg happen to hear what time the M.E. thinks he died?"

"No."

"Would you ask him, please?"

Janey snatched up my phone and called lawyer Greg at his office. Turning away so I couldn't hear, she murmured and listened a moment, turned back, whispered, "I love you," and hung up.

"They just released the report. He died between one and four in the morning."

"You didn't tell Greg about the note, did you?"

"No."

"Why?"

"I am trying to have a relationship with this man. I am trying to have a normal, decent love affair. I'm trying to live a life and maybe find a good man for my children."

"But the note—"

"Is your job. That's what I'm paying you for. To clean up the mess of my old life and let me get on with the new."

"No, you are not paying me to clean up your life. And you certainly are not paying me to bodyguard your children."

"They're not your problem. I've sent them to my mother's for the summer. They're out of here."

That was more fuel for the anger burning under her skin. "Is she far away?"

"Florida. Her new husband is head of security for a big bank. He has guns. They can't get to them. They're safe for the duration."

"What duration?"

"Till you clear Reg's name."

"And you get the insurance."

"If he was clean—"

I raised a hand. "The M.E. just said no."

"If he was clean, I have a right to the insurance, and so do my children."

I said, "You're not telling me everything."

She said, "Yes, I am," yanked a checkbook from her bag, and, wielding a ballpoint pen like an icepick, wrote me one for fifteen hundred dollars. "Twenty hours, Ben. That should get you started."

"Who are the 'they' who wrote the note?"

"How do I know?"

"Who *would* know?"

"Reg would know."

"Reg is dead."

"Bastard."

I didn't know if she meant me or Reg. She probably didn't either, as she stormed from my office, with every appearance of a woman about to wig out. In case she already had, I dropped her check in the drawer, thinking I'd test the water a little on my own dime before I obligated myself.

According to old Al Bell, a gatecrasher had stayed late for the indoor segment of the Fisk party. Now I wondered: Reg, by any chance? High on pistachio ice cream? As that rumor came from the same horny old gossip who had speculated that a stripper had jumped out of a cake and run into the swamp, I saw no profit in pumping Al on the subject. Not when I could tap a disinterested observer of Newbury's goings-on.

I found her with her roses, gardening in a blue cotton dress, narrow-brimmed straw hat, and a simple strand of pearls that China-trader Constantine Abbott had exchanged early last century for opium. She was kneeling on an old piece of carpet, working fertilizer into the soil around each plant with a hand rake.

"Missed one."

"No, I'm fertilizing half with systemic and half with organic. Look." She beckoned me closer. "Feel the soil."

The soil a foot around the rose was packed hard as clay. I'd noticed the same thing around my roses.

"The systemic is wonderful for killing aphids and white fly and a whole raft of horrible insects. But it drives out the worms so the earth just packs harder and harder."

"But look at your roses." Connie had Gallicas and Albas and Portland Damasks that the rosarians of the New York Botanical Garden made an annual pilgrimage to visit.

"I thought this year I'd experiment, to see if I can get by without the poisons." She snipped a piece from a long stick with her razor-sharp shears and marked the systemicked bush.

"Connie, may I ask you something?"

"Go ahead."

"I've been hearing rumors that there was a gatecrasher who stayed late at the Fisks' party. The later party."

"Fisks?"

"The later party. You know, the sleep—"

"I don't listen to gossip, Ben."

Her ice-blue eyes shifted from the roses to mine and we slowly stood up together, me offering a hand, which she ignored, pushing off instead with her trowel. I had parachuted into a minefield. True, she was above gossip, yet she somehow managed to know everything going on in town.

"The Fish Line," I ventured. "I was thinking maybe you heard something on the telephone."

"Well, even if I had, do you think I'd willy-nilly repeat it?"

"No, but I asked, so it's not willy-nilly. It's a request for information from your nephew—grand-nephew at that—flesh and blood."

"Do you think I want my nephew—my grand-nephew, my flesh and blood—developing a reputation as a gossip?"

There were times I could not tell whether Connie was laughing at me or deadly serious. I took a chance and guessed the former. "Better a gossip than a rumormonger."

"Is there a difference?"

"A rumormonger invents it. A gossip makes an effort to get the facts straight."

"So you're spreading rumors about a gatecrasher."

"Connie. Give me a break."

"Put away my things and I'll give you a cup of tea."

"Deal."

I loaded fertilizers—organic and systemic—into her wooden wheelbarrow, tossed aboard trowels and rake and shovel and carpet, trundled them to her barn, and put everything in its place. Then I wiped my feet carefully at her kitchen door and found her pouring boiling water. Pots, milk, sugar, cups, and lemon cookies were on a tray, which I carried, following her through her dining room into a seating alcove formed by a bay window that thrust into an old-fashioned garden. We sat on embroidered chairs, facing each other over a low table, where she poured for both of us. A soft breeze tugged the sheer curtains. The garden below was afire in peonies.

"A gatecrasher at the Fisks'?"

"That's what I heard."

"So did I."

"You did?"

"Apparently he—or she—stayed for the festivities." Born shortly after the century, Connie spoke a language rich in euphemism. Lovers were "dear friends." A guy looking to get laid was a "gentleman caller." A married woman hosting a boyfriend was "entertaining." She's influenced my language as well—how many guys my age say "hosting" for "screwing"?—and we both knew that "festivities" was the proper word for "orgy."

"You heard that? Who told you?"

She fixed me with an iceberg gaze.

I said, "This isn't idle curiosity," and explained about Janey Hopkins.

"Fifteen hundred dollars! Ben, you could make a living doing this."

"I'd rather sell houses."

"It never hurts to have a second arrow in your quiver. I'm glad you took the job. You get bored. And when you get bored you get in trouble."

"So who told you?"

"I've heard it in bits and pieces—oh, don't look so disappointed. Why don't you go to the original source?"

"Who is?"

"Who started all the talk about the Jacuzzi and the carpet and the mirrors in that 'party' room of theirs?"

"Who?"

"Marie Butler. Their cleaning woman. Marie was there for the installation of all the accouterments and must have been there to clean up afterwards. Use your head, Ben. The woman would have won a Pulitzer years ago if she worked for a newspaper."

So I called Marie Butler. Mike, her husband, who had retired quite young on a disability that didn't stop him from hunting, drinking, and bowling, informed me she was working at the Bowlands'.

I drove out to Rick and Georgia Bowlands', a 1980s neo-Victorian that sprouted numerous gables perforated by anachronistic Palladian windows. It was situated in a mini-development of a half-dozen houses of similar taste clustered around a cul de sac. Their nanny, a lonely Scottish woman, was sitting in the sideyard gazebo, rocking an English pram draped with mosquito netting. I waved and headed for the front door.

Rick Bowland, like his corporate neighbors, commuted downstate. They represented a small but growing faction of out-of-towners priced out of the traditional bedroom communities farther south. For half of what they'd pay nearer the Sound, they lived very well in Newbury, though the price was a long drive that got longer every year as more and more of them cluttered country roads.

Unlike most commuters, the Bowlands tried to fit in with local movers and shakers like the Fisks and the Carters; Rick worked hard as a volunteer on Planning and Zoning. I enjoyed them. He was a trifle too buttoned-down, and took more pleasure than I would in suburban toys like his totally tech gas-fired barbecue, yet we usually found something in *The Economist* to commiserate about. Also, I admired his bravery to flaunt even a small mustache on the executive floor.

Georgia was outwardly smooth and upbeat as any publicist. Like most of the breed, she could talk at length about anything, and with a couple of drinks in her she could be very, very funny. She was also fun to look at, as she had a beautiful eye for clothing.

This morning, of course, Rick was off at IBM. Georgia was apparently gone too, as the garage doors were open, with both bays empty. Marie Butler's rusty red Thunderbird of many years was parked in the drive. She let me in with a whooped greeting and a big hug. We'd known each other forever, but my twisted background gave me a special place in her gossipy heart. I reminded myself that whatever I asked I'd hear in the General Store by morning.

"What are you doing here? They selling? I'm not surprised. Everybody in this development owes more on their mortgage than their house is worth. I heard at the bank that two of them are six months behind in payments. So they're selling?"

"Not that I'm aware of." In fact, I'd always assumed Georgia had money. There was a quality to the furnishings a young couple did not purchase on a salary, while Georgia herself had a certain ease I associated with boarding school and a trust fund, or a doting father.

"Mrs. Bowland just left. She's got another meeting about Steve La France. You seen them bumper stickers? She is one smart cookie. Good thing for Steve. He's dumber than his old man, and we're talkin' dumb."

"Actually, I came to see you."

"Find me another job?"

I shook my head. The Bowlands' living room looked like a bomb had hit it: lampshades askew, vacuum hoses snaked like fire hoses in the blitz, paper towels and Windex spray everywhere. I picked up a double photo frame that had tumbled to the carpet. One side showed Georgia holding her baby like an unsolicited delivery from Federal Express, the other, Rick in a Brooks Brothers shirt grilling hot dogs at the Fire Department cookout.

"Yeah, you don't give me work any more. It all goes to your Mrs. Mealy. Well, let me tell you something, Ben. I don't need the work. I got plenty."

"Your Mrs. Mealy" lived in an apartment over my barn with her daughter, Alison. I'd found them hitchhiking and homeless and brought them home. Marie and her armies had a field day broadcasting their speculations upon our relationship, but gradually the stories had died down, particularly as I was seen around town with several other ladies, including the far more gossipable first selectman.

"I knew you had plenty of work. That's why I passed a couple of things Mrs. Mealy's way."

"So she could pay your rent."

Marie, a voluminous, outwardly jolly lady, preferred bad news to good news, dirt to joy. Offering no fuel on the subject of rent, I asked instead, "Are you still working for the Fisks?"

"Sure. Though there's things going on there that would curl your hair."

"Like what?"

"Where've you been? The party?"

"I was there."

"You were?"

"It was great. Duane did a marinated lamb he could open a restaurant with."

Marie looked at me with undisguised pity. "Not the cookout. The *party*. After. In the Jacuzzi."

"I didn't get in any Jacuzzi."

"That's 'cause you weren't invited."

"Who was?" I knew, of course, but I hoped to flatter her into my camp.

"The Bowlands. The Barretts. The Carters."

"Wow. The Bowlands? The Barretts? And the Carters? The builder Carters? Sherry and Bill?"

"You heard it here first."

"And the Fisks."

"You wouldn't believe the bathing suit Michelle bought for that party."

"But they've been in bed together for years."

"*What?*" Marie grabbed my arm in a powerful hand and jerked hard. "What do you mean? What do you know?"

"Marie. It's a joke."

"What do you mean, joke? What kind of joke?" she demanded, and I saw a lifetime of orgies pass unreported before her eyes.

"An expression."

"What are you talking about?"

"Rick Bowland and Ted Barrett are on the Planning and Zoning Commission. Right? They have to approve new construction. Right? Bill Carter is a builder. And Duane does drains and footings and septics and speculates in land. When you've got a bunch of friends all in the business of building or regulating building, you could say they're in bed together."

"Oh, I've heard that expression. Yeah, but you made a joke— Hey, that's pretty good, Ben." She laughed loud and long, with great relief, and slapped one ample thigh.

"So they stayed overnight?"

"It was one of those parties, if you know what I mean."

I said, "Oh, come on, Ted and Susan are the tightest couple I know."

"Yeah," Marie admitted. "You never hear nothin' about them. 'Course, they went bust. . . . Wouldn't put anything past Sherry Carter."

I shrugged. Personally, I thought Sherry was more talk than action; but I didn't want to argue with Marie, I wanted her to keep talking. Which she did, in a hoarse whisper in case the nanny was listening from the gazebo. "Mrs. Bowland? Wouldn't put anything past her, either, when she's drinkin'— You seen that party room the Fisks built?"

"Heard about it."

"Check it out, sometime. Heavy duty." She grinned, gap-toothedly. "Like a porn video."

"How would you know about a porn video, Marie?"

"Hey, you wouldn't believe the people who go in and out of that little side room at the rental. Your cousin Brian told me—"

"You said just three couples—four couples, counting Duane and Michelle."

"Plus the crashers."

"Who?" I asked.

"Somebody stayed late. From the cookout. Slipped into the Jacuzzi with the rest of them."

"Who?"

"Nobody knows."

"Lights out?"

"I don't know. Nobody knows. But the word is, there was somebody else and they ran off into the woods."

"Al Bell said they had a stripper who jumped out of a cake."

"Al Bell doesn't know his ass from a hole in the ground. What the hell would four couples in a Jacuzzi need a stripper for?"

"I wondered about that. But he said the stripper ran into the swamp."

"The man is a fool, Ben. He doesn't know crap. There was no goddamned stripper. And that's the truth."

"But there was a crasher."

"Right."

"I get it."

"At last."

I drove home and wandered over to Town Hall to chat up Vicky, who usually had her ear to the ground and had arrived at the cookout shortly before I left.

She was busy as hell and in no mood to chat, though she did hint she'd be available for a late beer and burger at the Yankee Drover. As I had some reason to hope that Rita Long might be up from New York, I weaseled out of it and asked, even as she edged me toward the door, "Do you know if any extras stayed on for Stage Two of the Fisk party?"

"No."

"No, you don't know, or no, no one stayed?"

"No, I don't know, and I doubt any did. Michelle was acting like a chaperone at a Methodist dance."

"Methodists don't dance."

"That's what I meant. Bye, Ben. I gotta—"

"Did you by chance see Reg at the cookout?"

"What?"

"I gather you stayed late."

"Not that late."

"But did you see Reg?"

Vicky hesitated, then closed the door she'd been attempting to hustle me through. "When I arrived," she said.

"I didn't see him then."

"He didn't come in. He was kind of driving by."

"Kind of? What do you mean?"

"I was coming from town, so I was about to turn left into their drive, when I saw Reg coming the other way, in his Blazer. I waited for him to turn right, but he just slowed down a second and then kept going."

"When was this?"

"About six-thirty."

"Did you talk?"

"No. I waved. But he just went by."

"Didn't wave back?"

"No. . . ."

"He didn't turn in?"

"I saw his face. He looked so sad. . . . Like he was going to cry."

"You didn't say anything Sunday, when I told you we found him."

Vicky didn't answer me. Instead, she mused, "It was like he was saying goodbye or something. Too bad he didn't come in; it might have been different."

"He wasn't invited."

"Why not?"

"They'd kind of drifted apart after Reg stopped drinking. You didn't see him later?"

"No."

"Okay. Thanks."

"Why do you ask?"

"Between you and me, Janey wants to prove that Reg wasn't doing dope."

"That's crazy. What does she care? They're divorcing, and besides, it's obvious he was."

I agreed it looked that way. She said, "Why not leave it alone then?"

"What do you mean?"

"I have enough problems fighting Steve without this turning into a bigger deal than it was. You know, 'Lax Government Encourages Newbury Dope Fiends.'"

"It's no big deal. I'm really just helping Janey ease into the idea that Reg ODed."

"And what if he didn't?"

"Then Janey has a right to her insurance."

"Of course."

I promised to stop by re-election headquarters above the General Store for an envelope-stuffing session and went back to my office, where I put my feet up and reviewed: After dressing and eating and gassing up, Reg had swung past the Fisk party before disappearing until eleven. Terrific. I'd filled in another ten minutes. And heard that he'd looked sad. Which was about how I would have felt if my former best friends hadn't invited me to a cookout attended by half the town.

It had just occurred to me that Janey Hopkins might have spent her money better on Marie Butler, when I heard a familiar scratching noise at the door.

"Do I hear a muskrat?" I asked over my shoulder.

"No."

"Otter?"

"No."

"Does it wear braces and a smile like an Oldsmobile?"

"You rat."

"Hello, Alison."

She scuttled in, dropped her book bag and flute case on the floor, and climbed into the client's chair, though at eleven she'd not be house shopping, and even less likely to know Reg's whereabouts Saturday night. From my desk I produced a mini-size Kit Kat, which she opened solemnly.

"Guess what?"

"What?"

"The music teacher?"

"Who has a name."

"Mr. Shipley. He gave me two tickets to the Newbury Friends of Music."

"Great!"

"The Ping Quartet."

"Really?" An inconsistent group, the Pings. Very good when they were good, dreary when they weren't.

"From Shanghai."

"Yes." They had in fact been living in Chicago for some years and were a regular feature on the Northeast concert circuit.

"Want to come?"

"Why not ask your mom?" I said, recalling insipid Brahms, bad Beethoven, and a grim dose of Ravel the last time the Pings had blown through town.

Alison's smile of gleaming braces closed like a zipper. "She won't come."

"Did you ask her?" Mrs. Mealy was a shy woman, painfully conscious of old New England class lines that few but the very poor honored anymore.

"No. But she won't come. Will you?"

"Only if your mother won't go."

"She won't."

"Ask."

"Okay. Then you'll come?"

"Sunday?"

"Three o'clock."

Our neighboring towns in northwestern Connecticut were known for sparkling art galleries or serious antique shops (blessedly light on Ye Olde, but heavy on the checkbook), but Newbury had a lock on good music. One reason was our energetic and old-money funded Friends of Music. The other was that the movie theater in Town Hall doubled as a rather splendid concert auditorium, a gift way back in 1930 from a young heiress. Its official name, engraved above the marble portico, was Leslie Town Hall—Leslie for Edgar Leslie, a World War I hero who died in the great influenza epidemic of 1918 and whose connection to my maiden aunt was lost in history, if not in her heart.

A big crowd was bustling in behind us.

"Where should we sit?" asked Alison, cute and squirmy in a little dress Connie had produced from her gigantic attic.

"Down front on the left."

We found two seats in the sixth row, behind Connie and a group of well-dressed elderly ladies discussing their recent trips to the Amazon.

The Pings, a handsome family of string players, took the stage.

I glanced at the program and groaned.

"What's wrong?"

"Ravel. The Friends of Music ought to set aside a Ravel Haters Room we could retreat to."

Aunt Connie turned around and told me to behave myself. The first violin stamped his foot and the Pings galloped into some fine

Mozart. I scanned the program notes, written with a flourish by Scooter's wife; Eleanor made the Ravel piece sound interesting, but when they got to it, it wasn't.

There's something about Ravel. Musicians love the guy. There's rarely a Friends concert without him, and barely a note of movie and TV music that hasn't been lifted from the Frenchman that critics more knowledgeable than I have dubbed "the musical self-abuser." I whispered to Alison that New Guinea headhunter pickup bands play Ravel on their neighbors' skulls at least once an evening.

Predictably, he cleared the hall like grapeshot. Only half the audience returned from intermission, which was a shame, because the Pings had grown to a quintet, procuring the services of a vast lady in red who played a showy piano. She bounced on her stool like a Jeep Cherokee on a washboard road and tossed her long black hair with such ecstasy that I had to wonder what it would be like to be on the bottom making love with her. After she took her bows, the Pings got real with a Corelli piece intended to make angels weep.

"Jesus!" Alison breathed when it was over.

" 'Gosh' will do, thank you."

"Why do you always correct me?"

I glanced at Connie's white head. She was applauding with enthusiasm. I said, "Because when I was growing up, Connie and my parents did it for me, and it helps me know now what's appropriate when and where. Makes you comfortable, no matter what the company."

"But Ben, it was a 'Jesus!' moment."

I admitted she had me there and wondered if ice cream at the General Store was a good idea. But we were being very grown up today, and Alison said, a little tentatively, as she does when she's afraid of being disappointed, "There's a reception to meet the musicians. Can we go?"

"Yeah, I want to meet the lady in red."

"Say 'yes,' Ben. Not 'yeah.' "

The lady in red turned out to be as jolly offstage as on, and Alison got a little jealous until the violinist paid some attention to her, which left her starry-eyed all the way home. I walked her to the barn door.

"Thanks for asking me."

"Thanks for coming. Hey, Ben?"

"What?"

"I heard you were asking about Mr. Hopkins?"

"Yes?"

"You should have asked me."

"Oh, really?"

"The big kids saw him that night."

"When?"

"Late."

"Where?"

She drew back, and I realized I had grabbed her shoulder and was squeezing. "Sorry." I stepped back. "What do you mean, hon? Who saw him?"

"I don't know. Big kids. They were riding their bikes real late and they saw him."

Bikes. When I was a "big kid" fourteen to sixteen, we walked everywhere. But nowadays they got around on bikes, which we had scorned as kid stuff as soon as we were old enough to start counting the years to a driver's license.

"Where did they see him?"

"The party that the Fisks gave."

"The cookout?"

"No. You know. The grownup party. The Jacuzzi party."

I bent down until we were eye to eye. "This is important. What time?"

"Late. Midnight, maybe."

"What were they doing out at the Fisks' at midnight?"

"Some of them rode out hoping to watch."

"Watch what?"

"You know. The Jacuzzi. The grownups in the Jacuzzi."

"And they say they saw Mr. Hopkins go to the party, at midnight?"

"I think so."

"In his Chevy Blazer?"

"Yeah. The blue S10 with the WindVents."

Just that once, I didn't tell her to say "yes" for "yeah."

I'd inquired of about fifteen people if they'd seen Reg. Who had the answer, but my little backyard neighbor? I thought immediately of going out and bracing Duane and Michelle, who had assured me Reg hadn't showed. But that was strong stuff to base on high-school stories. Better, maybe, to come at them sideways.

Bill Carter had been at the sleepover. And Bill had built a $600,000 spec house he couldn't unload, which gave a real estate agent some leverage.

# 7

It was one of those houses built for the builder's convenience. Bill Carter had plunked it smack on the required setback line, ignoring a lovely rise sixty feet deeper in the lot. The driveway, sporting a pretentious wiggle, invaded the property in precisely the spot that destroyed maximum privacy. The septic field looked like he had buried Moby Dick in the front yard.

"Sherry's sorry she couldn't make it, Ben."

That was fine with me. Flirty gazelles notwithstanding, Sherry was very much the brains of the Carter marriage, and I was grateful to have Bill to myself. I claimed I was sorry too and said, "Let's see your house."

Bill was proud of the kitchen, where he'd saved some money on Garland and Sub-Zero knockoffs, and prouder still of the downstairs powder room, which offered guests pushing the front door bell an unobstructed view of its fine porcelain commode.

"The entire structure," Bill beamed, "is architect-designed."

I told him we could work around that problem too. I'd always liked him. He was the kind of optimist you had to be if you wanted to raise spec houses for a living.

"I'm amazed, Ben. I thought she'd sell in a flash. Goddamned recession."

"It's a bitch, Bill." I wondered, not for the first time, whether "the economy" had become a secular society's "the Devil made me do it."

"So what do you say?"

"I don't know, man. You gave Fred an exclusive."

"I told you, Fred's history. I'm firing him."

"Yeah, but if Fred couldn't sell—"

"Fred's got his head in the clouds. Says I'm asking estate money for— You know what he called this? He called it a suburban house without a suburb. You believe the nerve of the guy?"

My ablest competitor had hit the nail on the head. Bill Carter needed a corporate buyer heading up the ladder so fast he didn't care where he lived for the next two years. But that sort didn't buy houses in the woods. They flocked with their own around cul de sacs like Rick and Georgia Bowlands'.

"Hell, Ben. You could sell this place in a week." He punctuated this compliment with a hearty slap on the back, which, from a former all-state guard, sent me reeling with camaraderie. Back in grade school, you could count on him to scare off bullies.

Doubting Donald Trump could have sold it in his best year, I said, "Not for six hundred thousand."

"Okay, I know that. Get me five-fifty."

"I don't get a lot of customers for such. . . . But I'll see what I can do."

"Advertising! You'll want to do a lot of advertising."

"Costly," I said.

"Blank check, fella. Pay you out of your commission."

"I don't think so."

His face fell. He knew better, but he'd been surfing on hope again. Frustrated, he grouched, "And I suppose you'll hold me up for the full commission, too?"

I'd been waiting for that opening and said, with a most generous smile, "No. I'll knock off a point. Charge you five percent."

"Fred was working for four!" he protested indignantly.

That was patently untrue, but I had no intention of alienating Bill by calling him a liar, so I said, "Ordinarily I charge six. Five for old times' sake."

Bill tried an ursine scowl, but he was too amiable to give it teeth.

I said, "Go ask Duane and Michelle what I charge 'em on their land deals. Or ask Janey Hopkins what Fred was charging Reg. Five for good customers. Five for friends."

Bill hunched up even more bearlike. It still didn't work, as the bear he was like could have entertained in a petting zoo.

I said, "Come on, Bill, you were in with Reg on that little office conversion you did on Church Hill Road. What did I charge you?"

"Five."

"Did I sell it?"

"Yeah. You sold it."

"How long did it take?"

"Three months."

"Did you get your price?"

"Yeah."

"How'd Reg look when he left the party the other night?"

"Oh, he was fine. No probl—"

"What time did he leave?"

"What are you talking about?"

"I just wondered what time it was when Reg left the Fisk party. Was it after midnight?"

The bear now looked like he'd frozen solid in a snowstorm. Only his eyes moved and they moved slowly, sliding at me, down at the knotholes in the number-three-grade maple floor, back up at me. "What are you talking about, Ben?"

I wandered away from him, into the family room. Bill followed, looming uncertainly. Outside the sliding glass doors was a handsome flagstone terrace set in stone dust.

"Did you lay the terrace yourself?"

"Yeah."

"Nice work."

A stone dust base cost less than a concrete slab, but it's one economy I applaud. Strong, yet porous, it makes a more forgiving bed.

There's nothing rigid for ice to crack—no small matter in New England winters—while in barefoot weather it lets the cold ground absorb the heat of the sun. You'd best be sure of your mason, however, as wide joints invite weeds. Bill's were narrow as Sherry's pinky.

"Did Reg leave after midnight, or before?"

"I didn't see him."

"You said he looked fine."

"I didn't see him leave, is what I meant."

"Oh." I shrugged and looked around for another change of subject. "Where'd you get that chandelier?"

"Sherry bought it at an auction."

Imagine Sherry picking her long-limbed way about a jumbled salesroom, then descending upon the auctioneer with a preemptive bid. I certainly could.

"Neat. Does something for the room— Listen, Bill. Go talk to a couple of other brokers. Try one of the franchise outfits. Maybe they'll find you somebody. Otherwise, give me a ring. I'll see what we can do."

He was staring hard. And for once he didn't look so amiable.

I said, "Just so we understand up front. I'd go multiple listing right away. I can't handle it as an exclusive."

Bill Carter said he'd think about it.

I drove directly to the Fisks' place on River Road, hoping he wouldn't telephone Michelle before I got there.

Their front lawn was littered with specimen trees. Kousa was blooming; pear, cherry, and crabapples had already leafed out. They'd planted them too close together and crowded the driveway, creating the impression of an overstocked wholesale nursery.

The house loomed, chockablock with architectural details from many eras, though its mansard roof allowed realtors to call it a French Colonial, despite the historical fact that in New England most French colonists had huddled in shacks on the outskirts of English towns.

In our cups one night at the Yankee Drover, Fred Gleason and I swore a solemn vow to slap a ten percent surcharge on any house that called itself a French Colonial. I don't know about him, but I kept my word, and the damnedest thing was, people paid it anyhow. So if Duane and Michelle ever decided to sell, their seven-fifty mansion would go for a cool eight twenty-five. It *was* beautifully kept. When they had finished the new party room they'd painted the whole joint; it all looked brand new, neat and clean.

Duane still drove a truck—a fully loaded deluxe PowerWagon—which wasn't in the drive. Michelle had gone European, tooling around town in an Audi Quattro that I lusted after, secretly. It was in the circle drive at the front door, red and delicious as an apple. I parked by the garage and knocked on the back door.

High heels clicked busily over the kitchen floor and the next second Michelle flung the door open with a whiff of perfume and makeup. She looked very pretty, dressed to go out for lunch in a little suit that hugged her hips and stopped just above her knees. If I had a chemical dislike of Janey Hopkins, I liked Michelle very much, chemically speaking.

"Ben. Hi. Come in. I'm just running out, but what's up? Hey, did they like Morris Mountain?"

She ushered me in and, waving at the coffee machine, said, "Coffee's still warm. I just shut it off."

"Thanks. Black."

She clicked to the counter and poured a cup, while I let my imagination drift toward her brimming Jacuzzi. She came back, dark eyes flashing, cheery smile ablaze—the nice-girl-smart-woman looks of a CNN newscaster—and who hasn't wanted to jump *their* bones on a slow news night?

"Sit, sit. It's just lunch at the club. They'll wait." We sat at a maple table. "Tell me: How'd it go?" She pushed sugar my way and offered a spoon. She had chubby little fingers, and with that Jacuzzi already bubbling, there was something erotically grasping about them.

"So? Did they like it?"

"They liked the view."

"Good. Good. So?"

"Unfortunately, they had brought a friend with them and the friend had some horror story about someone she knew who had had a terrible experience building a house."

"Did they *listen* to her?"

"Like a mosquito in their ears. It didn't help. Anyhow, they're coming back next week, so they still think I'm the one. Who knows?"

"Well, there's more where they came from. . . . New Yorkers?"

"That's where the money is."

"I love 'em. Listen, thanks, Ben. Drink up. I've really got to get down there. I'm on the Stand for Steve committee."

"I saw Georgia's bumper stickers. Are you really backing *Steve* La France against *Vicky?*"

"Time for a change, Ben. I know she's your friend, but she's out of step."

"She's done a spectacular job; we almost went under three years ago and you know it."

"She can't solve Newbury's problems throwing taxpayers' money at them; not while she undercuts the tax base." (Translation: Cut the school budget, again, and stop forcing builders to comply with zoning. Michelle, to her credit, uttered no sanctimony about crime and disorder; this was about money.)

Poor Vicky. The younger club ladies, women with time on their hands and plenty of energy, like Michelle Fisk and Sherry Carter and Georgia Bowland, could grab a lot of headlines in the *Clarion*. And with their smiley good looks, Scooter would give them plenty of picture space too. Lookers for La France.

"We're doing a fundraiser—a dance. What do you think of 'Stomp for Steve'?"

I started to say that "Stomp for Steve" sounded friendly as a drive-by shooting. But I bit my tongue. Vicky would find a better time to say it, publicly.

"Georgia thinks we should call it 'Dance for La France.' "

"Sounds elitist. I'd stick with 'Stomp for Steve.' . . . Listen, I was just talking to Bill Carter."

"Oh, good. You're going to sell his house. Boy did he get in a jam with that one. You'll save him, Ben. Come on, drink up. I gotta go." She took my cup and headed for the sink.

"Bill told me that Reg was at your party."

She got a funny little smile on her face, pivoted for a moment on her heel, and sat down again. Elbows on the table, chin resting on her chubby hands, she studied me with more puzzlement than irritation.

"What's up, Ben? I don't get this."

"You told me Reg wasn't here the night he died. Bill says he was."

"So?"

"Why didn't you tell me he was here?"

"I don't have to tell you the truth."

"I beg pardon."

"You heard me. It's not any of your business who was here."

"Reg was my friend. And he died that night. And his widow asked me—"

"His *widow*? His *widow*, Ben, dumped him. What the hell business is it of hers where he was that night?"

"Michelle."

"Ben, you're way out of line. Come on, we're friends. We go back a long way; and you and Duane, forever. But come on. You're crowding us something weird. I don't know what your problem is, but it's not right." She had taken her chin off her hands by then, and heat was flaring deep in her eyes, heat she contained as she stood up and said, "I really have to go."

"What time did Reg leave?"

"One-ten."

"Exactly one-ten?"

"By that clock." She pointed at a replica Regulator in a too-shiny oak box. "You want to know why he left at one-ten? Because I threw him out. You want to know why I threw him out?"

"Yes I do."

"Because in my kitchen. At my table. Where my kids eat breakfast. He was snorting heroin."

"You saw him?"

"I came in for ice. The icemaker in the bar ran out and here he was, sitting right where you are, with a foot-long line of heroin."

"How'd you know it was heroin?"

She gave me a look of burning gasoline, then surprised me with a subdued, "Actually, I didn't know. It was white powder. I thought it was coke. But later, when they said he died of heroin, then I knew what I'd seen."

"That's when you threw him out?"

"Of course. I'm not having anybody do drugs in my house. . . . Okay, now and then Duane and me'll smoke some grass. The kids working for him might slip him a joint. They get off on the idea of 'Old Duane and Michelle' getting stoned. But we sure don't go looking for it. It's illegal. Who needs it? If I want to get high, I can drink wine. Duane's fine on beer."

I nodded agreement. There was a simplicity to honest alcohol.

"Wha'd he say?"

"I don't know. I didn't hear him." She surprised me with a laugh. "I was screaming my head off. You should have heard me, Ben. 'Get out of my house. Get out of my effin' house'—believe the mouth on me?—But I was so upset. I mean, first he barges in and then he sneaks into my kitchen. It was disgusting. It was a really rotten thing for him to do."

"So he just left?"

"Scooped up his garbage and left. By then Duane came. He heard me yelling. He calmed me down and we went back to the party."

"Did you tell everybody what happened?"

"No. I mean, they saw Reg's lights as he drove away, but I didn't tell them the whole thing. It wasn't their business. Reg had a lot of problems, and he was our friend, and I wasn't about to start bad-mouthing him in front of the rest of them."

I said, "I see."

"Do you see why I lied to you?"

"To protect him."

"No one else will."

"But that's why Janey asked me to check him out."

"Janey wants the life insurance, for God's sake, Ben. Are you stupid? She wants the money. . . . Hey, if she can get it, more power. Right? She's got kids. They'll need it. So I'll tell you this, Ben: If you keep quiet what I told you and it doesn't get around, then maybe I won't have to tell it again to some insurance investigator. You know what I'm saying?"

"I hear you."

"Good. Listen, I gotta go. I'm sorry you got caught in the middle of this. I hope we're still friends." Tentatively, she extended a hand. I took it.

"Hopefully it won't come to an insurance investigator. But word around town is there was a gatecrasher here. If they start hunting, they'll hear it."

"If you'll stop hunting, now that you know what happened, maybe it will all settle down."

"Was Reg the crasher?"

"Beg pardon?"

"Look, Michelle. Everybody's talking about your party. Rumor has a bunch of people having fun and games in your Jacuzzi. Rumor also has a mysterious gatecrasher—possibly a woman—running into the woods. Was there another crasher, or just Reg?"

"I told you what happened."

"Yeah, right. . . . Listen, could the stuff you saw him snorting have been coke instead of heroin?"

"It could have been Sweet 'n' Low, for all I know. Except who snorts Sweet 'n' Low up a twenty-dollar bill?"

"Would you mind if I tried to find any traces of it on the table? I could take it to a lab."

"I cleaned the table twenty times since then."

"Maybe something in the cracks. Like here between the boards."

"Ben, you're really pissing me off. I want you to leave."

I stood up and left.

She watched from the kitchen door, arms crossed, face dark with anger. Just before I reached the car she yelled, "You really take advantage of being friends, Ben."

"Hey, did he snort up what was on the table or put it away?"

"Screw you!"

"Did he?"

"Every goddamned grain of it. Right up his goddamned nose. Satisfied?"

I was not satisfied. The sensible half of my brain believed Michelle. But I didn't want to. I suspected I'd be more sensible, though not happier, after I talked to Ted Barrett. But I couldn't do that until school let out, which left me three hours to go bother someone else. Debating whom, it occurred to me that since I was talking to everyone in town about Reg, why not try to touch base with Reg himself?

I drove out to his cottage.

Some vandal had knocked over Fred Gleason's For Sale sign. I propped it up, then stood back to admire Reg's handiwork. His thatched roof was an oddity, but oddity or not, the roof, stucco walls, and tiny deepset windows were proportioned so authentically that no one would have been surprised to see Richard the Lion-hearted bang on the door demanding *droite du seigneur*.

Fred's lockbox held the key.

The house had the cold feel empty houses get even in summer. Things looked a little messy, as if the state police had half-heartedly searched for a major stash they knew they wouldn't find. And it was clear that Reg had holed up in the combination kitchen-fireplace room in the back of the house since Janey took the kids. I found an empty box from Lorenzo's Pizza Palace on the counter, unopened bills and junk mail, and some of last week's newspapers.

He had mounted elk antlers over his fireplace, but the rack was a mite small to dominate the room. In fact, had the animal they bagged been any younger, the Rocky Mountain park rangers would have bagged Reg and Duane for statutory poaching. Their swordfish on the wall opposite, however, looked big enough to sink a Montauk charter boat and sufficiently irritated to shish kebab the crew.

I sat in a big lounge chair that faced a twenty-seven-inch TV. On the table beside the lounger was a coffee cup growing mold on the dregs, and an Eric Sloane book about barns and covered bridges, lying open, facedown.

I closed it so the covers wouldn't warp and in doing so found that Duane Fisk had inscribed the flyleaf on July 17, 1989: "Happy birthday, Old Buddy. Thatch this!"

I owned the book myself. My father had given it to me. Sloane had written it back in '55, when he was one of the first to realize that suburbs and interstate highways would steamroll nineteenth-century New England into oblivion. As a birthday book it was a hell of a reminder of mortality. But for a craftsman like Reg, what better gift than a story in words and pictures about the vanished skills that were once universal in these parts?

I hit the TV remote. He'd been watching CNN last. There was a telephone. I pushed Redial, listened to it tapdance Reg's last call.

"Lorenzo's. Laura speaking."

Brilliant. "Hi, Laura. Ben."

"Hi, Ben. . . . Do you want to order?"

"Hey Laura, do you remember when Reg came in for a pie last?"

"The Friday before he died. It was the last time I saw him."

One thing I continued to be brilliant at was *not* filling in the nearly five-hour gap between the time Vicky saw Reg cruise past the cookout and Dr. Mead fed him pistachio ice cream.

I wondered how he got all the way from Michelle's kitchen to the covered bridge before the hotload killed him.

For that matter, why had he gone to the bridge at all? I opened the book again. The pages fell to the spot he'd been reading. But it wasn't about bridges, it was about barn structure. In the margin, he'd sketched a framing plan. He was losing the cottage in the divorce, which meant he needed a home. Why not a hand-hewn barn?

Maybe what Michelle saw him snort wasn't the hotload that killed him. Maybe Michelle and Duane weren't the last people who'd seen him alive. Did he meet somebody at the bridge? A good question.

I levered myself out of his lounger, locked up, and drove out to the covered bridge.

Sloane had described it in his book.

It had been built in 1851—the third to span this ford, the previous two having been washed away. This time the farmers and iron miners had gotten it right, constructing a new patented lattice frame that had allowed them to build it longer, and therefore higher above the floodwaters that had wrecked its predecessors.

It was cool and dim inside. I estimated where the Blazer had been by the windows. I sat on a convenient timber and tried to imagine the moment he drove in and stopped. The problem was, no matter how I concentrated, I couldn't imagine why he had stopped. Old wooden bridges, even quaint covered bridges, are a little creepy. Who knows when they're going to fall down? Why stop inside, particularly when you'd block the road to the Indian reservation, whose oft-abused residents had every reason to be surly?

I mulled these and related inconsistencies while square patches of sunlight from the windows crept along the wooden roadbed. Had they troubled Sergeant Marian while she conducted her investigation? Had Trooper Moody grunted "Something's fishy"? Had Marian—a pro through and through— confirmed the old warhorse's insight with a startling piece of evidence?

Somehow I doubted that, particularly as she hadn't requested the state police Major Case Squad crime-scene truck. It was easy to accuse her of mistaking Reg's death as a cut-and-dry overdose. The difficulty lay in the fact that Marian had not risen to sergeant making mistakes. Maybe she hadn't needed the truck.

Scooter had published a good photograph of her and Ollie crawling beside the Blazer on their hands and knees—Ollie, shaped like a rhino that lost a contact lens; Marian, shapely. So I got down on my hands and knees and crawled beside where the Blazer had been. I found wood splinters, dried mud, dust and pebbles, all dropped and scattered by a week of traffic. I poked between the floorboards. And where a sun-square had moved, I saw a glint of reflection. I pried out a tiny chip of blue paint from Reg's Blazer.

It stood to reason that in their search, before traffic had passed through, Marian and Ollie had found similar chips, proving the S10 had received its scratch on the bridge. Still, I felt sort of proud about my little piece of evidence. Though not proud enough to cash Janey's check yet.

# 8

The acid scents of oak sawdust and nostril-searing molten aluminum rocketed me back to seventh-grade shop class. Old Mr. Tyler had retired and now Ted Barrett, the handsome failed builder turned teacher, sent boys and girls home to their mothers with pig-shaped carving boards, water-pump lamps, and sand-cast letter openers. As I stood in the doorway inhaling it all, he was instructing a group of Alison's classmates never to stand behind the table saw. *Never.*

Ted had a deep, commanding voice. "Once," he told them, "it threw a four-foot-long two-by-eight through that window." The kids turned and *ahhed* at the window some thirty feet behind the saw. "Through the shade, through the glass, through the storm window. It flew all the way across the parking lot and landed on the principal's car."

The kids gave him a giggle. The next instant the bell rang. I stepped aside and they were out the door like rabbits.

I had to admire him. Most contractors who went belly-up pulled a vanishing act, leaving the lumberyard and the hardware store holding the bag. Ted had had Tim Hall organize an orderly Chapter Eleven and was paying down his debts; tough on a teaching salary, even with Susan nursing in a New Milford daycare center.

"Ben." Ted nodded warily, and I knew Michelle had beaten me to him.

"Mr. Tyler told that same story when we were in seventh grade."

"Whatever works. That saw's lethal if it binds."

"Except for the part about the principal's car. That was a nice touch."

Ted turned and walked away. I followed him to a far corner of the shop. He sat at his desk and gazed a moment at Susan's picture, which hung on the wall. Scooter MacKay had shot it for the *Clarion*'s Christmas issue the winter that Susan chaired Newbury's Adopt-A-Family committee. Posing with a heap of stuffed animals people had contributed, she looked about as beautiful, and beatific, as you'd expect a God-sent angel to look on Christmas Eve—deep, warm eyes, a veil of platinum hair, cheekbones to convert for, and a mouth to write home about. (Those who didn't believe in angels assumed she was Santa's chief of staff.)

"I think we better have a talk, Ben."

"Great. I think so too."

He looked at the clock on the wall. The bell had rung the end of the school day. I had wanted to get to him before Susan did.

"Here okay?" I asked.

"I'm meeting Bill and Duane out at Gill Farm. Want to follow me?"

I'd heard they were dismantling an old dairy barn, intending to move it to one of the homesites Duane owned on Mount Pleasant. "Let me ride along with you, if you can drop me back at my car."

"No, you better follow me," said Ted. "I gotta stay and help out."

I hesitated. I'd do best alone with Ted, but I was due at Rita Long's at six for a drink, with expectations of dinner or something afterward. As she was both busy and mobile, it had been weeks since we'd gotten together.

"How late you going to stay?"

"We'll work 'til dark."

"I'll take my car."

Aware this was not the swiftest move, I contrived to excuse myself

on the grounds that I hadn't cashed Janey's check and didn't expect
to learn much more from Ted than Michelle had told me, anyway.
I was equally aware that when it came to Rita Long, my ethical
standards had degenerated to those of a starving man with a rock
discovering pheasant under glass.

Ted locked the shop and signed out at the principal's office, and
I followed his Honda out of town and up Mount Pleasant Road. He
drove sedately, more like a retiree than the hotshot contractor who
used to race his Corvette down to Long Island Sound where he had
docked a cabin cruiser. With his beautiful Susan at his side, they
had been one of the sights of the town.

They still were, for that matter: Susan Barrett didn't need Cor-
vettes and cabin cruisers to knock male socks off; driving a rusty
compact these days, she still stopped traffic; while to go drinking
with Ted was to have women whisper in your ear, "Who's your
friend with the blue eyes?"

An encampment of Amish folk, up from Pennsylvania in modest
vans and RVs, were building a brand-new ultra-modern dairy barn
for Gill Farm. The men had split into two crews—masons pouring
the perforated concrete floor and carpenters erecting the frame.
Their women were cooking supper under some maple trees.

I pulled up a moment to say hi to Fred Gill, who had recently
bought Ellis Butler's herd when Ellis retired. Fred was beaming like
a new father. The huge concrete basin behind the barn, he explained,
was a holding-mixing tank for a cow manure slurry, piped from
under the cows, that he would spread on his fields; by feeding them
indoors, he figured to double production and halve costs, as the
cows would be fertilizing their own corn.

I congratulated him and caught up with Ted's Honda behind the
old barn where Duane Fisk and Bill Carter were pulling nails and
stacking siding. I wasn't quite prepared for my initial reception.

When Duane saw me, he hurried over, calling, "Hey, Ben. Perfect
timing. Things are moving real fast all of a sudden."

Duane was broad and beefy, a little shorter than I, and making excellent progress on a beer gut. In fact he had been putting on new weight for several months. Now when he smiled his jowls got big and his eyes nearly disappeared in slits of flesh.

I got out of the car. He slipped his hammer through his nail apron and tossed his catspaw nailpuller on the grass so we could shake hands.

"You look happy. What's moving?"

"We're going to pick up Reg's half of the Mount Pleasant sub-division. Me and Bill and Ted. Rates low, the market's coming back. We'll throw up four houses to start; first one we sell we start two more."

"Terrific," I said, curious what bank owed Duane a favor, and somewhat glad for them. As I've noted, I had never liked the Mount Pleasant deal; but the damage had been done already, in the course of clearing the lots and building the road, so there was little point in the scarred-up hillside eroding further as it sat empty. The people who bought their houses would make their own mark planting new trees and gradually erase the bulldozer scars with lawns and gardens and barbecues.

In fact, I was so glad for them that I didn't see the bribe coming until it was wrapping around me like a gaucho's bola. "Thing is, Ben, we'd like you to handle it with an exclusive."

"That's a decent offer."

"You've got the kind of buyers we'll need. Right, Bill?"

"Damn straight," said Bill, and Ted chimed in with a less-than-convinced, "Absolutely."

This was absurd. I specialized in country homes—second homes for well-off New Yorkers—and I hadn't met one yet who'd buy a house in a subdivision, much less one with a gravel pit for a front door.

"You sure I'm the guy for you?"

"No question."

"Okay. Let me sit down with my Rolodex. I'll get back to you."

"Good man."

"In the meantime, can I ask you something?"

"Shoot," said Duane, though Bill was reverting to his earlier irritated-bear look, and Ted was turning dark.

"I got a little bit of a problem. You see, Janey Hopkins—"

"Poor Janey's a problem. But she'll deal. She wants out. Guaranteed."

"Good, but she also wants me to tell her that Reg really wasn't snorting heroin."

"But he was."

"Well, I know that now. Michelle told me."

"So what's your problem?"

"Well, aside from the fact that Michelle first didn't tell me—"

"Later, she did. So what's your problem?"

"My problem is, she doesn't know what Reg was snorting. It could have been Sweet 'n' Low—her own words."

"He's dead," said Duane. "Why don't you leave him in peace?"

Bill Carter said, "The autopsy said heroin. What do you want, Ben?"

"I want to believe that and I don't."

"Michelle told you what she saw. Why you bugging us?"

"How'd he look when he left the house?"

"I didn't see him," said Ted.

"Me neither," said Bill.

"I saw him and he looked stoned," said Duane. "Come on, Ben, I've known Reg my whole life. Believe me, he was stoned."

"Then how did he drive twenty miles—eight miles of dirt road —to the covered bridge?"

"Who the hell knows?" demanded Bill.

And Ted added, "Who cares?"

I looked at Duane. "You care, don't you? Your best pal. For crissake, you guys were like brothers."

"Ben, if you don't shut up about Reg, you're not getting this job."

"Or any other job," said Bill. "None of my houses."

Considering what I'd seen this morning, that wasn't the biggest threat to my happiness. Ted grew darker and quieter, mourning, I assumed, that he had no houses to take back from me now that he taught shop.

Duane stepped closer and started pointing with a finger he'd cut while pulling nails. "None of my deals. And none of my friends' deals."

This *was* a threat. Newbury Pre-cast had continued to prosper in the same economy that cost Ted his cabin cruiser and that Bill Carter blamed for his woes. Shrewdly bartering concrete work for a piece of the action, Duane had garnered shares in every new project in the county, as well as some dead ones recently rescued from grateful banks.

While it was true that I concentrated on selling country houses, there weren't enough of them to count on for my entire income, which Duane knew very well. So perhaps I spoke harshly.

"You've just reminded me of a piece of Newbury history. Mount Pleasant wasn't always called 'Mount Pleasant.' My great-grandfather changed the name to toney up the neighborhood. Sounds like your project ought to go back to the original."

"Yeah, what's that?"

"Slut Hill."

"What the *hell* is that supposed to mean?"

"Reg was my friend too. If the situation was reversed, he'd tell the three of you to shove your business sideways."

To my absolute astonishment, Duane balled his fists and told me that if I knew what was good for me, I'd back off. Big Bill Carter shouldered beside him, forearms up like a defenseman looking for blood.

I laughed.

"You're kidding— Come on, you guys, what are you doing?"

They lunged shoulder to shoulder. I couldn't believe my eyes. But it was suddenly clear to me that Duane was going to take a swing. I looked around. Bill appeared to be winding up to blow me into the next county. Ted was watching. Still amazed, I tried to catch his eye, but he looked through me like I wasn't there. The old barn blocked us from the busy Amish. Fred Gill was nowhere to be seen.

I slipped off my Academy ring, which would make an awful cut, and punched Duane Fisk in the eye. There's nothing quite so disorienting as a punch in the eye, particularly if a guy's not accustomed to getting punched. He reeled back, clutching his face.

Bill moved between us. "What the hell did you hit him for?" he asked, throwing a big arm around Duane's shoulder.

Sensing a rush, I went cold. Ted had picked up a two-by-four stud. Red with anger, he stepped into his swing like a long-ball hitter.

# 9

The prisoners waiting to become my friends and enemies at Leavenworth had organized a lively pool in anticipation of my arrival, betting on how long and in what manner the white-collar felon would survive. But all bets were off when they saw me go cold the first time my life was threatened. It took one to know one, and the sociopaths present recognized a fellow killing machine long before I did. It was sheer luck I didn't spend the rest of my life there for murder committed behind bars.

When I went cold, a survival genie slipped from his dark bottle. All thinking ceased and I made no conscious decisions. But while middle-class Benjamin Abbott III watched from a safe distance, the genie inventoried weapons at hand: another two-by-four; a jagged half cinderblock; the catspaw nailpuller Duane had dropped. My hand took the catspaw—twelve inches of steel rod with a claw at either end. My legs delivered me inside the arc of Ted's swing.

Ted had his own survival genie, a little more civilized than mine. He dropped the stud and backed away, muttering, "Jesus, what am I doing?" And then, when he realized that my survival genie was very reluctant to climb back into his bottle, Ted wisely turned and ran.

I started after him, measuring the long target of his back, cocked my arm, and threw the nailpuller with all my strength. At the last second, I got ahold of myself long enough to hurl the catspaw down instead of through his shoulder blades. It penetrated six inches into the soil. I stood over it, gasping, trying to expel the electric surge of adrenaline through my lungs.

As I became aware that my friends were staring at me in fear and disgust, I spread my hands wide. "I'm sorry. I'm really sorry."

"Sorry?" echoed Duane, still holding his eye. "You oughta be sorry, you son of a bitch." Bill muttered indignantly that I was crazy. But I wasn't talking to them.

Ted knew. He shambled toward me—his face burning with that particular delight felt when you're surprised to discover you're still alive—his hand extended. "I'm sorry, Ben."

"Me too." We started to shake hands but ended up in a clumsy World Series winners' hug, less out of love than a desire to confirm we both still existed.

It was very quiet. The carpenters had stopped hammering.

The air, already rich from the grass and blossoms of a summer evening, and the sharp cow scents of the farm, suddenly shimmered with the delicious odor of chicken frying in the Amish camp. For a moment so vivid it seemed to ache, Ted and Bill and Duane and I —and even Reg—could have been heading home twenty years ago after seven innings in Old Man Hawley's side yard.

"So what happened?" I asked. "Was Reg stoned when he left?"

"I don't know," said Ted. "I saw his lights when he drove away. He wasn't going particularly fast or slow. He didn't seem to be weaving. His brakes flashed at the road."

"Did he signal his turn?"

Ted thought a moment, while the others stared at us. "As a matter of fact, he signaled."

"Left or right?"

"Left."

"Toward Frenchtown?"

"Left."

"You guys see that?" I asked.

Bill shrugged. "I didn't see the car."

"Yeah, he turned left," said Duane.

"Was he stoned?" I asked Duane.

Duane hesitated. "No. Look, I think Michelle walked in on him before he got a chance to do anything."

"So what's the big secret? Why is she—"

"You upset her, Ben. You scared her."

I found it difficult to imagine scaring Michelle. I said, "And I scared you guys too?"

Ted said, "Ben, try to understand. You know this town. I teach school. I don't want word getting around that I was at a party where a guy ODed on heroin. With the Board of Ed cutbacks and the new budget—and worse if Steve wins the election—who do you think would lose his job?"

"I don't know," I said. "From what I hear, half the town thinks you were swapping wives in Duane's Jacuzzi."

"I went home."

"So did I," said Bill.

"So did Rick and Georgia," said Duane. "Goddamned old lady gossips. Michelle and I were alone by two o'clock."

"Reg left at one?"

"One-ten. And he wasn't stoned. But who the hell would have believed that if we admitted he was there? Ben, considering some of the crap you've been through, you oughta know something about loose talk."

I agreed I did.

Ted said, "There's something else."

Bill and Duane eyed him warily. He turned to me. "According to the paper, the cops said he died of a hotload. You know?"

"Super-strong dose," explained Bill. "Bad batch."

"I read that."

"Well, from what I've heard, the stuff hits you like a ton of bricks. You're gone in a second."

"That's what I've heard."

"Well, doesn't it stand to reason, Ben, that if he died of a hotload Reg couldn't have driven from Duane's to the covered bridge? He'd have dropped dead in Michelle's kitchen."

"Good point. Maybe the first stuff he snorted wasn't too strong. Maybe he took another hit in the car. I asked Michelle if I could check for traces."

"But either way, it's not *our* fault."

"True . . ." I admitted.

"You going to leave this thing alone now?" Duane asked. "Please?"

I gave that some honest consideration. The thing was, I'd filled in nearly two more hours of Reg's evening. But between one and three hours later, and twenty miles away, he was dead.

"Maybe," ventured Bill Carter, "maybe the medical examiner screwed up."

"How so?"

"You read about it all the time. They make mistakes just like anybody else. Maybe it wasn't heroin. Maybe he had a heart attack. Remember that thing in New Jersey last year? They said the guy had fallen on his head? Turned out when they dug him up and looked again, he had two bullets in his skull. Why don't you go check that out? Leave us alone."

"Better yet," said Duane, "why don't you let a sleeping dog lie. Nothing you do is going to bring Reg back."

"Right," said Bill Carter. "He's dead and gone. Why wreck our lives?"

"Too late to bring him back," Duane repeated bleakly.

"Michelle told me you came running when she freaked out."

"Boy, was she pissed. You know, she sees the kitchen table, she thinks of the kids. One thing I know, you can get in a lot of trouble messing with a woman's house."

Bill groaned. "Tell me about it. Every house we've ever had, Sherry's bananas until I built a mudroom for my boots. Man, you get inside those four walls, you better believe you're in *their* space."

Ted nodded. "Susan's the same way. Far as I'm concerned, my space ends in the driveway."

Duane offered a thin laugh of agreement. "Michelle'll cut me more slack in the bedroom than the kitchen."

This camaraderie took us men about as far as it deserved to. In the silence that ensued, I asked, "Did Reg apologize?"

"Oh, yeah. He was practically begging for her to forgive him. She's just screaming, 'Get out, get out.' "

"What did you do?"

"Sent her back to the party and walked him out to his car."

"What did he say to you?"

Duane stared off at Fred Gill's fields. It was milking time. A string of cows were plodding through a gate like a party of middle-aged ladies filing off a tourist bus. "Same thing he was saying to her. 'I'm sorry, I'm sorry,' I told him. 'Go home, sleep it off.' "

"Sleep what off?"

"Whatever was bugging him. He goes, Would I apologize to Michelle. I said I would. He got in the car and drove away."

"Did he thank you?"

"For what?"

"For interceding with Michelle."

"Oh, yeah. He was babbling apologies. 'I won't do it again.' All that stuff."

"But he wasn't stoned."

"I honestly don't think he was. . . . So where do we stand, Ben? You going to drop this? Tell Janey that's the way it was and let's get on with our lives?"

I gave a noncommittal shrug, little more than a twitch, and turned away from him to watch the cows come home. I wondered what exactly I'd say to Janey when she brought up the paste-up note threatening her kids.

"It would be great if you sell Mount Pleasant."

"Sure would. . . ." We all started shuffling in the direction of my car and soon I had the door open and my hands on the wheel.

"You guys really didn't stay the night?"

"Hell no."

"How come?"

They looked at one another. Ted said, "Sherry's mom called, Margy was throwing up."

"My mother was with our kids," said Bill. "They were fine, but *she* got sick."

I turned to Duane. "What about Rick Bowland?"

Duane glanced at Ted. Then, in lowered tones, "Just between us and the lamppost, Georgia got drunk as a skunk. Rick had to throw a hammerlock on her to get her into the car."

I looked at the three of them, watching me intently. "Hell of a night."

"A pisser," said Bill.

Ted shrugged.

Duane nodded. His eye was puffing up where I'd hit him and he suddenly looked weary and old, as he had at the funeral. "One thing I'll tell you."

"What's that?"

"It sure beat Reg's night."

# 10

Rita Long fed me grapes, gingerly.

Like a little girl slipping Milk-Bones to an eager Labrador retriever, she seemed less afraid of being bitten than drooled upon. Her blunt fingers smelled of paint (she had been working in her studio when I arrived). Her nails were spatular, an indication, according to the digital physiognomists, that she was a problem solver.

She was also an extraordinarily beautiful woman with long black hair and startling blue eyes in a heart-shaped face. Yet tonight, when I saw her for the first time in weeks, she was, as always, more beautiful than I remembered. Between grapes, I remarked upon that impression. Rita shrugged it aside: "That's just because you're in love."

Couldn't argue with that. Which was just as well because we found enough to argue about anyway, on a wide range of subjects, all circling and skirting my desire to be near her and her desire to be away.

Her grapes, sweet red imports, were the culmination of an array of treats she'd brought up from Fraser-Morris. Sated on smoked fish, marinated meats, asparagus, and chocolate—all washed down with Veuve Cliquot—I ate them more for taste than need, while plotting routes north and south of her fingers.

"Getting cool," I observed.

We were cozied up in her favorite perch, a bench in the top of a tall tower that climbed the southwest corner of her thirty-or-so-room stone mansion that we bedazzled locals had dubbed "The Castle." It commanded a hundred acres of Morris Mountain—a large estate by Newbury standards—and gorgeous views that sloped miles south and west to the river. An evening chill was moving down the mountain as the sunset burned itself out and it seemed like a fine time to go inside somewhere warmer. Her bedroom had a very nice fireplace.

But Rita said, "Run it by me again: Twice Duane Fisk claimed that Reg Hopkins wasn't stoned? But first he said Reg *was* stoned?"

"I think it's cool enough to build a fire."

"He sounds confused."

"He's upset. The two of them were like brothers."

"And Duane's wife—what's her name?"

"Michelle."

"Michelle said she saw him actually snort the heroin?"

"She happened to be screaming at me, but yeah, I think that's what she said."

"Screaming mad, so she could have been exaggerating?"

"Possible." As we were seated side by side, my hand fell quite naturally on her thigh.

Rita inched closer and put a warm arm around me when I complained again of the cold. "And the reason none of them spent the night at the Fisks as they planned was what?"

"A sick child. A sick mother. And a drunk wife."

"Give me a break."

"I wish to *hell* I had questioned them separately. I shouldn't have gone out there with Ted."

"The shop teacher?"

"I should have braced him while we were alone."

"The one who tried to hit you with the two-by-four?"

"He didn't mean it. Ted's not like that."

"Well, he was with the two-by-four."

"Yeah, but I—I just don't get what set him off like that. Actually,

I do. He's been through hell the last few years. Chapter Eleven, lost everything— Anyway, I don't know that their leaving early means a whole hell of a lot."

"Not that you'll ever know, since they've gotten together to compare excuses."

I explored the loveliest thigh in Plainfield County.

Rita bit my shoulder. "You know what I think about these neat little dovetailed stories?"

"What?"

"The leaving of Reg was a lot messier, louder, and more emotional than they're telling you."

I agreed, exploring further. "When the screams and tears were over and he'd finally gone, no one felt much like group immersion in hot water."

"Believe it. I mean, how would you feel?"

"That would depend on my fellow immersee. If it were you, for instance—"

"No groups."

"Christ no."

"So now what?"

"Why don't we build a fire?"

"I mean, what do you do next?"

"Let's sleep on it. I'll think about it in the morning."

"Obviously, you have to find out what happened *after* one-ten, when Reg left the party, because the missing hours between that first selectman woman at six-thirty and the ice cream shop at eleven were spent scoring his hotload of heroin."

Rita's "obviously" was stronger than I felt. But, willing to accede to anything that would speed us indoors, I nodded, adding only, "And God knows what other pharmaceutical oddities."

"Drugs sound so 'old hat' these days."

"They always hit later here. Acid and pot arrived in the 'Seventies, long after city flower children had cut their hair. Now 'Nineties Newburians snort 'Eighties coke. Come the millennium, they'll be smoking crack."

"So the hours *after* he left the Fisks' have to be your next goal."

She was probably right. The answer lay within that slot of time I'd narrowed between his life and death. "A goal I'll pursue tomorrow morning." I stood up, thinking I'd drag her indoors by the ankles. She jumped up too. "Ice cream."

"Huh?"

"We were talking about the ice cream shop."

"Yes."

"I want ice cream."

"Let's see what's in the freezer."

We ran down the circular stairs and up a long corridor into a kitchen a four-star chef would have been honored to perform in. Rita used it mostly for the storage of takeout menus, and indeed, neither of the Sub-Zeroes held any ice cream.

"Let's go."

"Where?"

"Dr. Mead's."

I followed her to the garage, where an old Land Rover and a shiny new V-12 Jaguar awaited her pleasure. She headed for the Jag.

"Hey, you want to drive?"

"No, you drive." I'd guzzled the lion's share of the Veuve Cliquot, and besides, being driven by a beautiful woman in a flashy car has always struck me as one of the joys of life. The garage door rose and the Jag fired up nine or ten cylinders. Rita cursed gently until eleven and twelve woke up. She lowered the top and soon we were tooling down her long and curvaceous driveway under a sky alight with stars.

"May I use your phone?"

Her hand went smoothly from third gear to the telephone to me to fourth. I dialed Painter Joe Pitkin, interrupting a television show. He found a quieter phone in the kitchen. His wife hung up, and I asked, "Let's say for a minute you decided—for whatever reason: stress, misery, lost love, divorce—decided you really wanted to get high."

"Yeah?"

"Such a thing could happen on a lousy day, right?"

"Or a wonderful day. What's the question, Ben?"

"Could you in such circumstances talk yourself into thinking: Since I'm an alcoholic and booze is my problem, it would be better if I got high on dope instead?"

"Are we talking about me or our friend who's passed over?"

"Our friend who has passed over."

"You're missing the point."

"I know, I know. Deck chairs on the *Titanic*. But—"

"The point is, our friend *has* passed over."

"But—"

"Ben, listen. You're emotionally involved in this. *I'm* emotionally involved. I spoke to a guy I know from meetings. A bigshot guy who knows everybody in Plainfield, okay? I asked him, I said, 'Could the coroner have made a mistake? Could maybe Reg have been kicked by a mule or choked on a candy bar or something?' Now this guy knows, Ben. He talked to the coroner—off the record, one bigshot to another—and there is no doubt in his mind that poor Reg died of a heroin overdose. Okay? No doubt."

He took my silence for disbelief.

"The reason they're all so sure is now that the cops are on to these 'hotload' things, they're double checking. They're taking samples of tissue and stuff to try to trace it to the seller."

"Lots of luck."

"Yeah, well, you know more about that than I do. But no doubt that Reg died of heroin."

He fell silent. I could hear the TV in the distance. Finally, I said, "I'm sorry."

"Not half as much as me. Good night, Ben."

I pressed the End Transmission button and watched eyes beside the road in the headlights. Rita glanced at me. I took her hand.

"I'm thinking maybe Reg bought his dope as backup, kind of a failsafe device in case the evening he had hoped for—like a visit with friends—went sour. . . . Everybody knows when they're not welcome." I pictured him crashing the party, meeting cold hostility, fading away to the Fisks' kitchen, spreading his stuff on the table. "I mean if he felt alone and rejected, he wouldn't be the first person to think, Why not get high? Right?"

"Right," said Rita.

"So who was the 'mystery guest'?"

"Reg was the mystery guest."

"But how do the gossips turn a guy coming in late, annoying everybody, sneaking off to the kitchen to do his dope, into a woman who runs off into the woods?"

"You should see the looks I get in the General Store. People want to believe everything. As long as it's bad."

"Beautiful widows fire the imagination."

"*Your* imagination." She laughed. Then, quite suddenly somber, she added, "You know, one of the reasons I go away so often is for plain, simple privacy."

"What are the other reasons?"

She glanced at me. By the glow of the Jaguar's instruments I saw a deep sadness in her expression. She looked back to the road without speaking.

No way I wanted to open the subject of where she went. Or with whom. Or even if there was a "whom." I said, "I wonder if *Reg* brought the mystery guest."

"Didn't the kids who saw him say he was alone?"

"At night, behind the tinted windows? What could they see?"

"Are you saying maybe she left with Reg? Hey, maybe Reg delivered the cake the stripper jumped out of."

I shook my head. "He couldn't fit a cake that big in the Blazer."

"Sure he could."

We argued the relative dimensions of Chevy Blazer cargo space and the size cake a stripper required. Rita was convinced such a cake would fit. I wasn't so sure. We devised a formula where either the cake came in two parts, to be assembled on site, or the stripper was a tiny woman.

"Five-one or -two. Hundred and five pounds."

"A petite."

"I always think of strippers as big."

"That's because of presence. They look big on stage."

"You've seen strippers on stage?" I asked. "Hey, I got an idea. Let's get a bunch of cake mix and kind of bake one around you."

"I'm not petite."

"For comparison."

"If you want petite, I'll drop you at Town Hall."

Sometimes, when Rita was in a particularly kind mood, she did me the courtesy of acting jealous. I did her the courtesy of protesting innocence and my undying love, which was essentially true, despite my recent half-hearted attempt to talk Vicky into snuggling on Scooter's lawn tractor. Unfortunately, protestations of undying love were no sure route to Rita's heart. If anything, they scared her off.

I changed the subject. "Assuming Reg did not deliver the stripper in the cake, was the guest already there when he arrived, or did she come after?"

"You keep saying 'she.' "

"The rumors say 'she.' "

"Maybe 'she' gave him the heroin."

"He already had heroin."

"Maybe he gave her a ride," Rita mused. "Maybe he offered her his heroin."

"As an inducement out of the woods and into his car?"

"No. She needed a ride and they probably knew each other. Everybody does. Then they drove twenty miles to the covered bridge and snorted up together and he died and she ran home."

"Twenty miles?"

"Maybe she lived near the bridge."

"Ah. He gave a ride to somebody who lived out near the bridge." We looked at each other, and Rita nearly ran into the flagpole at Church Hill Road.

She slewed around it on screeching tires. I saw Ollie parked in the shadows of the Congregational Church. I thought for a minute he'd come after us, but he was either uncharacteristically mellow or lazy that night and he let us go.

At the bottom of Church Hill we found Dr. Mead alone in his shop, gearing up for the end of the first movie at Town Hall. Rita had a single cone of her favorite coffee. I had pistachio in a cup and we retired to the Jag to eat in splendor.

"But so what?" said Rita. "What good would it do you to find a witness to Reg Hopkins dying of an overdose? It wouldn't help your client. What is her name?"

"Janey."

"Mrs. Hopkins. Other than satisfying your curiosity, what good would it do?"

"Earn my fee from Janey," I said with little enthusiasm. "And, uh, I don't know, put her mind to rest, at least."

"Who lives out that way?" Rita asked. "Isn't it just woods?"

"The Indians on the reservation. . . ."

The Jervis clan, a renegade family of petty and not-at-all petty criminals, inhabited the remote and empty land that adjoined the reservation. Aggressively opportunistic—ferocious if provoked— they specialized in cigarette smuggling, dope deals, car theft, and supplying uppers at the truck stops, as well as anything else profitable that struck their fancy. But they didn't mingle with regular people and I couldn't for the life of me imagine any of them hanging around the Fisk party; these were people who regarded my cousin Pinkerton as effete.

They *could* have supplied Reg's heroin—though they tended to run bigger deals above the retail level, and not in Newbury. I had one friend among them. But were I to ask Gwen Jervis what she knew about Reg's heroin, much less his death, I'd receive as warm a response as from a Russian asked if she had been a KGB informer under the Communist regime. Besides, Reg had brought his own dope to the party; and in the unlikely event he'd bought it from the Jervises, he certainly wouldn't have invited his supplier to join him at the party.

"This isn't getting me anywhere."

"Well, maybe you're looking in the wrong place," said Rita, engulfing the remains of her cone. She licked her lips, started the car, put my hand back on her thigh, and scattered Dr. Mead's gravel on the way out of his parking lot, into the night.

I woke up at two in the morning. Rita was thrashing around, and when I reached to soothe her, she drew back.

"I can't sleep."

"Here, I'll rub your back."

The fire had died down to a glow that lit the ceiling. She threw off the light quilt and sat up, rubbing her face. "No, don't—I'm sorry. My head's running in circles."

"I'll make you some warm milk."

"No, I can't—Ben, can you go home? I'm just lying here, feeling you, and I just can't sleep. You snore."

I groaned myself to my feet and stood reeling a moment, trying to remember where I'd find my clothes.

Eventually, to my discomfort and amazement, I found myself driving home to Main Street, with something Rita had said earlier ringing in my ears.

"You worship sex, don't you?" she had asked.

I could have answered in all truth that I worshipped sex with her. Or I could have said that she too had partaken of the sacrament with extraordinary reverence. But it had seemed at the time, and so much more now, like a question with no happy answer.

As I drove by the General Store I saw windows lit upstairs where Vicky McLachlan had commandeered part of Tim Hall's law office for re-election headquarters. Tim's Subaru was parked below, and a couple of other cars belonging to the volunteers slogging away at a late-night envelope-stuffing and strategy session. Not only was Vicky tireless; she had a true leader's gift for inspiring others to drive themselves too. I felt a sudden empathy, or sympathy, for the first selectman—an awful insight that she felt about me the way I felt about Rita.

Dead tired and deeply depressed, I parked the Olds outside my barn so as not to wake Alison and Mrs. Mealy. Then I walked through my dark house, straight upstairs, dropped my clothes on a chair, and climbed into my own cold bed. I lay there awhile, trying to think up reasons why I wasn't losing Rita, and eventually fell asleep.

When I awakened, foggy-brained, to a noise, I thought she was telephoning me. But when I snatched up the phone, all I got was a dial tone. While, downstairs in the dark, whoever had clanged metal against the crystal bowl on the foyer table caused the first tread of the stairs to sigh beneath his weight.

# 11

I owned a formidable gun collection I had inherited from my father: sidearms that included nineteenth-century horse pistols, several dozen revolvers, one a sweet little .38 the old man had kept in the night table, and a Navy-issue Colt .44 capable of blowing holes in a battleship.

They were all registered: When I got out of prison I applied for relief of civil disability so I could get my real estate license. Aunt Connie helped speed the process, with the aid of old Judge Kinsolving, who owed her his appointment. While we were at it, I took out permits so I could keep my father's guns, which seemed at the time of his death like an important link to him. As a mere white-collar criminal, I even had a license to carry.

Unfortunately, when little Alison moved into the barn and got comfortable enough to bring her little friends over to watch my TV or bang on my mother's piano, I locked the entire collection in an iron safe.

The key was hidden in the top of my clothes closet. But the safe was down in the cellar, built into an old brick furnace, two floors and one housebreaker from where I lay in bed, listening to him come up the stairs.

As it was likely that he had at least part of his own gun collection on his person, I picked up the telephone and punched up Trooper Moody's number on the lighted keypad. Three-thirty in the morning, Ollie picked up loud and clear: "What?"

"Ben Abbott. Somebody's broken into my house."

I could imagine the conflict in Ollie's mind: On the one hand, what a nice idea that a burglar would rob Benjamin Abbott III while he cowered in his bed. On the other hand, the housebreaker had invaded Ollie's turf, and had had the nerve to do it three hundred yards down Main Street from the trooper's own residence.

"Where are your guns?"

"Locked up."

"Mrs. Mealy?"

"In the barn."

"You upstairs?"

"In bed."

"Stay there."

We hung up. I eased out of bed and headed for the door, trying not to creak on the old chestnut floorboards. One of them groaned as if I was pulling nails with a claw hammer. I froze, listening. An answering creak drifted up the stairs. I glided forward again, reaching through the dark for the black iron key that protruded decoratively from the lock.

I missed, brushed it with the back of my hand. It rattled like a sack of horseshoes. There was a thud in the hall and a gleam of light under the door. I twisted the key. The lock probably hadn't been used since my parents had made love when I was four years old. It was like trying to turn a nail in a stump. I twisted hard with both hands. The key turned. The bolt shot into place. And I was locked in, safe as houses, until the door exploded inward, slamming me across the bedroom, over the bed and onto the floor.

I got up fast; my skull was thundering where the door had smashed me and I felt like my life had been divided into two parts—before and after the pain. The beam of a penlight crept across the wall, stopped on the lightswitch. A hand brushed it. The lights came on. My survival genie took one look and slunk back into his bottle.

There were two of them, broad, squat Hispanics, powerfully built, wearing baggy pants and tight T-shirts. The one in back might have been Italian, but I didn't care, because their bulging arms were speckled with blue-green prison tattoos. Gang symbols, I knew, but what really chilled me were the tears tattooed down the lead guy's face. Where I'd done time, those tears represented murders, sometimes in increments of five to avoid crowding.

I wondered how they happened to have strayed so far from their natural territory. Waterbury, the blighted old "Brass City," was the closest gang town. But it was thirty miles from Newbury, as the crow flew, and a hell of a lot farther for a ghetto crow that had to drive country roads across countless borders of language, culture, and inclination.

I said, "The money's downstairs."

They said, "What you got up here?"

I said, "There's a fifteen-thousand-dollar wristwatch in the attic." There was, a gold Piaget moon watch I'd accepted, unwisely, from an arbitrageur, back when people wanted to do me big favors. It resided in the pocket of a rapidly dating mothballed Armani suit I used to wear while encouraging clients to steal other peoples' corporations.

The Hispanic filling my bedroom door said, "Bullshit."

The Italian, still behind him in the hall, said, "What, you got a gun up there?"

Trapped, naked as the day I was born, in the space between the bed and wall, counting the minutes for Trooper Moody to get dressed and over here, my only hope was to get out the door and lead them on a chase through my dark house.

So far as disabling them with a punch in the eye, à la Duane Fisk, was concerned, guys like these had started breakfast most mornings since they were kids with a punch in the eye. The fact that they were still alive at the ripe age of twenty meant they had won more fights in any given month than I had in my life—prep school boxing, Navy hand-to-hand, and Leavenworth shank duels combined. That there were two of them and one of me complicated matters further. But my main disadvantage, I learned at the price of first blood, was that I had not fully recovered from the door slamming my head.

Everything had slowed a beat behind.

I escaped the corner behind the bed by running right over the bed. That move caught the Hispanic by surprise, but not the Italian. He stepped right into my path, swinging a ring-studded fist at my face. I launched a body blow and slipped his punch—or thought I did. My moves were right, but so slow. My fist bounced on a boilerplate belly. His rings raked my cheek and nearly tore my ear off.

I got past him—barely—stunned and bleeding.

Halfway out the bedroom door, one of them brought me down with a flying tackle; my head banged the wallpaper across the hall. The other started kicking, allowing his partner to stand up and kick me too.

In the hemmed-in space of the half-hall outside my bedroom, they got bored and decided to drag me into the open, which was their only mistake. My head was still muddy, but the moment's respite allowed me to figure out where each of them was. When they dropped me in the main hall at the top of the stairs, and the one nearest my head aimed a kick at my nose, I seized his foot with both hands and twisted.

A yell of surprise—punctured by a sharp crack—leaped in key to a shriek of pain. Still twisting, I braced my legs wide for purchase and tried to heave him down the stairs. And it would have worked, if his buddy hadn't ruined it by kicking me in the groin.

It was my turn to yell and yell I did, convulsed into a ball of pain, only dimly aware that one was cursing I'd broken his ankle and the other was grunting with the effort of each kick and then punch as he knelt down to work on my face.

Bashing my skull in the hall hadn't cleared my head, but the pain between my legs did and I never fully blacked out as he tore at me. In resisting I'd provoked them to administer what the street gangs, from Waterbury or Bridgeport or Hartford or whatever miserable ghetto had spawned them, called a beat down. With that realization, the survival genie slipped out for another look. Problem was, he didn't have much to work with.

A streetlight shining through the stairwell window revealed the Italian hopping on one foot holding his ankle with one hand and pawing into his pants with the other, while his partner kept trying to get to my face, which I was resisting both with my hands and the occasional weak kick. Happily he wasn't wearing as many rings as the Italian holding his foot. But the Italian was reaching for a weapon. I prayed it was a knife. Turned out to be a gun—one of those glitzy semiautomatics tricked up to look like a machine pistol.

"I'm bangin' him, man."

"No!"

"He broke my foot."

The Hispanic rose to block him. On the theory he was going to lose that argument, the genie levered me off the floor and drove a fist deep into his kidneys. He grunted and I thought I'd killed him. But he turned and backhanded me with a fist that had traveled through a hundred and eighty degrees and carried all his weight and considerable enmity. A long while later I heard the gun go off.

I hurt so badly I didn't know where they'd shot me. After a while, it appeared that maybe they hadn't. If that were the case, they'd shot Trooper Moody. In a flash of pain-filled epiphany, I realized I deeply hoped that Ollie was not bleeding to death on my living-room floor. I headed downstairs to look and got there faster than I had planned, by losing my balance on the top step and tumbling to the bottom.

When I opened my eyes again, Ollie was standing over me, shining his Mag light into them.

"Look what happened to you."

"You get 'em?" I asked—or slurred—through puffed and bloody lips.

"Shot my tires out."

"Sons of bitches."

"Want an ambulance?" he asked cheerfully.

I started to say I didn't really need one. Before I could, the Mag light turned red, and then black. I had the weirdest feeling that Rita Long had gently draped her jet hair over my face. But when I woke up, I was in a sunlit hospital room and the woman holding my hand was Vicky McLachlan.

I took in the room, the curtain around the bed beside mine, the view of a cemetery from the window, a hanging TV, Vicky's pretty face and neat little legs crossed at the knee. Later I woke up again and asked, "What happened?"

"You have two concussions," she said, speaking very slowly.

"How did I get concussions?"

"You don't remember?"

I shopped back in my mind. "I fell down the stairs."

"Yes." She nodded, encouraging me to go on. "Do you remember how you fell down the stairs?"

"Drunk?"

"No, dear. Don't you remember?"

"I remember Trooper Moody's light in my face. Did Ollie—"

"No. You telephoned him at three in the morning."

"Rrrrright." I snapped my fingers, or would have if an IV weren't taped to my hand. "There was somebody in the house."

"Oh, thank God. They said you might not remember anything."

It was coming back in a rush. "I have a feeling I'd just as soon not— What's that?" I pointed at the newspaper in her lap.

"*Danbury Republican*," she said, offering it to me. "Scooter got a byline."

"Good for him."

It was open to page five and I saw the headline: "Prominent Newbury Real Estate Broker Hospitalized in Burglary Attempt."

"That sounds like I'm the burglar."

"Not in the context."

"Oh, wonderful. . . . Give me that thing."

"Special to the *Danbury Republican*," Scooter had written. "Benjamin Abbott III, prominent Newbury real estate agent, was hospitalized early this morning after a burglary attempt on his Main Street home."

"For crissake, he makes it sound like I'm robbing my own house."

"Scooter said they edited him."

"Jeesus . . . Oh, here it gets better. . . . 'Abbott foiled the burglary when he awakened and challenged the burglars later described by resident State Trooper Oliver Moody as "Swarthy individuals possibly of Hispanic descent." According to Trooper Moody, Abbott "put up a pretty good fight and scared them outside where they pegged a couple of shots at me, disabling my cruiser so I could not give chase." Trooper Moody radioed the Plainfield barracks, where, according to a State Police spokesman, it was discovered that due to continuing budget cuts, "We had no more cruisers anywhere near the Newbury area." ' Great. My house gets broken into and Ollie gets the story and the cops complain about their budget. . . . Oh look, you're in it too. 'Newbury First Selectman Victoria McLachlan, in response to a charge by re-nomination challenger Steve La France that Newbury is rapidly becoming unsafe for decent families, replied that . . .' The ink blurs here. What did you say?"

"According to Scooter, I said, 'Newbury is still as close as you can get to heaven in modern America.' "

"You said that?"

"I don't know. I was really upset."

"What happened?"

Vicky stared long and hard. "You were lying here unconscious, you stupid bastard."

"What did I—"

She got up. "I'm glad you're awake. Goodbye."

"Thanks for coming."

"No problem."

She left. A while later somebody brought me lunch. Then an elegant Indian resident physician strolled in and asked me some questions. Later Steve Greenan stopped by with the resident, who, I was pleased to see, treated Steve with enormous respect.

The next day Dr. Mahadevan said to me, "Do you know that old man is a real GP? I hardly ever meet one."

"He delivered me."

"That explains it."

"What?"

"They say he rode with you in the ambulance."

"At three in the morning?"

"Not easy for such an old man. Ah, I see you have another visitor."

"Another?" Hoping Rita.

"Yesterday you had the first selectlady."

Today it was Janey Hopkins, looking just about as crazed as last time I'd seen her.

"Are you okay?"

"Fine."

"It wasn't burglars, was it?"

"What do you mean?"

"It was about Reg. Wasn't it?"

"I don't know."

"I told you. I warned you. They're trying to stop us."

"Who?"

"Whoever killed Reg."

"Janey."

She looked away.

"Janey. Give me your hand. Please."

She stood nearer the bed and extended a rough, dry hand. I held it in both of mine, rubbed the backs of her fingers. "Janey. From everything I've learned, the medical examiner had it right. Reg died of an accidental overdose. My advice to you is try to force the insurance company to settle. Let Greg try to negotiate something."

"Who beat you up?"

"Trooper Moody had it right in the paper. Two swarthy individuals. They looked like they'd done hard time." I hesitated sharing my fleeting impression—spawned in the heat of battle and less real now—that they'd come after me specifically. It was just a feeling and bound to set her off down one of the increasingly weird paths her mind was exploring.

"I see you didn't cash my check."

"It's in my desk."

"*Why?*"

"Don't want to rip you off."

She jerked her hand away. "Then give it back to me. I'm going to hire somebody else."

"I'll give it back, of course, but I really wish you'd drop it. You're making yourself a target for somebody who will rip you off."

"Someone will help me."

"Well, at least get Greg to recommend a detective. Lawyers know who they are."

"No. This is between me and—and them. Not Greg."

I reached for her hand again, and her blocky face screwed up in tears. "You don't know what this has been like."

"Of course I don't."

"It isn't fair."

"What isn't fair?"

She stared at me. Her mouth twisted with the same expression of distaste it had had the first day in my office, and for a long instant I thought she was about to spring a huge confession. Instead, she gently withdrew her hand and said, "Tear my check up. Mail me the pieces. Save me the hassle at the bank."

I said, "I'm probably out of here tomorrow. Give me a couple of days—a week. My head's killing me. Give me a week, maybe less."

"What for?"

"Just to check out one more thing."

# 12

Ollie came by the next morning with a suspect file of burglars who worked northwest Connecticut. It was a thin one. And while I recognized several of the criminals pictured—including a cousin by marriage into the Chevalleys—I was not surprised not to find my tattooed attackers. Neither was Ollie.

"None a these mutts have the balls to shoot out my tires. Fact, probably none of 'em even carry."

"Tires? The newspaper said they shot at *you.*"

"Scooter MacKay oughta write comic books. When I called him on it he blamed the Danbury editor. Tell you, Ben, the worst of these scum"—he pounded the file with a finger the dimensions of a normal forearm—"I'd trust farther than the media assholes running this country into the ground."

I looked at him and he stiffened with embarrassment. It was the first personal view he had shared with me in the twenty years we'd been at each other's throats.

"You got a gang file?"

"What for?"

"I think they did time. And they were young enough so they probably did it right here in Connecticut."

"You telling me we had a prison gang in Newbury?"

"Well, obviously not the whole gang, or I wouldn't be here talking to you."

Ollie gave me a hard look. "I was afraid of that. I don't know everything you've been getting into, Ben, but I'm telling you right now, you draw the wrong element into town and you'll answer to me."

He misinterpreted my open-mouthed gape as a guilty plea.

"I was wondering why we'd suddenly see a pair of hard cases. These guys weren't locked up in Connecticut. You pissed 'em off in Leavenworth. Finally got paroled and came to even up the score. Well, you tell your slammer friends for me, if they want your ass they better make plans to meet you in New York."

"Ollie, nobody's coming after me from Leavenworth." In fact, I'd gotten the occasional late-night telephone call from guys between convictions asking me to wire a fast hundred. The one or two twisted souls who'd want my blood would not see parole in a thousand years. And no one had escaped the joint since 1910.

"I knew it the second they opened up with that automatic. Said to myself, 'Ben Abbott's pissed 'em off and they're shooting up my town.' I won't stand for it, Ben."

He stood up, towered over my bed. I had to put some effort into not flinching. "And you tell your friends for me. Leave their guns at home, or I'll show 'em firepower they'll never forget. Shootin' up a street of wood-frame houses. People sleeping in their beds. What do they think we live in, some goddamned housing project?"

Shaking with anger, he loomed a long moment, then stalked out. A liver-spotted hand tugged the curtain around the bed beside mine and the patient within asked, "Was that a peace officer?"

"Sort of."

A navy blue Mercedes limo was waiting outside Danbury General, uniformed driver holding the door. "Good morning, sir. Ms. Long regrets she was tied up in New York." My heart fell; I'd been hoping to find her in the back seat.

On the seat was a note, redolent of Anaïs Anaïs. "Hospitals give me the creeps. Talk to you soon."

I tried the telephone, got her New York machine, said, "Thanks for the ride," and sat back to enjoy it as much as I could, considering that every bump and sway irritated some part of me that ached, and that a fairly deep depression was one of the effects of getting pounded in the head.

Halfway to Newbury, I said, "Charles, would you have time to swing through Plainfield?"

"My orders are to take you anyplace there's a road—but I gotta say, Mr. Abbott, you look like you ought to get straight to bed."

"It looks worse than it is." My bruises were yellowing and they'd removed the bandages from most of the cuts on my face; one ear looked like Dr. Frankenstein had sewed it on with a turkey needle.

In fact, I felt terrible, but that was the head stuff—a pair of minor concussions that healed enough to let me out of the hospital but still required rest. Basically, I'd had a headache since I woke up two days ago.

"The state police barracks," I said, "right next to the county jail."

"Oh, I know where it is, sir."

Of course he did; Rita had spent a few nights in the lockup before her then-husband sent enough Park Avenue lawyers to effect a hostile takeover of Canada.

"Is Sergeant Boyce around?" I asked the trooper guarding the front desk.

"No sir. She's due in at sixteen hundred. That's four o'clock. Want to wait?" He stared curiously at my bashed-up face.

"How about Sergeant Bender?"

"What's your name?"

I told him. He asked me to sign in and shortly Arnie Bender, a smallish man for a trooper, came out to collect me. He extended his hand warily. "What's up, Abbott?"

"I read in the paper you got a federal grant to computerize your gang files."

"Yeah?"

"I'd like to see them."

"By what right?"

"Crime victim."

"I heard you got the face in a B and E."

"I couldn't find the sons of bitches in Trooper Moody's burglar file and I was thinking maybe we were looking in the wrong place."

"It's Trooper Moody's investigation. Tell him."

"Trooper Moody is a farmer."

Arnie Bender might have smiled if he were a smiling man. Like Marian Boyce, he was city-bred. He'd grown up in Hartford; Marian, in Bridgeport. Neither detective was at their best on grass. But put them on asphalt sprinkled with broken bottles, and they shone like icebergs in the moonlight.

Bender had been Marian Boyce's boss until, in the course of a case I got involved in, she caught up. His basic take on me was that I was a jailbird—his and Ollie's word—who had gotten in the way of his career. On the plus side, he was a decent guy with his head on fairly straight, for a cop. I'd seen him do the right thing in the past and I was hoping he'd do it now. Also, he was a good detective, and good detectives like to lock up criminals.

"They had prison tattoos. One of 'em had tears."

"What the hell were they doing in Newbury?"

"I'd love to know."

"They come at you out of the slammer?"

"Farmer Moody already asked me that."

Bender noticed the front desk trooper pressing his ear to the armored-glass air holes. He took my arm and led me into the detective room. It was a well-lit office like a real estate agent's—a modern, national franchiser's, not a quaint-and-musty shop like mine. He offered a chair beside his desk and coffee from a burnt-smelling maker. Figuring my headache couldn't get much worse, I accepted, with half-and-half and sugar, and while he stirred, answered his question. "No one has any reason to come at me out of Leavenworth. Besides, these guys did state time."

"How you figure that?"

"Frankly, they weren't that tough."

Bender pointed at my ear. "How tough you want?"

"They were local. Bridgeport, Hartford, Waterbury—Waterbury's closest to Newbury. I thought we could start there."

"Makes no sense. These 'gangstas' have a pretty narrow world view. They're not climbing in cars to raid small towns in the country. They don't even know places like Newbury exist."

"These guys knew."

Bender leveled at me a marble-eyed state trooper stare. "This is not about you returning the favor to these whacked-out criminal thugs. This is about helping the police solve a crime."

"I'm not into revenge. I'd like very much to see you lock them up so they don't come back to Newbury next time they're short of spending money."

Bender liked that answer enough to log onto the state police gang task force file and swivel his monitor so we both could read the screen.

The faces pictured made Ollie's burglars file look like greeters at the shopping mall. None had been in a very good mood when asked to pose. Most looked so scary you had to admire the photographer's courage. And yet, up close, under the scowls and behind the dead stares, many were almost children. Dangerous children, heavily armed, but children, who, had they been privileged to grow up in Newbury, might at worst be high-school dropouts.

When we'd finished with Waterbury, Bender scrolled files for Hartford and Bridgeport. By the time I'd slogged through them, my headache had ballooned to the proportions of a hangover steeped in discount bourbon.

"Want to see Norwalk?"

"Okay."

"You look like hell."

"Truth in packaging. Let's do Norwalk. Then I gotta crash."

We ran the Norwalk file, quickly, as its subjects were mostly black Jamaicans. I stood up, clutching his desk for support, and declined his invitation to peruse the Stamford gangs.

"Go to bed."

"Thanks for your help."

"I hope you're not driving."

"My limo's waiting."

Bender looked at me closely. "I'll have somebody drive you home. Pick up your car when you feel better."

"No, I'm serious. I really have a limo."

Bender walked me out to the street where Rita's driver was buffing an already-gleaming fender. "How'd—"

"Don't ask."

In the car, I said, "Excuse me, Charles," then raised the partition for privacy, telephoned Information, then Waterbury Hospital.

"May I speak with John Martello? He's a patient."

My Hispanic hadn't made the Waterbury gang file, but my Italian had: John Martello, alias Little John, alias Large John, alias Latin John.

Martello had owned a string of assault charges before some armed robbery landed him at Somers Correctional. There, probably, he had joined a Hispanic-Italian gang called the Latin Popes. According to Bender's file, the Popes were big in Waterbury.

"No, sir, we have no patient under that name."

"Martello. *M-a-r-t-e-l—*"

"No John Martello, sir."

"I was sure he was in. He hurt his foot pretty bad—could you switch me to Emergency Room?"

She switched me. Early afternoon must have been a slow time in Emergency, because I was answered by a resident who sounded unharried. "Martello," I said. "John Martello. They told me he's not checked in the hospital, but he came in with a broken ankle Saturday night."

"Hold on. . . . Nope. No John Martellos this week. You state police?"

I figured that an affirmative mumble couldn't really be construed as impersonating a police officer.

"Like we told you: The only ankle-foot injuries are a couple of old ladies, a construction worker who fell off a roof, and a ten-year-old who got his foot caught in the tracks."

"What construction worker?"

"Middle-aged guy. Nothing like what you wanted."

"Thanks."

I hung up and closed my eyes, still wondering how a ghetto gangsta had found my house to rob in a small town on the far side of his planet.

I woke up in my driveway with Charles murmuring, "You're home, Mr. Abbott."

Alison came running down the driveway and demanded to prop her little shoulder under me. Between the two of them, I got in the house and up the stairs. "Mom cleaned up the mess."

"Thank her for me."

"She couldn't get all the blood off the hall carpet."

"Well, it's an old Persian. They look bloody anyhow."

"You're disgusting, Ben."

I sat on the bed. "Muskrat, would you please take Charles down to the kitchen and find him some lunch and a cup of coffee? Charles, thanks for the ride."

Alone, I sagged back on the bed and worked up the energy to take off my clothes. I wasn't too surprised Martello hadn't shown up at the hospital; having sprayed gunfire at a state trooper, even the most mentally blighted would reason that the cops would be canvassing emergency rooms all over the state. Also, despite the satisfying crack when I twisted his ankle, young bones didn't snap that easily, and I very likely just tore some cartilage or popped out the joint, which his friends were quite capable of popping back.

The gang file had listed all sorts of known particulars, including hangouts. Martello's local watering hole was Ramos's Bar on Foundry Street. One of these days, when I felt a lot better than I did now, I would stop in Ramos's for a quick one.

# 13

"Knock, knock? How are you?"

Late-morning sun was pouring in my bedroom's side window. My head still hurt, but I was getting used to it, and Vicky looked fresh as the day in a scoop-neck cotton dress, so I said, "Fine, except I'm truly and totally and completely baffled."

She bounced into the room, gave me a little peck on the cheek, and made me lean forward while she fluffed my pillows. "Want coffee?"

"Not yet. How are you? Who's running the town?"

"What baffles you?"

"The Fisks' mystery guest."

"Oh, Ben. Not that again."

"It's bugging me."

"Drop it. You have to get better and sell some houses."

"I'm not showing any houses till they take the stitches out of my ear. I look like I'm made out of spare parts."

"Not to mention coming over to headquarters to give me a hand."

"I'll be on my feet tomorrow. But somehow . . . somehow."

"Drop it, silly."

"Can't."

"Or won't."

"Won't."

"Why? Why are you doing this?"

"Why am I doing this? . . . Friend of mine, back in the Academy? Matt Titus. Best sailor you ever saw. He *hated* any boat that wasn't going as fast as it should. He'd do sail changes until the winch grinders were vomiting. The way Matt was about slow-moving boats, I am about wanting to know what the hell is going on."

"In other words, you're a gossip."

"I am not a gossip."

"A typical small-town gossip. You're as bad as Marie Butler."

*"I am not!"*

"Okay."

"I mean that, Vicky."

"Fine."

"Gossips spread it around. Not me. I don't live off it. But point me at something like poor Reg and I want to know it all."

"Please stop."

"Why?"

"Ben, you're so goddamned selfish sometimes. Steve La France is this close to taking the nomination away from me. Every f—goddammed thing that goes wrong in town is my fault and right now you're turning a simple tragedy into a big deal."

"I am not."

"Everyone is talking about you going around asking stupid questions. Maybe *you* don't mind being taken for a fool—"

"Doesn't bother me in the slightest."

"But you're wrecking things for me.— Wait two weeks? Just two weeks. Shut up for two weeks. Let me lock Steve back in his Liquor Locker and then you can go around and ask every stupid question you want."

"Yeah, but after you get the nomination you'll be bugging me about the election in November."

"There isn't a Republican in Newbury I can't paint the walls with. But a conservative Democrat like that bastard—like my worthy opponent in the Liquor Locker—will split my party and get one of those goddamned Republican Butlers elected and then where will we all be? If you don't care about me, think of Alison."

"Alison?"

"She's a kid. The Republicans would rather send their kids to private school. Steve La France would prefer volunteers from the National Rifle Association teaching classes in a tent. I'm the only person who can convince people to pass a decent school budget and keep this town alive."

"Relax. You'll be governor before you know it. Do it by fiat."

"If I can't get re-nominated at this level, I'll never get a shot at governor and you know it. So back off. Okay?"

I didn't say anything, but I felt my head sort of nodding. Then the telephone rang. Vicky walked to the window and stared out at Main Street. Her dress dipped in back too, and I could see she was breathing hard.

"Hi, Ben. Greg Riggs over in Plainfield. How are you today?"

"Pretty good, Mr. Riggs. How are you?"

I have an old-fashioned stiff and prickly side to my personality that I blame on my Aunt Connie: I don't like people I've never met calling me by my first name, particularly on the telephone and especially when I have a splitting headache and am losing an argument with the government of Newbury.

"I guess you know who I am?"

"I've heard of you."

"And you're probably aware that I'm representing, or was, Janey Hopkins in her divorce action."

"I assume Reg's death moots that."

"I'm calling for a favor and I can imagine you can guess what that favor is."

"I'd rather not guess."

"It's this detective thing." Riggs waited for silence to loom, but in my day I'd paid for too many lawyers' Mercedes Benzes to fall for that one, so I waited, too, filling the time by admiring the sweet line of Vicky's back. Eventually, Greg Riggs broke his own silence.

"Look, Ben. Janey is really upset."

"I agree with you there," I said. "I don't know her as well as you, of course, but I think she's on the verge of falling apart."

"Well, with what she's been through, you're not surprised, are you?"

"Like I say, you know her better than I do."

"The thing is . . . Look, I'll level with you. I wish you'd drop it —she told me about hiring you. I'd be extremely grateful if you'd take your expenses and return the rest of her money and just let's all get on with our lives before this turns really messy."

"Messy?"

"You said it. The woman is ready to flip out."

"I already tried to return her money. She made it clear she'd hire somebody else. Figuring he might not be as marvelous a fellow as I, I told her I'd take another shot."

"I appreciate your honesty."

"Call it loyalty in this case."

"You mean Reg?"

"We were friends."

"I appreciate your loyalty as well as your honesty, but the fact remains this 'investigation' of yours is dragging out and delaying the whole process of recovery Janey's got to go through.— Look, I want to level with you."

I slid a little lower in bed and moved the phone from my ear, on the theory that when a lawyer offers twice in one minute to level with me I'm about to hear the sounds of silence. He confirmed my fear, after a dramatic pause, by stating even more dramatically, "Man to man, Ben?"

"Go, Mr. Riggs."

"A number of, shall we say, 'important' people are of the opinion I should run for public office." He didn't say which office. I didn't ask. I didn't want to sound hostile. I didn't want to annoy the man. He was destined to become a power in the county and it's bad business to alienate powers in the county.

"Without going into too many details on the telephone . . ."

"You're welcome to come over," I said.

"No, I see no reason why we can't wrap this up on the phone. What I'm trying to say is . . . When Janey hired me to handle her divorce, I wasn't exactly an unknown quantity. If you get my drift."

"Uh huh." Was I hearing right? Was this lawyer really stupid enough to plead his own mistress's divorce?

As if sensing my astonishment, he said, "I really love her. Very much. If this tragedy were allowed to fade away as such things do —as such tragedies should—I wouldn't have to face questions based on loose talk, if I decide to run for office."

No stranger to love and stupidity, I said, "Let me think about it. I've made her certain promises I can't break."

"I think I can control Janey."

"Well, I'll still have to think about it."

In a brisk, let's-wrap-up-this-meeting voice, designed to secure a tacit commitment, Riggs said, "Thanks, Ben. I know you'll see sense."

"I beg your pardon?" Empathy notwithstanding, and in spite of powers in the county, I was in no mood to be patronized by a sharpie from Plainfield.

"I mean I won't forget you've been sensible. I'll make it up to you, Ben. Throw something your way."

"How about a bone?"

"What?"

"Screw you." I slammed my phone down on the night table, with an impact that seemed to shatter my skull.

Vicky jumped.

"You told *Greg Riggs,* 'Screw you'?"

"Son of a bitch."

"He's hosting a fundraiser for me."

"I'll mail a check."

"Ben!"

"Did you know that Janey Hopkins's live-in divorce attorney had something going with her *before* she left Reg?"

"You *are* a gossip."

"Screw you too."

"*Ben!*"

"Sorry. Sorry. I didn't mean it."

"What did he say to get you so mad?"

"I'm going to find that woman in the woods if it kills me."

"Ben, you promised."

"No. There is something going on here I'm not getting." I sat up in bed, pounding my fist into my palm with a thud that made me wince and squeeze my temples. Vicky looked torn between sympathy and a desire to tear my heart out. So I winced again.

She came and sat beside me on the bed. Laying a cool finger on my brow, she said, "Ben. Listen to me."

"I promise I will do it quietly. More quietly than I have so far. But I am going to find out if she was at the party, if she was a she or he, and what he or she saw of Reg."

Vicky pressed a little harder. "Can I tell you a secret?"

"Sure."

"Really secret. You can't tell anybody."

"Cross my heart and hope to die."

"I'm not kidding."

"I give you my word."

"Guess who ran into the woods."

"Oh, no."

# 14

I was surprised the sun was still shining. It seemed to me as if Vicky and I had sat silently staring at the sheets for about ten hours.

Finally, I asked, "Did you see Reg?"

"Let me tell you what happened."

"And then maybe you'll tell me why you haven't told me before."

"Maybe I will," she said, coolly, in a clear announcement that, having bit this particular bullet, it was her bullet and she would chew it up or spit it out as she pleased.

Vicky stood up, circled the bed, grabbed hold of one of the posts, and hugged it to her chest. Her dress was snug on top, loose below her waist. She had pretty knees and perfect calves and Cinderella feet. Her arms were bare and shapely, her skin white, as she'd hardly been outdoors since the nominating challenge started. She had a few freckles with which, on occasion, we had played "connect the dots."

Most of her story, she told to the bedspread. Now and then she shook her curls, as if to rattle certain memories loose. Once she looked me full in the face, with an expression that said she was on her own and expected nothing from me. I felt I wanted to help her and then I felt guilty, realizing I'd had my chances to help her and hadn't.

"I was surprised when you left the cookout so early," she said.

"You inhaled some lamb and you were gone. I'd kind of thought you'd stay 'til nine and then maybe we'd hook up and go someplace."

"Yeah, well I had—"

"Whatever. Anyway, you were gone by seven. I had a couple beers. Three or four, actually, and I figured what the heck and drove back to town."

"You left too?"

"I went up to headquarters to get some work done."

Vicky came from a large Irish family. While they didn't drink beer for breakfast, she could call upon a certain capacity when in the mood. As I knew she could function clearly on four beers, I wondered why she mentioned the count.

"Tim was there."

If Tim Hall had his way, he'd marry Vicky and they'd live happily ever after, with Vicky running for higher and higher office while he managed her campaigns. His was both a romantic and practical dream, but Vicky was not cooperating.

"Tim wanted to go to the cookout. I realized I was starving; I hadn't eaten anything there. So we drove back out to the Fisks'. His car, because I shouldn't have been driving. The beers were hitting me on an empty stomach. We got there about eight-thirty.

"It looked like the whole town was there. All the burgers and sausages were gone and Duane had maybe one *morsel* of lamb left. Tim and I split it on a piece of bread and had a couple of beers.

"Duane and Michelle started trying to shut it down. People started sort of milling toward the cars. Tim and I ran into the Meadows brothers. They had a cooler in their pickup truck, and they're really generous and I was feeling no pain, so we had a couple in the driveway."

"We're up to eight beers."

"No, the Meadows had a Margarita mix. It was after nine o'clock. I've been really stressed for various reasons and I was finally feeling relaxed. Tim said he wanted to go. He was starving. He thought we ought to get a pizza. I thought I ought to have one more with the

Meadows. Tim couldn't, he was driving, but I wasn't, so why shouldn't I have one more? It was a beautiful night, warm and soft. And it's so dark out there. The Meadows were trying to show me the Milky Way and Tim got really bent out of shape. He's usually so damned *nice.* But not that night. Anyway, we had a few words and I finally told him to leave me alone.

"Tim went tearing off in his car. I didn't care. I could catch a ride with the Meadows. So we were standing there; there were still a lot of people, and Duane and Michelle were beginning to look put out.

"I decided to have another Margarita. The Meadows, not driving, joined me, and the three of us lay down on the lawn to check out the Milky Way some more, which didn't work too well because of all the headlights as people started driving home."

Vicky, still hugging my bedpost, shook her head. "Part of me was saying, 'This is kind of fun, lying in the grass between two handsome young fellows.' What are they, Ben, twenty-two?"

"Somewhere at that virile stage."

"I was having a ball. Another part of me, of course, was praying no headlights illuminated the candidate for renomination sprawled on the lawn with the Meadows brothers. And a third part was saying, 'Once all these headlights have gone, I'm possibly going to have to deal with these two handsome young men.' But with six beers and three Margaritas, I decided I'd cross that bridge when I had to. So I was watching the Milky Way and the Meadows were chatting away on either side of me, when I gradually began to hear what they're saying: They're wondering if I would give them a—"

"A what?" I asked.

"Guess."

"I don't want to."

"A contract to mow town lawns. Can you believe that?"

"Well, they are in the mowing business."

"Ben, am I ugly?"

"Not at all."

"Am I that *old?*"

"Still south of thirty."

"I asked myself both these questions, and as there was no one else I could ask, I decided, How about another Margarita? The Meadows ran and got it. There were just a few people left by then. It must have been almost ten and I suddenly had to pee. I noticed Duane and Michelle saying goodbye to another carload, so I headed for the house, trailing the Meadows, who were explaining why they deserved such a contract."

"Well, they do," I interjected. "They're the best mowers in Newbury."

"Yeah, well, they're not the best diplomats, and I suddenly said, 'You have some nerve getting me drunk to talk business.'

"They slunk off. I felt terrible, 'cause they're so young, but I had to pee so bad I thought I would die. So I ran to the house and slipped in the back door.

"Somebody was already in the mudroom bathroom. I headed for the front powder room. But I heard people talking and suddenly realized I might look slightly smashed."

"And grass-stained?"

"Let's just say I was not looking very First Selectmanish. It's a *big* house. They have a back stairs. I ran up it and found a guest bathroom."

Vicky straightened up, let go of the bedpost, and rubbed her face. "Boy was I blitzed. The walls started circling like sea gulls. I thought I was going to get sick. But it passed. And I guess after a while I fell asleep."

"In the bathroom?"

"It had this wonderful thick carpet. The *money* they spend!"

Nobody straight ever got rich in Newbury politics. Vicky's own home was a cute little cottage hidden behind the Congregational church. A New Yorker would recognize it as a smallish studio apartment partitioned into a one-bedroom.

"Nobody tried to use the bathroom?"

"I heard voices in the guest room. I quick crawled over and locked the door. It was a guest-room bathroom, inside the guest room, if you know what I mean."

"I've heard of such an arrangement."

Vicky was getting so distracted, she took no notice of my smart-assedness. "Two people were talking—a man and a woman."

"Recognize the voices?"

She gave me a none-of-your-business-you-filthy-gossip-and-besides-it's-not-germane look and grabbed the bedpost again.

"What were they talking about?"

"Tombstones."

"Okay, don't tell me. All I meant was were they talking about Reg."

"Tombstones were a drink Duane was mixing in the party-room bar. Brandy, vodka, bourbon, heavy cream—"

"Stop!"

"I almost threw up. Anyway, after a while they stopped talking and—figure it out for yourself. I was trapped in the bathroom, so I lay down again and I must have fallen asleep again. Next thing I knew, I was dreaming a jet was landing on the house."

I looked at her. "A jet?"

"It might have been a vacuum cleaner—one of those central vacuums? I heard yelling and doors slamming. Finally, I really woke up. I looked at my watch. I couldn't believe it. Three in the morning!"

" 'Wake up, little Susie!' "

"I lay there thinking, 'Oh God, oh God.' Finally it occurred to me, at three in the morning they'd all be asleep. I could just slip away. Right? *Wrong.* As soon as I opened the door I heard voices. A lot of voices. 'Oh God. Oh God!' So I said to myself, 'Vicky, you've got to be cool, got to be smart. Find out what's going on.'

"I listened real carefully. All the voices were coming from the kitchen. And they were all women's voices. No guys. So I thought, okay, like too many parties around here, the guys are in one room, the girls in the kitchen. That put the guys in the party room, 'cause

I couldn't hear them, and it's far away in that whole new wing they built.

"The women were talking really loudly. Michelle was practically screaming. And Georgia was crying. Susan was comforting her. And Sherry was arguing with Michelle, but not very hard."

"Arguing about what?"

"I couldn't tell, at first. It was just noise, downstairs. I thought maybe whoever snuck off to the guest room got caught."

"Wait. Wait. Wait. Three o'clock. They told me they all went home at one-ten."

"Three."

"Is it conceivable that maybe the Meadows Brothers rolled on your watch while entering their bid?"

"This is a perfect example of why people shouldn't keep guns in their house. If I had access to a gun right now, you'd be dead meat."

"Did you see three o'clock on any other clock?"

"Yes. There was a lighted alarm clock in the guest room that said three. Okay?"

"Okay."

"Jeez, Ben. If I didn't know better I'd think you were jealous."

"Okay, so at three o'clock the women are arguing in the kitchen. And the guys are in the party room."

"I *thought* they were in the party room. I snuck past the back stairs, down a hall to the front stairs—you know, that big, wide, open staircase with all the whatever you call that stuff."

"Banisters and balustrades. Some poor carpenter owed Duane a fortune. The way I heard it, they locked him in the house until he built that staircase."

"Well, he did a lousy job, because it creaked. And all of a sudden I heard Michelle yelling, 'Who's that?' And she and the rest of them came tearing out of the kitchen. Thank *God* the front door wasn't locked. They would have caught me if it was. But I got out the door and through the screen."

"They didn't see you?"

"No."

"Are you sure?"

"Positive."

"Not even a glimpse of your hair?"

"Well, maybe when they turned on the floodlights, but I don't think so, because by then I was quite a ways down the driveway."

"Running."

"That's when I remembered my car was at Tim's office."

"Is it possible you were still a little high on Margaritas?"

"For God's sake, Ben, I was high, sick, dead-tired, and scared. I mean, look—why was I running at all?"

"Good question."

"I just thought, 'I can't let anybody see me like this.' You know, I'm in a fishbowl. Then a car came along River Road. I thought, 'Jeez, I can get a ride.' Then I thought, 'Maybe I better not.' While I was debating, it turned into the drive."

"Did the driver see you?"

"No. As soon as I saw it start the turn, I ran into the trees. I thought, 'Oh God, what if it's one of them, went out for cigarettes or something?'"

"Who was it?"

"The men. Duane and Bill and Ted and Rick."

"All of them?"

"It was almost funny. They pulled up to the house, and Michelle and the rest were running around the lawn going, 'Did you see anybody?' So they turned the car around and pointed the lights at the woods. I heard them yelling, 'Quiet! Quiet! Listen!' So I stopped, and of course they never really got quiet enough to hear.

"And then I heard Michelle screaming—really screaming—there was somebody in the house. And the others are going, 'No, no, no,' and Duane is going, 'Get a grip,' and Michelle's screaming, 'Don't tell me to get a grip, you stupid bastard.'

"And then I heard Ted, real calm and slow. You know how his voice gets real low. Ted's going, 'Relax. It's over. It's over. All taken care of. Just calm down.'

"And Michelle's going, 'There was somebody in my effing house!'

and Ted says, 'Did any of you girls see anybody in the house?' And it's like, 'No, Ted. No. No.' All except Michelle, who goes, 'There's somebody in my effing house,' et cetera, et cetera, 'til finally Duane says, 'We're going to search the house.'

"They all went inside, looking over their shoulders, and I finally snuck through the trees and around the lights and onto the road and walked home."

"How long did that take?"

"Two hours. Every time a car came along I jumped into the bushes. It was almost light when I reached Main Street. I thought, 'Great. Just the image, First Selectman McLachlan stumbling home in a torn dress at five in the morning.' If anyone asked I figured I'd say I was up for early mass."

"You'll need more than the Catholic vote to win in this town."

She had gotten into her house without bumping into any early risers, stood under a hot shower for a while, slept a few hours, and made nine o'clock mass.

"*That's* why you were wearing sunglasses?"

"I had the hangover I deserved."

"And why you were so worried when you saw Trooper Moody head out of town?"

Vicky hugged the bedpost. "What do you mean?"

"I mean you were afraid something was up."

"What are you getting at?"

"Come on, Vicky. You knew *something* was up."

"*You* know as well as I—or ought to—that anything that would send Ollie charging out of town on Sunday morning was potentially a problem for me."

"I thought that at the time. But now, I think maybe you suspected some sort of special problem because of what you saw the night before."

"Like what?"

"Or heard in the kitchen."

Vicky picked up my night-table lamp, turned it on, tilted the bright bulb on her face. "Does this help, Officer?"

"Come on."

"Want to slap me around in the back room?"

"Go to hell."

"You have some nerve."

"*You* have some nerve. You watched me running around like an idiot and you never helped."

"I'm helping now. Aren't I?"

"Thank you, Vicky. What were the women talking about in Michelle's kitchen?"

"Listen, you've got to promise me something."

"I will not betray your trust. I will not use your name. I will not expose you in any way. I promise."

"That's not what I mean."

"What do you want me to promise?"

"Promise you won't hate me."

"For what?"

"For anything I tell you."

"Vicky, you're Catholic. You're already carrying more guilt than I could ever lay on you. I promise nothing you could tell me would make me hate you. Except if you killed Reg without a good reason."

"Don't even say that. I couldn't kill anybody."

"Did you see Reg?"

"Only at six-thirty, like I told you."

"So what's the big guilt?"

"Promise."

"Vicky, you're the most principled person I know, except for Aunt Connie. I promise I won't hate you."

"Okay. First, you've got to believe me that when I saw Trooper Moody that morning, I didn't know what he was going to find. Because I didn't understand what I'd heard in the kitchen. Even after we heard the radio, I didn't know. But when you came back to the Drover and told me about Reg, I knew."

"Knew what?"

She took a deep breath and slowly, coolly, told me what else she had heard. As she had said earlier, Michelle was doing the yelling, Sherry was mostly quiet, and Georgia Bowland was crying. Finally Ted's wife, Susan, the nurse, cut Michelle off and said, "I guarantee you he was gone. We did the only right thing."

"That's what I'm trying to tell her," shouted Michelle.

"Michelle, calm down. Georgia. Listen to me, Georgia. Nobody did anything wrong; it just happened. It's not our fault. We shouldn't have to pay for it."

"I'm goddamned not paying for it," said Michelle.

"None of us are," said Susan.

"We'll get caught," sobbed Georgia.

"No we won't. No one's going to get caught."

Vicky said, "Susan had the most soothing voice. A wonderful go-to-sleep-and-everything-will-be-okay nurse voice. It was remarkable. I've seen this in meetings—one person rises to the occasion and becomes the voice of reason. Well, that was Nurse Susan. Georgia stopped crying. Sherry stopped her mumbling—I never could hear what she was going on about. And Michelle began to taper off. At least until stupid me stepped on her creaky stairs."

"Pay for what?" I asked. "Sounds like somebody broke a vase."

"I'll let you figure that out, Mr. Investigator."

"I don't have to. You figured it out for me. If you didn't, you wouldn't feel so guilty."

"Doesn't it sound like Reg died at the party and the guys dumped his body in the covered bridge?"

"Sounds that way."

"The thing is, Ben, you wouldn't know any of this if I hadn't been there."

"That's for sure."

"And a lot of it is guessing. I mean, they could have been talking about something else. I mean, when I first heard Susan saying that thing about guaranteeing he was gone, I thought she meant one of the guys. Like one of the couples had had a fight."

"Like the couple, part of one of which was humping in the guest room?"

"Right. . . . But the main thing is—"

"The main thing is, First Selectman McLachlan was never there."

"It's probably a crime for me not to say anything. I'm a public official. I'm supposed to operate on a higher standard than everybody. Already, I've screwed up and maybe broken the law. But all I did was wake up drunk. Ben, I could lose everything. . . . Even if it's only an ethical lapse—Jesus, listen to me—'only.' I'm disgusting."

"Go to confession or something. I'll deal with the real stuff."

"Really?"

"Really."

"How can I thank you?"

"According to the doctor, it's going to be a week before I can participate in sincere thanks. Maybe we'll celebrate your renomination."

"What are you going to do?"

I looked out the window for a few minutes and then I said, "I think I'll go drinking with Pinkerton Chevalley."

# 15

Until my head got better all I could drink was club soda, which would be no problem, as Pink would be happy to drink for both of us.

"Your tab?" he asked, when I stopped by Chevalley Enterprises to make my offer.

"On me."

"Betty," he yelled. "I'm outta here."

Mechanics looked up, smiling. Pink noticed. "I'm still waiting for my screwdriver. . . . Let's go, Ben."

Outside, I said, "Before we go drinking, I'd like a quick look at Reg's Blazer."

"It's to hell and gone over in Plainfield."

"Won't take long."

"But it's locked up at the troopers'. I can't get in without a tow job."

"Put my Olds on the flatbed."

Muttering that we'd waste an hour and a half and maybe miss Happy Hour, Pink winched my Olds onto his flatbed wrecker.

"You got an extra cap?"

He found me a Chevalley Enterprises baseball cap drenched in transmission fluid.

We drove to Plainfield at a high rate of speed, yellow flashers blazing, and when the compound guard saw us coming he obligingly opened the gate. Pink wove through rows of confiscated automobiles, wrecked automobiles, and automobiles held for evidence in upcoming trials. Reg's was way in back, coated with pollen from a towering hemlock hedge that screened the lot from its neighbors. Heat shimmered from the sunbaked hood.

"Make it snappy."

The scratch that ran the length of the passenger side had grown a line of rust already. I inspected it fore and aft. Pink blew his horn.

The door wasn't locked. I opened it on an oven blast of hot air and looked inside. The glove compartment and the console hatch were empty. No sign of Reg: no drug stuff. Everything seized, presumably, for evidence. I found a discarded wrapper for latex surgical gloves, size eight and a half. Probably Doctor Steve's. Pink leaned on his horn again. I ran back to the wrecker. "Go."

Pink roared for the gate, but the guard had already shut it. He came out of his shack, eyes busy. "You forgot to unload the car."

"Goddamned winch broke," Pink growled. "Can't get the 'sucker off 'til I fix it."

"Where's the sticker?"

"Huh?" Pink loved a good scam, but he wasn't very quick. The missing orange state police sticker that should have been pasted to my Olds threw him badly. Pulling my cap low, I leaned past him and said, "I saw something blow off on 361. Looked orange. Thought it was a bird."

The guard wasn't that quick either; he wasn't a trooper, just an old guy with enough pull to get the job. He grumped.

Pink said, "Come on, buddy, I gotta get my truck fixed."

He grumped some more and opened the gate.

"All right!" Pink exulted.

We drove back to Chevalley Enterprises, offloaded my car, and transferred to Pink's pickup. I'd have preferred to drive on this outing; but Pink preferred his truck because it had a cooler in the cab for beers between stops.

"What were you looking for?" he asked as we headed for the White Birch.

"I wanted to see which end that scratch started on."

"Which end?"

"It was deepest in front, so I figured the guy with the church key started in front and walked toward the back."

"Makes sense," said Pink. "So what?"

"Tells me he was crossing the bridge leaving the reservation. Know any Indians?"

"Couple. Crazy 'suckers. How you know it was scratched on the bridge? Could have been done anywhere."

"Could have," I agreed. "Except I saw paint chips on the bridge."

We made Happy Hour with time to spare.

Pink bellied up to the bar. "Beer and a shot. On my father, here."

I told Wide Greg to run a tab.

Under such circumstances, your average guest would be eager to show his gratitude. He'd respond to attempts to make conversation and rise to every opportunity to please. Not Pink. He was Chevalley through and through: free drinks was an opportunity to be seized at speed before the fool buying regained his wits.

A big man, even bigger than Oliver Moody, Pink's capacity was enormous. And yet it was a relatively inexpensive afternoon, evening, and night as the ginmills he favored—and Wide Greg's biker bar was the toniest we patronized—catered to fortunes pegged at the minimum wage. He was known in each, and welcomed by management with the same weary resignation with which farmers greeted hail storms.

As darkness fell on our peregrine route—which I edged ever northward toward the Jervis woods and the Indian reservation—Pink encountered other large, taciturn, solitary men. Neither party seemed to find his mirror image particularly pleasing, and more than once in my concussed and scabbed condition I felt like a wart hog strolling the elephant walk between rival bulls.

At first, Pink ignored all of my small talk and most of my questions. But as his spirit intake mellowed him over the course of many hours, he revealed that he was stressing out at Chevalley Enterprises. Hardly surprising. Sustained work and a willingness to make decisions were not the hallmarks of Chevalley men, who, traditionally, left the thinking to the women and acted on impulse.

Once he did surprise me, harkening back to an earlier conversation: "That weren't no Indian."

A very long silence followed this announcement. Finally I asked, "Who weren't no Indian?"

"Scratched Reg's S10."

"How you figure that, Pink?"

"Son-of-a-bitchin' vandal was *leaving* the reservation. . . ."

"Yeah, Pink?"

"Kinda late for Indians goin' *out*— Drink up, Ben. Let's blow this joint."

Club soda, he noted at every refill, was a "pussy cure" for a concussion. His own prescription was tequila, until, up north on a dirt road off Route 7, we arrived at the River End Bar.

The River End was owned by Matthew Jervis, the only adult Jervis without a police record, which made him front man for the clan's forays into legitimate enterprise. House brew was a Newfoundland rum called Screech, aged aboard the same truck that delivered untaxed Canadian cigarettes. Screech, my cousin assured me, would fix what ailed.

Matthew agreed, claiming that Canadian fishermen subsisted for days on Screech.

"And never need no solid food," a bearded giant down the bar put in his two cents.

Pink Chevalley, red in the eye by now, stared hard.

The other patrons—a grandmother with a baby, and some car thieves arguing the merits of popping the lock cylinder versus smashing a window—looked over with interest, hoping the big guys would liven things up by removing each other's tattoos. Just then some pickup trucks pulled into the parking lot bearing customers I did not want scared off by a fight refereed by the state police.

"How about a round of Screech?" I asked.

Matthew Jervis hurriedly filled every glass on the bar. It tasted about the way it sounded, and appeared to crinkle the varnish wherever Matthew had splashed it in his haste. But it did make everyone friends of a sort, which was my intention. People started piling in and by ten-thirty, the joint was jumpin' as they fed the jukebox and danced to what came out.

The bearded giant turned out to be the Jervises' Canadian truck driver, and a dirt-track jockey like Pink. Soon they were locked in monosyllabic conversation punctuated by spontaneous bouts of arm-wrestling, which Pink won, while hinting over his shoulder that his glass was getting dry.

I had my own arms full with the car thieves—who had had a lot to drink and were demanding I settle an argument about removing The Club by bolt-cutting the steering wheel—and the babysitting grandmother venting her dissatisfaction with a daughter who "partied way too hard." As none of them knew anything new about a Blazer in the covered bridge, I excused myself and worked my way across the jammed-up dance floor to the jukebox, where an angular redhead in a tight blouse and tighter jeans was hesitating over her final selection.

"How about 'I Got Friends in Low Places'?"

Gwen Jervis moved her Bud bottle an inch from her lips.

"It's Benjamin Abbott III. What are you doing here? What in hell happened to your ear?"

She drowned my answer in a long, wet kiss which I returned with pleasure and one eye on the rapid approach of a broad-shouldered, sunburned guy flashing a gold nugget bracelet.

Gwen murmured into my mouth, "Buddy's home."

Her common-law husband and father of her two grown children worked as an oil-rig roustabout. His long disappearances allowed Gwen an independence enjoyed by few Jervis women. The fact that her villainous father, Old Herman, was clan leader emeritus and her brothers managed the criminal activities fortified her position.

Buddy had put on weight and lost hair. "Hi, Buddy. How's the Persian Gulf treating you?"

He ignored my hand and my greeting. "Next time you say hello to my wife, 'Hello' will do."

"For Godsake, Buddy, Ben's my cousin. . . . Well, almost. He's Pink's cousin—right, Ben?—and Pink is my cousin, so it stands to reason." She gave me a sexy smile, replaying the night many, many, many years ago when Pink had bought me a six-pack and propelled me in her direction for a sexual initiation that set a standard I'd aspired to ever since.

"He's no more your cousin than I'm your cousin," Buddy retorted.

"You *are* my cousin," Gwen reminded him. "And you're drunk," she added with some affection.

Buddy ran a callused hand over his mouth. "Oh yeah. Well, I don't give a damn. Seems to me, Ben, you ought'nta kiss a man's wife that way. And you watch your ass," he said, nudging her hard.

Gwen returned the steady gaze of an eagle grading woodchucks. She was missing a front tooth that Buddy had knocked out years ago. Buddy had spent the rest of that night in the care of a surgical team that specialized in puncture wounds. After which, the couple had declared a truce on the rough stuff.

"So, what happened to your ear?" Her people lived in a house-trailer encampment in the deep woods and tended not to subscribe to the *Danbury Republican.*

"Couple of guys broke into my house."

"That why you're here?"

"What do you mean?"

"Looking for them."

"No, they came up from Waterbury."

"So why aren't you in Waterbury?"

"I have to get back in shape first."

Gwen took a pull on her Bud, tongueing the bottle and enjoying my reaction. "So what are you doing here?"

"I'm wondering who might visit the Indians late on a Saturday night."

"Like the night your pal Reg ODed?"

"Yeah."

"I have no idea— Hey, Buddy! Dance with me."

She glanced back, just once, to make sure I was staring at her jeans, which I was, and disappeared onto the dance floor.

I returned to the bar, disappointed, but not particularly surprised. Gwen owed me little, and what she did she would never pay with information about her neighbors, much less her own.

In fact, after eight bars, a lot of driving, and a hundred bucks' worth of booze and club soda, the day and night were beginning to wear thin. What had started with promise—an easy look at the impounded Blazer—had deteriorated to a headache in a loud, smoky joint full of people having a better time than I was. All I wanted to do was crawl into bed. But first I had to pry my cousin off a stool he appeared welded to.

"Matt wants money," Pink welcomed me back to the bar. "We had another round—hell, Matt, while he's got his money out might as well pour some more. *Matthew!* More Screech! 'Less you want me and Zeke to come back there and get it ourselves—no, I didn't think so." He and the bearded Canadian shared a laugh, which was suddenly drowned out by loud cheers at the door. Shouts and whistles followed the newcomer across the room.

Pink stood up, peered over the crowd. "Son of a bitch, it's old Smokey."

"Who?"

"That's the Norfolk dude that chainsawed the Hitching Post bar." (We had stopped at the Hitching Post earlier, found it boarded up.) "Hey, Smokey! Haul ass over here and let me buy you a drink. Buy him a drink, Ben."

"Is that Freddy Butler with him?"

"Yeah, the little weasel— Pour fast, Matthew, if you don't want another exit. That's Smokey coming— Hey Smoke." Big palms smacked together and Smokey, clearly enjoying his new celebrity, greeted Pink like an old friend. They weren't old friends; it was more a matter of the Alien extending Godzilla professional courtesy.

Freddy Butler, oozing in Smokey's trail like a pet snake, gave me a condescending nod. We'd gone to grade school together, where the bicepally challenged Freddy always made friends with the bully. He was a Jervis hanger-on with no obvious job, though he drove a new truck. Now he'd palled up with a case-hardened woody from the north.

I heard Pink say, "Ben, my cousin, here," and Smokey offered a double-wide hand. "Nice to meet you. I worked for your dad on occasion; came down, cleared some lots for him. I was sorry when he passed away." Smokey was a weather-wrinkled forty or so, back-woods lanky, long arms like braided wire. His hazel eyes were opaque, which would mask what I imagined would be abrupt changes in his mood.

"Thank you. Pink thought you might enjoy a drink."

"Yup. Yup. That's not a bad idea at all. Hello, Matthew. Got any of that Screech left?"

I asked Freddy what he'd have and he wanted Screech too.

"Let the little bastard buy his own drinks," Pink rumbled in my ear, but the Hitching Post wasn't that far from the covered bridge, and, the way I heard it, Smokey's alterations had been executed after closing time the night Reg died.

Everyone threw back his Screech and no one protested when I suggested another. "All right," said Pink. "I've heard seventeen versions of what happened that night. Now I want to hear it from the horse's mouth."

"You shoulda been there," piped Freddy Butler. "It was neat."

"If I'd been there I wouldn't of asked," Pink growled. "So what happened, Smoke? Bastards wouldn't serve you? Too drunk?"

"I wasn't that drunk. But the bartender said it was five past one."

"Closing is one," Freddy noted.

"I said my watch must have stopped."

Smokey held up two bare wrists, and everybody laughed.

" 'How about a quick one?' "

"So the bartender goes, 'We're closed,' " said Freddy.

"So I say, 'Okay, I know you're closed. All we want is one drink.' "

Freddy said, "The bartender goes, 'The cash register is locked.' "

"So I say, 'Put the cash in a coffee can until the morning, only pour me and my friend a drink.' This is one surly son of a bitch." Smokey's eye fell on the grandmother with the baby. "Excuse me, ma'am," he touched his cap.

"So the bartender goes—"

Smokey cut Freddy off. "Can it. The bartender says we gotta leave. I said, 'I'm leaving as soon as I get a drink.' "

"You gotta be firm with these people," Pink agreed.

"Bartender says, 'Get the hell out.' Picks up one of them little sawed-off baseball bats. I said, 'Look, everybody in this piss hole is still finishing their last drink. It's not going to hurt to give me and my friend a drink.'

"He waves his bat in my face. I didn't like that, but I figured, okay, maybe the sorry 'sucker's had a bad day. So I say, 'Tell you what. We're going visiting anyhow'—I got an Indian gal I'm buddies with—'so sell me a couple of six-packs we can bring as a house present. Like decent, well-brought-up people do.' Man bangs the bat on the bar and says next time it's going to be my head."

Smokey drained his Screech and looked around expectantly. I motioned Matthew, who came quickly.

"Thank you, Ben. . . . Now, I should explain he's doing this in front of people some of which I know personally. Couple of little Freddy's cousins, and their buddy Pete Stock. So he's not only threatening me, he's embarrassing me. Well, I blew my stack."

"I'd have blown it a lot faster," said Pink.

Smokey nodded. "Yes, you would. Anyway, I told Freddy to stand by the door in case the son of a bitch—excuse me, ma'am—tried to lock me out, and I went out to the truck to get a saw."

"Which one?" asked Pink.

"I would have preferred my Stiel, except it had a brand new chain, and I expected I'd run into nails. So I grabbed my old Husqvarna."

"Good tool," said Pink.

"The Husky's a quiet tool, yeah, but the Stiel is your better saw. 'Course, these days a lot of people go for the Jonsered."

"I won't buy a foreign tool."

"Where you think the Husky's made?"

"Alaska."

"Anyway, when I get to the door, poor Freddy's on the wrong side and it's locked."

"He hit me with the bat," said Freddy.

Everyone looked at Freddy; no one believed him.

"Not only was the door locked, it was one of them steel ones Stanley makes. So first thing I had to do was cut a new door. That didn't take long and I walked through the wall and there was the bartender on the phone to the cops, so I sawed the phone off the wall and then I got busy on the bar. Boy, you should have heard the noise. It was *loud* in there."

"Thought you said the Husky's a quiet tool."

"I forgot my earmuffs."

"Sawed it in half," yelled Freddy. "Right in half."

"I made two cuts thirty-six inches apart, to make Freddy a path. Told Freddy to grab a couple of six-packs and drop some money on the register. I mean, I wanted it clear we weren't talking robbery here."

"Entirely different situation," said Pink.

"Tell you one thing."

"What's that?"

"Since then, I never recall so many friendly bartenders. Second I'm in the door, there's a glass waiting."

"Was your lady friend grateful?" I asked.

"What's that, Ben? Oh, my Indian gal? She was pleased. I left Freddy to sleep in the truck and had a couple of beers with her. Left her the rest except one for the road."

"Wasn't that the night Reg Hopkins died?"

Smokey laughed. "Well, that was the funniest damned thing of all." He looked around.

The jukebox was screeching Mary-Chapin Carpenter and the car thieves had joined the dancing. Smokey's immediate audience included Pink and Matthew, the grandmother, Canada Zeke, and me, working hard at maintaining an appearance of casual interest.

"Don't pass this on, but this is the funniest thing you ever heard. Freddy and I start home, but when we get to the covered bridge, the 'sucker's blocked. There's this Chevy S10 sitting inside. Okay?

"Freddy here sticks his head out the window and yells, 'Move that goddamned truck.' Nothing. I notice the headlights are on, burned down to cats' eyes. Battery's dying. Freddy yells again, 'Move that goddamned truck or we'll saw it in half.' I say, 'Hold on, Freddy. First of all, I'm done sawing tonight. Second, man who parked there probably had a reason. We're just going to leave him and go around the long way.' 'Long way,' yells Freddy. 'That's twenty miles.' Well, it ain't, but it's a ways."

"I left my car at the Hitching Post," Freddy explained. "I thought the cops might take it."

"Freddy starts arguing with me. I said, 'Son, if you want to cross that bridge, you can walk, but I'm driving around.' Freddy starts yelling, 'Push it off the bridge. Push him out of the way.'

"Why didn't you?" asked Pink.

"You know, Pink, sometimes you reach a point of an evening when you just don't feel up to it. I just wanted a peaceful drive, finish my beer, and fall asleep. Nice warm night, I didn't want the aggravation. And like I say, I had a feeling the fellow in the Blazer wanted to be there."

"What time was that?" I asked.

"Three-thirty, maybe four, four-thirty. Hell, could have been five."

"But it was after three."

"Huh? Oh, had to be, counting the time at the Hitching Post and the time with my gal. Right, Freddy?"

"I was sleeping."

"Well, I wasn't. Anyway, Freddy decides he's going to walk to the Hitching Post. Not that anybody was thinking that clearly by then.

I said suit yourself. So I turned the truck around and the last I see of Freddy, he's walking across the covered bridge.

"Now get this. Next day I'm up early. Never made it home. Fell asleep in the truck. So I drive back down to Newbury for some breakfast at the White Birch. Some dude comes in and says the cops found poor Reg Hopkins dead in the covered bridge. Don't you see? That was *his* Blazer. Reg was in it. Dead. So I call up Freddy and ask his mother to wake him and he gets on the phone and I say, 'Hey, turkey. You know that Blazer you wanted to push? There was a dead body in it.' "

"I thought he was shitting me," said Freddy.

Smokey winked a hazel eye. "I said, 'Freddy. I hope you didn't leave your fingerprints on that Blazer. 'Cause if the cops find 'em, you're in deep trouble.'

"Freddy starts crying. 'I didn't do nothing. I didn't do nothing.' Pink, you should have heard him. He's begging me, 'Don't tell I was there. Don't tell I was there.' And I said, 'I don't have to tell if you left your fingerprints. They'll call you.' 'I didn't touch it,' says Freddy. 'I swear I didn't.' "

"I didn't," said Freddy. "But I was scared until Smokey started laughing. You really had me going there, Smokey."

While everyone was laughing, I asked Freddy, "What did you scratch it with, a can opener?"

"Car keys— Hey. What? *What?*"

"Wha'd you say, Ben?" asked Smokey, and Pink looked puzzled.

"You crossed the bridge into the reservation about two and there was no Blazer on the bridge. When you came back between three and five, it was blocking the bridge."

"The devil are you talking about, son?"

"I'm wondering when Reg arrived at the bridge."

"What scratch?" asked Freddy. "I didn't scratch nothing."

"What scratch?" asked Smokey.

Pink glared uncertainly through a haze of Screech. Finally, he said, "Oh, that scratch," and fell silent.

"You are making me jumpy," said Smokey.

"How's that?" I asked.

"You been following me around or something?"

"I saw a long scratch on Reg's Blazer."

"What were *you* doing there?"

"Heard the police call on the scanner. Drove out for a look. Anyway, Pink towed it into Plainfield pound and we were talking about the scratch. Now you tell this story and I figured it was Freddy who scratched it, being in a bad mood because he had to walk home."

Smokey clamped a big hand on my shoulder. Matthew Jervis found spills to wipe at the far end of his bar and the grandmother shielded her baby. The last thing I needed was another hit in the head, so I glanced at Pink, who said, "Let him go."

"When he explains what the hell—"

I heard an explosion like a gunshot point-blank. Smokey flew off his stool and landed on his back, motionless, his face red as a tomato where Pink had slapped him.

"Let's go, Ben. Man's got a lot of friends here."

We walked unhurriedly, but resolutely, across the dance floor, toward the door. We got some looks, but nobody made a move, except Gwen Jervis, who blew me a kiss.

In the parking lot, I said, "Thanks for the help."

Pink tossed me his keys. "Needed the ride home. I'm too shit-faced to drive."

I woke him outside his trailer in Frenchtown. He belched Screech and groaned, previewing his hangover.

"By the way, what can I tell Aunt Connie about the rattle in the Lincoln?"

"You gotta know now?"

"I'm going to have breakfast with her in the morning. I'd like to give her some good news, before I hit her up for a favor."

Pink swayed like a Sequoia in an earthquake. "Tell her . . . Tell her I'm going to tear that 'sucker down to the rocker panels if I have to. Tell her when I'm through with that mother—"

# 16

"Chevalley Enterprises stands by their warranty," I said, ladling a third portion of Connie's raspberry preserves. "Pink guarantees he'll fix that rattle."

"He's been guaranteeing for months now and it still rattles. Now for *whom* do you want me to give a dinner party?"

It was seven-thirty in Connie's morning room. Warm summer air drifted in the french doors. Yellow walls reflected sunlight dappling through an elm tree. House finches and chickadees nattered at a feeder.

Connie had already walked to the General Store for her *Wall Street Journal,* which she had been reading in neatly folded sections when I arrived. Coffee, tea, and toast were spread on a sideboard, and it appeared to me that Pink had been right about the medicinal qualities of Screech: My headache had diminished to the growl of a backhoe chewing on the other side of a hill. Which was just as well, as I had run into resistance.

"I told you. The Fisks, the Carters, the Bowlands, and the Barretts."

"But I don't know them."

"Of course you know them. Duane and Michelle Fisk own Newbury Pre-cast. Bill Carter the builder. Ted Barrett's the shop teacher—you know, the builder who went broke. The Bowlands are new; Rick works for IBM. He was cooking with me at the cookout. Remember? Button-down? You said he reminded you of *The Man in the Gray Flannel Suit.*"

"I don't *know* them."

"You've known Duane and Bill and Ted since they were kids." Newbury boys learned the work ethic raking Connie Abbott's lawn.

"You *know* what I mean, Benjamin."

I did, of course, know what she meant. Although she was a fierce democrat in the small "d" sense—her commitment exceeded only by her generosity toward charities and institutions that championed equal opportunity—Louis XIV would have felt right at home at her dinner table, where guests had to be known by family, long acquaintance, laudable achievement, or sterling introduction. Wealth was not considered a laudable achievement and, in fact, fortunes accumulated since the Civil War were a liability.

"I really need a favor, Aunt Connie. I'm betting eight people can't sustain a lie. At a dinner party I could trap all four couples in one place at the same time. If I can shake them up so they think I know more than I do, they'll fill in the empty spaces."

I had kept my word to Vicky. Not even to Aunt Connie would I name Vicky as the mystery guest, although I had filled her in on everything else I had learned since our last chat when she recommended I query gossip-queen Marie Butler.

Connie returned a shrewd look. "I looked up the word *nepotism* the other day. Did you know that it means, literally, favoritism shown to nephews?"

"It's a wonderful word, Connie. And I'm willing to pull nepotistical rank to settle up with whoever dumped Reg in that bridge."

"Perhaps you'd better explain why you can't give this dinner party in your own house."

"For one thing, it's pretty hard for a single guy to serve eight people alone. Beer and pizza won't lock them up the way you could in your dining room."

"Victoria McLachlan would be delighted to act as your hostess."

Connie held Vicky in high regard and followed her career with keen interest, while on the personal side, she thought Vicky was an ideal candidate to take me off the streets.

"They won't come to my house. They'll know right away I'm still chasing Reg."

"I can't very well invite them here, only to reveal you lurking under the tablecloth."

"They'll know I'm coming, but they have to accept your invitation."

"Oh, Ben, nobody cares about those old rules any more. Least not these people. Though Ted Barrett was an especially well-mannered young fellow—and quite handsome— No, if you want them to accept my invitation knowing you'll be here, you'll need juicier bait than dinner with what passes for *grande dame*dom in these parts."

"Like what?"

"What exactly do you want out of this evening?"

I told her.

"To what end?"

I told her that, too.

"Excellent. Either way you'll do justice. I suggest the following. I'll invite them—"

"Thank you. Thank you. Thank you."

"And you will spread a little white lie. Not a real lie. Just a hint that will make it impossible for them not to accept."

"You're reading my mind."

"Of course." Connie fixed me with her blue-eyed gaze like a buck in headlights. "What does that crowd want more than anything?"

"Land."

"That's why you want *me* to host your party. . . ." She smiled with genuine affection. "You're reasonably intelligent, when you put your mind to it."

"Are you by any chance patronizing me?"

"Do you think they'll bring cocaine?"

"*What?*"

"I'm joking, Nephew. I've heard drugs are not unknown in their set."

"I thought you don't listen to gossip."

"I didn't say I was deaf."

The next day I was drinking midmorning coffee outside the General Store when Michelle Fisk pulled up in her red Audi and tennis togs that revealed suntanned thighs firmer than I would have guessed. She tossed a sheet of Connie's pale green fold-over note paper on my table and demanded, "What in hell is this?"

"It's a dinner invitation. I got one too."

Aunt Connie had had them hand-delivered, kindness of Alison Mealy's girls-only Main Street bicycle gang.

"What's it supposed to mean?"

"Dinner on Saturday night. Cocktails at seven."

"Why would 'Miss Constance Abbott' invite us? We're not in her circle, in case you hadn't noticed. What are you up to, Ben?"

"She invited me, you and Duane, Ted and Susan, Bill and Sherry, and Rick and Georgia. I see a pattern. I'm surprised you don't— and I'm not talking about your Jacuzzi party."

"Then what?"

"Just because she's old doesn't mean she doesn't keep up. She knows who does subdivisions in Newbury."

Michelle sank to the bentwood chair beside mine. "Jesus, she owns more land than God."

"God panicked when the market collapsed. Connie bought."

"But years ago we tried to buy some and her lawyer, that old judge, told us to take a hike. He wasn't even nice about it."

"I don't know what to say. She's not getting any younger. Looking at probate. She supports a ton of charities, maybe she and the judge figure liquidating would make it easier to give it away."

"So where do you come in?"

"Well, I'm a grand nephew, and I *am* a real estate agent."

"Big bucks commissions."

"Not if I know Connie. She'll knock me down to three percent, if I'm lucky."

Michelle laughed. "Wow. Oh, wow. I hope you're right."

"Hey, I'm just guessing. But when she told me the guest list, that's what came to mind."

"Oh my God," she breathed. Then, suddenly: "Ohmigod what'll I wear? Ben, what do you wear to her house?"

"Good question. Saturday night . . . Written invitation . . . Dining room . . . Four or five courses. I mean, you could wear anything neat and clean, of course, but if you want to please her . . ."

"We do."

"Right. Well, I, for instance, will probably wear a light-colored sports coat, shoes, socks, pants, long-sleeve shirt—she *hates* not seeing cuffs—and a pleasant necktie."

"I can't get Duane in a tie."

I frowned. "Similar party last year—Saturday, written invites—this artsy fundraiser showed up dressed like a janitor in a flag factory."

"What happened?"

"Connie was perfectly polite. But he'll never be invited back; and the charity he represented received a strong hint they should review their hiring practices. Last I heard, he got transferred to Minneapolis."

"Are you putting me on?"

"Only a little— Hey, listen, maybe this is genuinely social. She likes young people, likes staying in touch. It could have nothing to do with her thousands of acres. But, whichever, I'll tell you this: You'll have a very interesting time. She's done it all and she knows everybody. But whatever you do, don't push the land thing. Let her do it her way."

Then I said something that under any other circumstances would have been just plain cruel: "She's always enjoyed stylish women."

Michelle drove off, somewhat pale, and I settled back, confident the guests would arrive tense.

"Oh my," said Connie. "Aren't they lovely?"

We'd been sharing dry sherry in the living room, and debating who'd show first, when Ted and Susan Barrett came up the walk like the wholesome vision of a lost America: Ted dark and handsome, Susan blond and beautiful. They were tall and slim, dressed with the understated care parishioners put into their Sunday best, and holding hands.

Halfway to the door, Susan stopped and faced Ted and struck the universal how-do-I-look pose. Ted stepped back and studied her. Whatever he said pleased her; he took her hand again, kissed it, and led her proudly to the door.

"Good luck tonight," said Connie.

We were old hands at hosting dinner parties. Like Masai hunters tracking lion, we worked by glances, nods, and long-established understandings. She took her place, perched upright, dead center, on a green velvet recamier. I went to the foyer.

Through the sidelight I saw the Barretts exchange wary looks that changed to party smiles as the door swung open.

"Come in. You look lovely, Susan. Hi Ted."

He and I shook hands a little self-consciously, the near-murder of each other at Gill Farm still fresh in our minds. Then I took Susan's hand.

Most women friends I would kiss on the cheek; but Susan Barrett's beauty could be off-putting. I would no sooner kiss her without a clear invitation than finger a Botticelli at the Metropolitan Museum of Art. Tonight I noticed a difference in her deep, warm eyes, a sort of shield raised by the other Susan—the nurse trained to be ice when shrapnel flew.

I led them to Connie, who drew them effortlessly into what had to be the most interesting conversation they had ever had about the uncommonly dry weather. Susan had brought her a little bouquet of rosemary and tarragon. Before the doorbell rang again, Connie had Susan describing her garden and both Barretts enthralled by a history of the West Street cottage they had moved to when Ted filed Chapter Eleven.

I opened the door to Rick and Georgia Bowland—Rick nervous and overdressed in a dark business suit, Georgia a little fragile in a silk blouse, a flower in her honey hair, and a whiff of expensive gin on her breath.

"What a beautiful house, Ben. You're so nice to invite us."

She handed me an antique perfume bottle filled with fresh lavender blooms. "Our nanny turns out to be a gardener."

She had done something very soft with her hair, perfect for a summer evening. When Rick started tugging his little mustache, she stopped him with a hand on his elbow and inquired in her pleasantly low voice, "To whom does one make lewd overtures to get a drink around here?"

I suspected that Georgia, too, was nervous. She didn't broadcast it like Rick, but she seemed almost frightened. What I didn't know was whether they were anxious about meeting Connie, or swinging a land deal, or had something to hide.

"Come meet Connie."

Georgia took my arm and stage-whispered, "Are there any *verboten* topics?"

"Beg pardon?"

"I too have an elderly aunt. We do not discuss Democrats or shopping malls."

"I'd avoid your 'I Believe in Steve' campaign, unless you want an earful about the La Frances. She thinks the world of Vicky."

"Got it. Thanks."

Connie welcomed them into the living room, exclaimed over the pretty bouquet, and assured an anxious Rick that she preferred "Connie" to "Ms. Abbott." Georgia had done her homework and Connie beamed when she dropped the name of one of her old friends from Greenwich.

I poured white wine for Ted and Susan, gin and tonics for the Bowlands, and hurried back to the foyer as Bill and Sherry Carter and Duane and Michelle Fisk piled out of Michelle's Audi. Duane handed over the keys and they came up Connie's broad walk, two by two.

Observing through the sidelight, I had the distinct impression that both Duane and Bill had been hogtied by their women to be shaved, hair-trimmed, and cravatted. Just before they reached the steps, Michelle turned Duane briskly west, straightened his tie by the light of the setting sun, and gave his shoulder a firm pat.

Sherry did much the same for her husband, although she ended her inspection with a kiss on Bill's nose. Bill returned a friendly swat to a behind rendered doubly intriguing by snug white slacks and a filmy jacket.

I opened the door. "Hi, everybody. Come on in."

Michelle led the way. She looked alert, though not as wary as the Bowlands and the Barretts.

"Are we the first?"

"No, the last. Come on in." I kissed her cheek. "Neat dress."

"You think so?"

"Perfect." I was really beginning to get a thing about her amiable roundness and snapping black eyes. She seemed confident that a dress for Saturday night at the country club, toned down, would pass muster on Main Street.

"Duane, how are you?" *His* black eye was healing nicely, a lot faster than my various wounds, but then I hadn't received mine from a considerate friend. It didn't seem to trouble him as much as the dress code.

"I'm fine, except this goddamned tie feels like a boa constrictor." An O-ring of neck fat squeezed by his collar suggested that his dress shirt pre-dated his recent weight gain.

"Hurts to be beautiful, Duane. How are you, Bill?"

"Doing great!— Here, we all chipped in." He thrust a magnum of Moët in my hands. "Real nice of your aunt to invite us."

"Come on in and tell her yourself. She'll love your champagne." In fact, she did not approve of extravagant hostess presents. "Hi, Sherry."

Sherry pranced up the steps, proud as a cat. It seemed she always put me in mind of animals—tonight a cat; an egret at an auction; a gazelle in the Grand Union. These images had less to do with my own predilections than Sherry's unabashed delight in herself. It was just possible that she flirted out of kindness, confident she was doing men a favor. Maybe that was why Bill never seemed jealous.

"Ben." She gave me the secret picnic smile.

I kissed her pretty cheek, took her hand, and said, "You look lovely."

"I cut my hair."

"Very appealing." I was a long-hair man myself, but she had a shapely head.

"Bill says I look like a boy."

"No boy I ever saw."

"Hear that, Bill? Ben doesn't think I look like a boy."

"I didn't mean *all* of you. Just your head."

"Come on in and meet Aunt Connie."

Bill lumbered after us, grinning happily, and emitted a low whistle when he caught sight of the living room. Connie's decorating technique was, simply put, to arrange artfully loot brought home by generations of sea captains.

She was on her feet, in the midst of the Bowlands and Barretts. (She had taught me when I was thirteen that the only reasons to ever sit during cocktails were either the insistence of your hostess or a grave need for medical attention.) I made introductions and drinks: white wine for the ladies, rye and ginger for Duane, and a beer for Bill; and topped up our sherries.

I jump-started conversations, refilled glasses, lit candles as the night came down, and passed the skimpy hors d'oeuvres. Connie didn't hold with the modern concept of lavish hors d'oeuvres. Green olives stuffed with pimento, peanuts, and smears of anchovy paste on cucumber had sufficed for President Coolidge and they would suffice tonight.

It appeared she was right. The room came alive with talk and laughter. Our guests grew expansive, shedding the tensions of the work week, which began to seem long, long ago. Connie sparkled: the color rose in her cheeks; her white hair glowed like a tradewind cloud.

Phyllis—who had served dinner for Connie since before I was born—caught my eye from the dining-room door. I nodded to Connie. She wound up an anecdote about an irascible old farmer who had sold her his pastures, and asked Ted if he would take her in to the dining room.

Arm in arm they marched off, and arm in arm the rest of us trailed. Sherry Carter said, "Ben, this is so neat. She's terrific."

"She's having a great time."

"Is she really *ninety?*"

"We tend not to home in on exact numbers, but my dad told me she ran away from boarding school to nurse the boys in World War One."

"Wow." She squeezed me tight. "Hey, this is fun. Thanks for asking us.— Oh, God. Look at the table."

Connie's dining room was ablaze in candlelight from a chandelier, wall sconces and a forest of candlesticks. We'd set placemats instead of a tablecloth for a summer night, and the polished cherry wood reflected the flames like General Washington's campfires.

Serious discussion had gone into the placecards. Connie sat at the head near the kitchen door, of course; I took the opposite end. She had demanded Ted Barrett on her right, insisting, "The least you can do is allow me a handsome man." In that spirit, I had opted for Michelle and Sherry on my right and left. She took Rick Bowland on her left, because he was new to her acquaintance. That put Susan beside Rick, then Bill. Across from them, Georgia sat beside Ted, with Duane between her and Sherry.

Phyllis served cold leek soup and then a salad the rabbits had overlooked in my garden. I helped clear, and poured red wine while she brought in the main course.

There was a standard dinner party menu in town, which I'd always called Newbury Stew, although the actual name and recipe varied socially and generationally. The older, well-fixed crowd served up a standard—very standard—*boeuf bourguignon* at its parties, where talk was always more important than the food. The graying and fraying yuppie generation cooked their Newbury stew with veal and oranges and called it marengo. While if you were invited for Newbury Stew at the Chevalleys', you'd encounter possum, woodchuck and anything else that couldn't get off the road fast enough. Connie's Newbury Stew was of the first variety and tonight's had turned out characteristically dry.

It didn't matter. Watching our guests' faces—the women savoring the beautiful room, basking in the glow of old silver and ancient china, the men loosening up on good wine and full plates—it struck me that this gathering of suspects had turned into the best party of the summer.

The long clock in the front hall struck ten.

"Well, my dears. It's time for an old woman to go to bed."

Our guests rose hastily.

"Please don't rush off. There's port and brandy in the library, after you sort out your designated drivers. Ben, I had Mrs. Mealy lay a fire; you'll light it if the ladies are cold. Good night, everyone. I'm delighted you could come."

During the chorus of thank yous, Duane and Michelle exchanged a puzzled look that I interpreted to read, What about the land?

"We'll talk in the library," I whispered to Michelle.

She gave Duane a reassuring nod. Connie concluded a grand retreat with an ascent up her curving stair. I started herding my mob toward the library when halfway to the landing Connie turned to say, "Susan? The Dufy I was telling you about? Come up for a quick look."

Susan glided up the steps like a woman born to Federal mansions and boudoirs hung with renegade Impressionists. Ted followed her with his eyes. He saw me notice and said, "I'm the luckiest son of a bitch in town."

I agreed to that. Then, worrying vaguely what Connie was up to, I guided the others into the library. "Oh, I love this," said Georgia. "Is it okay to light the fire, Ben?"

I opened the flue and touched a long wooden match to the newspaper Mrs. Mealy had crumpled under the kindling. The old chimney usually smoked, but tonight it was on its best behavior and the flames enveloped the logs with the thinnest whiff of sweet black birch.

My guests had dispersed into twosomes, peering at the calf-bound volumes, inspecting Connie's ornate Chippendale secretary, delighting over the brass fittings on her father's old captain's desk.

"So what was this about brandy?" boomed Bill Carter.

"Who's driving?"

"We'll ride with Duane. Ted and Susan walked, right Ted?"

"It's a short crawl," said Ted.

"We'll call our babysitter's boyfriend," said Rick.

"Duane?"

"I'm driving," Michelle answered for him. "I'll just have some more coffee, if you've got some."

I poured for her from a silver pot on a warmer and pressed brandy on Bill and Sherry and Duane. Georgia's request for "something with a kick" elicited a worried glance from Rick.

"I've got the makings of a mean Tombstone, if Duane'll mix it for you." Duane gave me a doubtful look and shared another with Michelle. Georgia opted for Bailey's Irish Cream. Ted asked for port and thought Susan would have some too. She came in a moment later and joined me at the desk where Connie had arranged the bar on a tray.

"Did the Dufy pass muster?"

"She just needed help with a zipper. I really like her."

"She seemed to like you too."

"She invited me over for tea. It's so funny. She's older than my grandmother, but it's like we could be friends."

"Port?"

"Thank you." She touched my arm. "Ben?" she said quietly. "Ted told me what happened out at Gill Farm."

"No problem. We worked it out."

"He came home shaking. He was so afraid of what he almost did."

"It's not a problem. It's over."

"Jesus," Bill cried from across the room. "What a life! You ever think what it's going to be like when you live here, Ben?"

"Billy!" said Sherry.

"Ben knows what I mean. She's a great old lady, but she can't live forever. Ben's her only relative, right?"

"I'm afraid I'll have to buy my ticket like everyone else."

"Huh?"

"She's giving it to the town. It's going to be a museum."

Rick Bowland wanted to know if the painting in the dining room was a Whistler. I told him it was.

"What's a Whistler?" asked Duane. "Hey, Michelle, can I take this goddamned tie off?"

"Go ahead."

"The Whistler is a portrait of Connie's Aunt Martha."

"What about the landscapes in the living room?"

"The one with the buck is Landseer, an English painter. The really neat Hudson River job is by Church."

"Tell me the birch trees in the foyer is Levinson."

"More likely school of."

"What kind of security does she have?"

"If you touch the frame, electric shocks are delivered direct to Trooper Moody's mattress and car seat."

Bill Carter laughed. "A museum? Why not? Share it, right?"

"I'd keep it," said Michelle. "Wouldn't you, Sherry?"

"I'd open it for the house tour Christmas week and maybe for Newbury Days, if we ever get that off the ground."

"Me too," said Susan. "If Ted didn't mind."

"Long as they wipe their feet."

I eased over to the mantelpiece, propped an elbow, squire-like. Now that I had them, I had to figure out what to do with them. "Okay, gang. Let's get down to it."

That sounded a little clumsy to my ear, but they didn't notice. They thought I was talking about land.

"Yeah," said Duane. "What's she selling?"

"I want to guess," said Michelle. "It's that two hundred acres on Morris Mountain, isn't it? The Fulton place?"

Duane said, "If she'd let go that stretch on Church Hill Road, we could throw up a six-screen multiplex. Have to widen Main Street for the traffic. Zoning'll go nuts, but hey— Ben, you get Ted and Rick to go along on a little variance and you'll have commissions up the wazoo."

Half in the bag on merlot and decent brandy, Duane was probably speaking louder than he meant to. Everyone turned to me for my reaction.

To my surprise, I heard myself talking about land too—talking in the stern tones of my ancestors.

"Neither Connie Abbott nor I would desecrate Main Street."

"Just a few trees."

"No way."

"Then what the hell are we talking about here?" Duane asked. "Wha'd you get us to this dinner for?"

I was half a mind to ask him what he was complaining about. He had scoffed down double portions of high-class Newbury stew, and exerted a near-tidal force on Connie's wine cellar; but Michelle, too, looked suspicious, and Susan and Sherry seemed disappointed. Ted's face was a solemn mask. Bill looked at Rick and shrugged his big shoulders.

I said quickly, "I didn't mean to get your hopes too high."

"Is she selling land or not?" Michelle demanded.

Good question. I pretended to give it my full attention and a funny thing happened. Suddenly I was acting the part of a real estate agent and spewing out fiction with a ring of truth: "Too bad Reg isn't here. We were batting around an idea about Connie forming a land trust."

"A *land trust?*" echoed Bill Carter. Not a phrase to make your average builder happy, conjuring visions of acreage off limits to backhoes.

Duane growled, "Reg never said 'land trust' to me."

"It didn't have to do with you. It had to do with Connie. This is Connie's deal. She's concerned with the future—not today, but tomorrow. We're talking long term here."

Another phrase far from the hearts of Bill and Duane.

"What kind of long term?"

Winging it—within the context of serious problems Newbury would face in a future without Connie Abbott—I said, "She owns a lot of land, much of it undeveloped. Her resources are not bottomless. Nor is her estate totally immune from death taxes. A trust requires funds to preserve it. If you guys could offer some sort of package, where you'd get a small part of her holdings in return for helping to protect the vast majority, you might find her amenable."

"Really?" asked Michelle.

"She'd particularly like to see some of the old farms kept going."

"Gee, I don't know," said Bill.

"Listen—you guys are the future. Newbury will pass out of her hands. We live here. We make our livings here. We've got a chance to preserve it. At least think about it."

"We'll think about it," said Michelle.

Duane said, "I can't believe Reg never said a word about this."

Now was the time: and I said quietly, almost gently, "Reg Hopkins died in your house, Duane."

"What—"

"I'm sorry. He ODed at your kitchen table."

"He left alive."

"Every one of you saw him dead."

"No!"

I looked them each in the face. "I don't blame you for panicking.

You were high on Duane's Tombstones. You were scared you'd be implicated in a *heroin* death. Christ, who needs that in Newbury? So instead of calling the cops, you decided to dump his body."

"That's not true," said Michelle.

"Duane, and Rick, and Bill, and Ted threw him in his Blazer and drove him out to the covered bridge."

Duane said, "You are out of your *mind*, man."

"And while the guys were dumping him, Michelle and Georgia and Sherry and Susan cleaned up the house. The men got back at three-fifteen. Michelle, you got a bit jumpy and thought somebody was in the house. You all searched, found no one, and by four or so everyone had split."

The only sound in the room was the fire crackling. I prayed one of them would ask a question I could turn to my advantage. But all eight stared at me, silent and accusing, as if I had done them wrong.

# 17

Back when I played timber wolf to the bulls and bears, investors who failed to study the prospectus might see their stock sink like an anvil in a pond. The trick to writing a prospectus, wherein the law required disclosure of any and all bad news, was to lose the bad news in a blizzard of facts. Thus had I blitzed my friends with every detail I had learned and guessed about their night with Reg.

Unfortunately, I was pledged to protect my main source—Vicky —while almost nothing from the chainsaw wizard would withstand close scrutiny.

"You are full of it," said Rick. He glanced at Georgia, who was shaking her head.

Ted was silent, dark eyes watchful. Susan had drifted near him.

Sherry Carter snaked an arm around Bill's shoulder. Bill said, "Jesus, Ben, you are all hosed up."

"Am I, Bill? Why don't you run that by the guys who chainsawed the Hitching Post?"

"Huh?" He looked at Duane, in apparent amazement. Duane shrugged.

"After they renovated the bar, they went over to the Indian reservation to celebrate. When they tried to get off, you guys were blocking the bridge."

No one did me the favor of retorting something stupid, like, Nobody saw us. For an eon or two I leaned on Connie's mantel while my brain chanted, Eight people can't sustain a lie.

But the silence deepened. Eyes averted, faces turned inward, they had time to think, to wait me out, or guess I had no more bombshells to drop on them. Had I lost the momentum? I felt their resolve hardening, like a chill penetrating the old house.

"No way," Duane said.

Then, when I thought I'd lost them, Georgia Bowland started to cry—God love her gin-addled soul. She sniffled at first, like a child. Then her body began to heave. Tears trickled through her makeup and splashed dark stains on her blouse.

They all looked at her, protests dying on their lips.

"I told you we'd get caught," she sobbed. "I told you. I—"

"Shut up!" said Duane.

Georgia cried harder. Duane moved toward her, his beefy frame in a threatening crouch. I went to block him, but Rick got to his wife first and laid a protective hand on her shoulder. "Leave her alone."

Georgia sank to the couch, crying, "I told you, I told you."

"Shut up!" Duane shouted at her. "Jesus, you're the one who told Ben."

"I did *not!*"

*"You told him!"*

Rick shoved the bigger man away. "Back off, Duane."

Duane straight-armed him. "Just try it, Rick. Give me an excuse."

Bill crossed the room like lightning, hands high.

I stepped among them. "Let's not break up Aunt Connie's furniture."

For an awful while, Georgia sobbed and we all stood around like spectators at a car wreck.

Duane recovered first. "I'm outta here. Come on, Michelle— Don't try to stop me, Ben."

"Can I tell Trooper Moody you're going straight home?"

"You son of a bitch."

"I told you," wailed Georgia.

*"Will you stop that goddamned crying?"*

Georgia sprang to her feet, pushed Rick aside, and yelled into Duane's face. *"You* cried, Duane. You cried like a baby. You're the only one who can cry? Screw you."

Duane got red. "Yeah, I cried. . . ." Then he sighed and the life seemed to drain out of him. "You're right, Georgia. I'm sorry. I'm sorry, Georgia. I really am. Reg looked so . . ."

Georgia sat back down on the couch. Duane sank beside her and stared at the carpet.

I said, "Just for the record, I never talked to Georgia."

Michelle was gazing at Duane with a strange, almost weary expression. Now she turned on me, eyes flaring. "Ben, what are you doing to us?"

The rest of them stared at me.

"What are you doing to us?" she said again, louder.

"Did you ever think of taking him to the hospital?"

"He was *dead.*"

"Were you afraid to call 911? Couldn't call an ambulance? Try to save him?"

"Susan said he was dead."

Susan stepped close, crossed her arms, and looked me in the eye. "Ben, I'm a nurse. The man was dead. He wasn't breathing. His heart had stopped. I tried to CPR him anyway, but I knew he was dead. When we found him his irises were dilated like saucers."

She sounded absolutely positive, but I kept thinking, What if Reg had had one more breath hiding in his body? I felt I owed him these questions. "I thought irises *constrict* when you're on dope."

"Only when you're alive. When your *brain* dies they open wide. Believe me, Ben. He was dead."

Duane spoke at the carpet. "I couldn't believe it. I kept thinking all we had to do was artificial respiration or CPR or something. Susan shined a light in his eyes. It was like looking down a hole."

I didn't know what to say.

"The guy was gone, Ben. He just died in my kitchen."

I'd hoped this evening would bring some sensible answers about Reg. But all I was hearing was stuff they'd already gone through looking for their own sensible answers. And there was no satisfaction in that.

"What are you going to do, Ben?"

What was *I* going to do?

"I'm going to start by advising *you* guys to go to the cops before they come to you. Fess up. Tell 'em what happened. Hire a good lawyer. It'll be messy, but better than waiting for all sorts of obstruction-of-justice charges landing on you like a ton of bricks."

"What about Janey?" asked Michelle.

"I've got to tell Janey that Reg did indeed definitely die of a heroin OD. What else can I tell her? I wish to hell I could give her better news."

"Are you going to tell her about us?"

"Don't you think she'll figure that out on her own when you go to the cops?"

"Do we have to?" asked Bill. His plaintive abused-bear expression reminded me of fourth grade, when, for some infraction, we were sent out on a cold day to beat erasers.

"Do you have to what?"

"Go to the cops?"

"If you don't I will. Cause now you've got *me* in this damned mess. I know *exactly* what happened. I have a certain responsibility to report what sounds a lot like a crime."

"Ben," Ted said quietly, "no one knows but us." He took Susan's hand.

"*I* found out."

"No one else is asking questions," said Rick Bowland. He was trying to sound indignant, but he was rubbing his mustache like poison ivy.

"Ben, please," said Sherry, nervously crossing and uncrossing her legs, smoothing her slacks over her knees.

"No. I have to ask *you*, please. I didn't do it. You all did. I'm just trying to help out Janey and I end up in the middle of this mess."

Rick, again: "If you'll stop feeding Janey Hopkins false hope, she won't push the insurance company and they'll have no reason to investigate."

Michelle waited until the others ran down. She contained her earlier anger and appeared almost subdued as she ran her fingers through her short black hair.

"Ben, there is nothing to be gained by turning us in. Like we said before, Reg is dead. Putting us through hell won't bring him back."

"That's right," said Rick. "Ben, IBM is firing people by the thousands. I stand a chance to be *promoted*—up above it. You know what the guys competing would do with my picture in the paper? They'll fax it to every district manager in the *world*. Please. I'm telling you I'm dead if this gets out."

I looked at Ted.

"I already told you what'll happen to me, Ben," he said quietly. "Same goes for Susan at the daycare."

"Just when we were getting back on our feet," Susan whispered.

Bill Carter said, "There isn't a son of a bitch born who can fire me; but I gotta wonder what my banks will do if they think I'm facing charges."

"I don't wonder," said Sherry. "They'll call in our loans and shut us down."

Duane was still staring at the floor. I looked at Michelle, who was worrying the fringe on one of Connie's reading lamps. She gazed back, her eyes brave.

"I'm not worried about the business. Duane's done a hell of a job getting us established. Anybody gets high and mighty with us, they'll wish they hadn't. And I really don't give a *fuck* about my reputation in Newbury. But my kids have to ride the school bus and sit in class. Kids are cruel, Ben. My children'll pay the price— It wasn't our fault! Reg crashed our party and died in our house. The ultimate party crash. Funny, isn't it? He checks out and ruins our lives at the same time. I wonder if he planned it."

Duane looked up. "Give the guy a break."

"We're still his victims," Michelle retorted. "It doesn't seem fair. Jesus, every time we gave a party, every time we had people over, *he'd* show up!"

"Hey, the guy was my best friend. Your best friend's allowed to drop in when he wants. I did the same with him. Okay?"

"No, it wasn't okay. I couldn't do anything without him showing up. He spoiled—"

"Will you let him alone, for God's sake. He's dead."

"Yeah, he's dead. And now he's killing us— Ben . . ." She looked back at me again, pleading, fighting to build a smile. "Ben, isn't there something we could work out? . . . Like maybe me and Sherry and Susan and Georgia could sleep with you for a night."

Seven jaws dropped—eight, counting mine. Sixteen eyes popped wide. Connie's library hadn't been so quiet since her father died at his desk.

"Okay, a weekend."

Sherry, Susan, and Georgia edged nearer their husbands.

Michelle raked her hair.

"That was a *joke*, everybody. I'm just trying to lighten this up a little so we can work something out. Oh, shit, now I've made things worse. Georgia, *please* stop crying. . . ."

By this point I was feeling sorry for everyone. I didn't know what I would have done in their situation that night. I *hoped* I would have dialed 911 even if he seemed dead as ice. But, half in the bag and shocked and frightened of the consequences—and more than a little angry at Reg for dumping the mess of his life on mine—I might have done just what they did: screamed and carried on and eventually got ahold of myself and taken charge and schemed to save my innocent skin.

"I have a question," I said. "It's a tough one, but I've got to ask it."

"What?" Michelle asked, when the others failed to respond.

"Who sent Janey Hopkins a picture of her children with a threatening note?"

Jaws sagged again, and even lower when Michelle raised her hand and said, "Guilty!"

"*You?*"

"It was stupid, foolish, dumb, and all the other things I do when I get scared. I really was scared. I thought—stupidly—it would make her go away."

"Michelle?" Sherry wailed. "How could you?"

"What did you write?" Susan asked, clearly appalled.

"I don't remember. It wasn't really threatening, like I'll kidnap them or anything. Was it, Ben?"

"I don't believe you did that," Georgia sobbed. Then, swatting with both hands at her tears, she shouted, "You're terrible! How could you threaten children?"

Michelle hung her head, stared at the floor, and in the deathly silence struggled to regain her composure. Her voice trembling, she said, "I didn't threaten them, Georgia. I didn't say anything like I'd hurt them or anything. Did I, Ben?"

"No," I admitted. "Nothing like that. On the other hand, you figure out how you'd react if it was your kids in the picture."

"See? I didn't *mean* it."

"I'd kill you if you did that to my child," said Georgia. "I'd kill you." Rick laid a calming hand on her shoulder. Georgia flung it off.

Michelle faced her. "Georgia, I hate myself for doing that. Please understand. I'm sorry."

"You should be."

"Ben?" Michelle asked. "Will you tell Janey I'm really, really sorry?"

"I think you better tell her yourself."

She hung her head again and hugged herself. "It was the worst thing I've ever done in my life. If I could do anything to undo it . . ."

"I'll let you tell her."

"But what about the cops?" asked Bill Carter.

Ted let go of Susan's hand and moved close to me, his usually strong, sure face wracked by a twitching eyelid. "Ben," he pleaded, "we are innocent of everything but stupidity. Can't we convince you of that?"

All I could do was shrug. "You don't have to convince me. It's hard to imagine eight dumber people. Though if I put myself in your shoes—tired, drunk, scared, and shocked—I'd probably do something as stupid. Fortunately, I'm not the one who has to live with it; you do."

"Live with what?" shouted Rick. "We didn't do anything wrong. Anyone who stopped to think about it would have done the same. It wasn't stupid. It was the only way out of a mess that wasn't our fault."

"Help us, Ben?" said Georgia. "Please."

"I don't know how to play God."

"I wish somebody would," growled Bill Carter. "Then we'd get a break."

I wandered back to the mantel, scuffed the granite hearthstone with a twelve-year-old Gucci loafer—spoils of a past life—and looked up at their worried faces. I saw lots of fear, but damned little guilt. They all had plenty to lose, but none seemed to believe they deserved to.

"Why don't we sit down, everybody, and let's talk— Would anyone like more coffee? Brandy, anyone? Georgia, how about another Bailey's?" I presided over refills and passed a tray of mints, and got them comfortable.

I wanted them clumped together in the el of the two couches so I could see all their expressions at once. But there wasn't room for eight, so I had to settle for Bill, the biggest, standing behind the couches, and Michelle lowering herself crosslegged to the carpet in front.

"I'll make you a deal."

"Name it," said Bill. "Anything you want, except Sherry."

"Michelle was kidding. I'm not."

Rick Bowland broke the silence. "Where are you going with this?"

"Call this blackmail, if you like."

That got looks, some wary, some hopeful, all intense, focused directly at me.

"But first, one more tough question: Who here knows John Martello?"

# 18

I had an offer in mind—a proposal fair and just that fit the situation—but first I wanted to make damned sure no one had hired a pair of beat-down specialists to drive me off the case.

Eight expressions are tough to read all at once. The women looked blank, the guys puzzled. All but Bill Carter, who said, "Yeah, I know him."

"You do?"

"Sure, he's a stonemason down in Westport. I haven't used him in years. Hell of a mechanic, but really expensive. Bids like he's making Tiffany watches and won't come down a cent."

"I'm thinking of John Martello from Waterbury."

"No, he's from Westport—'less he moved. His kind of work is mostly high-end stuff down on the shore. You know, Greenwich, Darien. But what does he—"

"My guy's about twenty, twenty-five years old."

"No way. John's gotta be fifty by now. He had a grown son."

"Where does *he* live?"

"Got killed by a backhoe. Jumped into a trench and the bucket crushed his skull."

"What is this?" asked Duane.

I returned a sour look. My bright idea was dying on a coincidence.

"What's this got to do with a deal?" asked Rick.

"Yeah, what are you talking about, Ben?"

"John Martello—alias Little John—was one of the sons of bitches who broke into my house last week. He seemed an odd candidate for a Main Street burglar, and I just wanted to make sure he hadn't been nudged in my direction by somebody who wanted me to stop asking questions about Reg."

"You're accusing one of us?" Duane asked.

"One of you sent the note to Janey. Why not one of you trying to shut my big mouth with John Martello's fist?"

"You're paranoid."

"Paranoid? These guys almost killed me. Want to see my X-rays?"

"Don't blame us. Next time lock your door," said Duane.

As they complained and I defended, I studied their faces. Not one appeared even mildly guilty. Duane and Michelle Fisk seemed outraged; the Barretts, the Bowlands, and the Carters were obviously most worried about my "deal" to save them from exposure.

The indignation died down, the accusations trailed off. Finally, I entered a silent space. "Here's the deal: You cut Janey in on the Mount Pleasant development. Set it up as a trust fund for the kids. What would have been Reg's piece, if he were alive to work with you, goes to the children."

Ted Barrett said, "That's not enough money to change their lives, Ben."

"It's not the money. It's so the kids'll know Dad's partners and friends respected him enough to look after them. No matter what they hear about Dad and dope—and they'll hear plenty, growing up around here—they'll always know that some important people in Newbury were proud to be his partner."

Duane looked at Michelle, then Bill. With a shrug, he said, "Sounds good to me."

"Me too," said Bill. Ted nodded. So did Rick.

"Yeah," said Michelle, "though we better put some sort of a cap on the money, in case it really takes off."

An expression of raw hatred flashed across Duane's face. "Michelle. Shut up."

They left quickly, avoiding one another's eyes. Only Georgia murmured a ritual Thank you. All but Michelle Fisk seemed relieved; she looked sullen. As we said goodnight, I gave Duane a sympathetic slap on the shoulder. He could not have been looking forward to the rest of the evening. The other couples hurried home holding hands—though in Rick's case it was an effort to keep Georgia upright.

Phyllis had cleared the dining room and cleaned up the kitchen.

I rescued half a bottle of merlot she had corked in the refrigerator and carried it and a wineglass into the library, where I wandered, browsing titles. I settled for a while in front of a tall bookcase home to Emerson, Thoreau, Alcott and the Channings, and a priceless complete collection of *The Dial.*

Vaguely dissatisfied, I felt in no mood for romantic insight. Like the Transcendentalists, I'd been playing fast and loose with logic, and leaning too much on intuition.

Doctor Greenan had warned me that bangs on my head could stir up some bouts of depression; made to order beside the Transcendentalists sat the often comedic Melville. I started to pry *Moby-Dick* loose from its neighbors, when I heard a loud creak and felt the wall move.

I had had a couple of dizzy spells, and thought this was another, as Ralph Waldo and Henry David appeared to sway into the room. I backed up and steadied myself on a couch, then jumped and nearly fell over it. The bookcase was pivoting outward on rusty hinges.

Through the hole it made in the stacks stepped Aunt Connie, saying, "I thought it went quite well."

She had changed into a quilted robe buttoned to the chin, a little sleeping cap, and airline slippers on her tiny feet.

*"Where did you come from?"*

"This house was a station on the Underground Railroad," she

said, swinging the bookshelf door shut before I could see into the hiding space. "I thought you knew. We were on the line to Canada."

"For runaway slaves?"

"My grandfather was an Abolitionist, you know that."

"How'd you get inside?"

"A stairway from my dressing-room closet."

I felt a funny sense of rejection. "How come you never showed me when I was a kid? Kids love hiding places."

"It's not a playroom."

I shrugged. "So you heard what happened?"

"Yes. I heard. I'm curious: What would you have done if Duane had walked out? Would you have told Trooper Moody?"

I shook my head. "I'm not a snitch."

Her lips pursed in annoyance. "Must you use jailhouse talk? Couldn't you say—oh, I don't know—tattletale?"

"Okay, I'm not a tattletale. Would you like a brandy?"

"No, thank you. I'll heat some milk."

"I'll do it." I brought back warm milk in a cup and saucer. (Connie wouldn't keep a mug in the house.) I sat with her on the couch while she drank it.

"But what about your *legal* responsibility?"

"Bluff. There is no legal responsibility to report a crime."

"Are you quite sure?"

"Absolutely. I checked with Tim Hall. You have to answer truthfully if questioned, but there is no obligation to volunteer."

"Well, there darned well should be. . . ."

"All I know, Connie, is their basic claim is solid: Why should they take the heat for what Reg did wrong?"

"Would you have gone along if you were there?"

"I think I would have called the ambulance. But that's easy for me to say. I don't teach school. I don't work for a corporation."

"It would have an effect on your business."

"I can't judge them."

"But you *have* judged them, by letting them off the hook."

"You knew I planned to."

"It was your decision. Yours to sleep with. . . . You know, dear, I take back what I said about your second career. To do it well, you must lie and dissemble. Maybe you ought to stick to selling houses."

"I didn't go looking for this."

"Well, anyhow, it's over. Isn't it?" She cocked her head to observe my reaction. "Isn't it?"

"What do you mean, 'isn't it'? Of course it's over."

"Then why are you sitting there like a puzzled beagle?"

"I beg your pardon?"

"You look like a dog in a washtub, wondering how he got there."

"I'm kind of tired. And a little headachy. And a little down."

"Go get some sleep. I'm tired too." She rose with her empty cup.

I took it. "I'll lock up. Talk to you in the morning. Thanks very much for the party."

"Thank *you*. I had a lovely time. I really must try and get out with more people."

"Connie?"

"What is it?"

"Did anything anyone said strike you the wrong way?"

Connie considered my question. "Not that I can recall—except, of course, that awful Fisk woman. Can you imagine! Frightening those children's mother? Good Lord."

"Did you believe her reason?"

"I believe there are people who can justify *any* behavior. Absolutely appalling. You will *not* invite her back." She paused and added, "She's definitely the powerhouse in *that* family."

"They're a pretty good team. Newbury Pre-cast is earning a fortune."

"One has to feel sympathy for Susan Barrett. What an awful position they put her in, being a nurse. I thought she handled herself very well."

"I gather you enjoyed Susan."

"Lovely girl. Ethereal. She might have floated out of Keats. There is something so compelling about a woman in love with her husband."

"What did you think of Sherry Carter?" I had meant her behavior in the library, but Connie said, only, "She has a roving eye. Of which, I imagine, you're aware."

Hastily, I asked her opinion of Georgia Bowland.

"Georgia will lose her looks to drink." She yawned. "Her husband strikes me as the sort that hides in his work."

In the front hall, at the bottom of the staircase, I kissed her soft cheek.

"I had such a good time," she said. "You know what made me happy? The Newbury boys. Ted and Bill and Duane. Exactly the same boys they were when they were ten years old. It's remarkable how little they change. I've noticed the same with Scooter. I see him walk down to the paper in the morning. But if I blinked my eyes he could be pedaling his bicycle to school."

I waited for her to tell me I hadn't changed either, that I was still whatever I was when I used to run across Main Street for our weekly afternoon tea. But Connie was done with the past.

"Good night, Ben. I hope you're not too keyed up to sleep."

I washed her cup and locked the kitchen door. A flashlight was plugged into a charger by the door. I took it with me and, turning off lamps in the dining and living rooms, worked my way back to the library. I found a latch in the kickplate under the Transcendentalists and eased the hidden door open slowly, to quiet the hinges.

Inside a cubbyhole that smelled of dry rot, I saw a narrow, rough wooden staircase spiral into the dark. I pulled the door shut to get a sense of what it felt like to hide in it, and sat on the only place to sit, the second tread of the stairs. By the flashlight I saw a candle sconce and a smoke smudge on the wall. Beside it were the words, written in lampblack: "Joshua Morgan—Christmas 1857—Bound for the promised land."

Others less literate had smeared crosses and Xes. I sat awhile, playing the light over them, and adding up the years. The presence of a secret room seemed odd. The house had been built in 1784, seventy-three years *before* lucky Joshua Morgan's escape.

The Revolution had been won, the British oppressor banished, and there hadn't been a peep out of the poor Indians for twenty years. So I doubted the space had been intended for hiding people. Stolen property—pirate loot—was more like it.

Did my ancestors include Newbury's leading fence?

Back when Main Street was muddy Newbury Pike, had pirates and highwaymen tied their horses behind the barn and knocked on my door with stolen lockets? Had Abbotts presided in my kitchen over those meetings between comfortable and poor which, like muggings, evictions, and dope scores, engendered no love even though both parties were bound as lovers to meet again?

As these were not questions I intended to take up with Connie, I poked the light into every nook, hunting evidence of ancestral malfeasance. I found instead a Magic Marker-ed peace sign from the Vietnam War, drawn in the trembling hand of a draft resister seeking sanctuary in Canada.

I went home to bed, marveling that Aunt Connie's Abolitionist grandfather would have been proud—secure in the knowledge that Great-aunt Connie couldn't show little Benjamin her Underground Railroad while there was a train in the station.

She was right. I was too keyed up to sleep. At one-thirty I took a chance and called Rita and got her machine at both numbers. At two-thirty I went downstairs and tried the milk trick. By four I had read the *Manchester Guardian Weekly* cover to cover, including the cricket scores. At four-fifteen I began to think that if this didn't end before the first bird sang I'd get up and brew some coffee. And indeed, as a summer dawn bathed Main Street in a blue-violet glow and the birds took up choral works, I found myself shivering over a mug in the back yard, wondering why I hadn't felt this off-balance since a woman who had worked for me on Wall Street—and whom I'd loved—had unburdened herself to a United States attorney all too eager to grant absolution in exchange for her confession of my sins.

It was Connie's fault, her "It's over. Isn't it?" remark. She had lived so long she was almost clairvoyant. She had picked up on some doubt bugging me. "It's over. Isn't it?" She was usually awake at dawn. I could go over and wring her neck. Then maybe I could get some sleep.

I ambushed her as she came up the street with her Sunday *Times* and asked her what she'd meant.

"Nothing."

"Nothing?" I echoed.

"Nothing. Except, they did have time to prepare a united front after they accepted my invitation. Didn't they?"

# 19

Had I been hustled?

I remembered my first days on the Street. There were guys who trolled for new kids—who took them under their wing, showed them the ropes, offered them a chance to sell a few million bucks of bonds at a price the new kid might not realize was just a little inflated. Or they would offer an opportunity to *buy* a security that an older hand might recognize by its resemblance to a boulder rolling toward a cliff.

Maybe I was just dodging a final chore. I hated to confront Janey Hopkins and say "Sorry. He hotloaded. He's exactly what everyone says. A poor lonely alcoholic who ODed on heroin."

Janey was done fighting. I knew the instant I walked into the Hopkins Septic office, and saw her hunched over a desk strewn with bills, that somewhere along the line she had finally accepted the truth. She greeted me as if I were a landlord come to evict her.

I gave her a check for nine hundred dollars, keeping seven hundred and fifty to cover my time. I told her what she already knew, that there was no doubt what had killed Reg. She nodded glumly. But she perked up when I told her that Duane and the rest planned to funnel Reg's share of the Mount Pleasant development into a trust fund for her children.

"That's wonderful! Did you make them do that?"

"No, no, no," I lied. "They have kids too. I think they thought through the implications. Don't count on a lot of money but—"

"That's okay. It's the thought— But who sent that note?"

"It was harmless."

"Harmless?"

"There was no danger to your children. Trust me. When you find out who sent it, you'll almost laugh."

She shrugged. "The kids will be better off with my mom this summer."

I got up to go. "I'm sorry about the insurance."

"So am I. It would have made such a difference."

"What are you going to do?"

She started to say, I don't know, but instead suddenly straightened up and asked out of the blue, "Do you know Peter Stock?"

"Very well."

"What do you think of him?"

"As what?"

"A worker."

"I don't think he's going anywhere pumping gas for Buzz, but he's young. He's got time. Last year he did night school for his diploma."

"He used to help Reg. He's good with machines. Never beat 'em up. . . . I'm thinking of hiring him."

"What for?"

"Maybe I'll get the business going."

"Excellent. You have the rep, Janey. If you can just hold it together, hire a few good people . . . Pete's a good start. Good luck."

She smiled the first smile I'd seen on her since the funeral. "Like Reg used to say, we'll never run short of product."

"It's a *great* idea."

"Greg doesn't think so."

"Tell Greg if he wants to go into politics it can't hurt to have a rich wife."

"Rich? I just want to pay my bills." She looked at my check. "Did you charge me enough?"

"Plenty."

"I don't want favors. You were very supportive."

I said, "You can do me a favor."

"Name it."

"Let me see that telephone bill."

It was still in the SNET envelope, unopened. Janey picked it up. "Why?"

"Just curious about something."

She looked a little skeptical, but she did hand it over. I slit it open with my penknife. Out fell all the extra paper the Southern New England had stuffed in, and the bill itself.

As Hopkins Septic was a local business, there were few long-distance calls.

The phone rang. Janey answered it. I motioned toward the Canon fax machine. She nodded and I ran the long-distance sheets through it, producing a curly but legible copy. Then I waved goodbye and walked back to my office.

On the day Reg died—after disappearing from six-thirty at night until a little after eleven, presumably to score heroin—he had placed no calls to Hartford, no calls to Bridgeport, no calls to Waterbury, and three calls to a number in Norwalk. I dialed the Norwalk number, wondering how a heroin dealer answered the phone. I got an answering machine with a recording by a man with a big voice:

"Norwalk PVC Pipe. We can't come to the phone because we're loading the truck. Leave your name and number and we'll call you back when we're done loading the truck."

I looked up Norwalk PVC Pipe in the Yellow Pages. The phone number matched. They sold pipe.

The only other long-distance call that Saturday was a 212 New York City number. Reg had called it at noon. I called it. A harried voice I couldn't understand said something against a background of restaurant noise. I yelled Hello, he yelled Hello. I asked could I make a reservation. He said Hold on. Four or five minutes later, another busy person picked up and asked politely if he could help. I told him I was waiting to make a reservation. He asked when.

"Tonight."

"Nothing before nine-thirty."

I said I'd take the nine-thirty, knowing full well I'd be fortunate to sit before ten if the joint was as successful as it sounded.

"Where are you exactly?"

He rattled off a Washington Street address.

"What is that, West Village?"

"Tribeca."

"And how exactly do you spell the restaurant's name?"

"B-r-a-s-s-é-e."

"Brassée? What does that mean?"

"I don't know. I just started here."

I looked it up in Cassell's. It meant "armful."

The round-trip drive to New York would explain the two hundred miles on the Blazer. He wouldn't have had time for much of a dinner, much less time to score his dope. The last time I'd been in Tribeca it hadn't struck me as a place to do that, but the nice thing about New York is that there's something for everyone everywhere.

I telephoned Rita, got her machine at both numbers, and left the same message: "Would you like to have a late dinner in New York, tonight?"

Then I went to the bank and cashed a check for a stack of crisp new twenty-dollar bills—tips for tips—which I folded into my money clip. Back in my office, I cut Reg's photograph from the *Clarion.*

Duane Fisk telephoned. He spoke not a word about last night but went straight to business. It was like breakfast with a stranger, afraid to ask, Exactly what happened before we passed out?

Was I still interested in handling the Mount Pleasant subdivision? I told him I was, and spent a little time writing up an advertisement for the local papers, which I faxed to his Newbury Pre-cast office. Duane called back, wondering whether I intended to run the ad in the *New York Times*.

Gently, I explained that my New York customers didn't buy country houses in subdivisions. Michelle picked up an extension. She too acted as if last night were last year. "We're talkin' four-acre lots, Ben."

"It doesn't fit their fantasies."

"It can't hurt to try."

"Trust me. . . . And speaking of which . . ."

"Yeah?"

"I think you should put some serious consideration into dressing up that gravel pit in front."

"What gravel pit?"

"The trap rock you dumped on the slope."

Duane said, "No way grass would hold that grade. Besides, the town—"

"I was thinking about stone walls."

"You know what stonemasons get a running foot?" Michelle protested.

"I prefer not to begin a sale with an apology. Think about it. You're asking for serious bucks. These days, that means quality."

They agreed to think about stone walls.

I stretched out on the sofa and slept soundly for two hours, awakened somewhat caught up on the long night, showered and dressed, and walked down to the general store for a cup of coffee.

Rita Long came by in her Jaguar, top down, a sight that stopped traffic like a jackknifed horsebox.

She climbed out, oblivious to screeching pickup trucks, and hurried to my table on the front porch. She was dressed for New York in a pale green silk jacket and skirt, and a peaked driving hat to protect her hair. "I thought you might be here. I stopped at the house."

"Terrific. We can drive in together."

"No."

"Aren't we on for tonight?"

"No."

"Oh. I'm sorry. I thought it would be fun."

"Ben, we have to talk."

"Sit down. Coffee?"

"No, I'm late." She took off her sunglasses and said, "Actually, *I* have to talk."

A cool steel C-clamp began to tighten around my heart. "So I guess I'll listen."

"I need some space."

Certain clichés never lose their impact.

In the event that I didn't fully comprehend, she added, "More space than you can give me."

I protested that I could give plenty of space and noted that we hadn't seen that much of each other lately as it was. I heard the empty echo of a one-sided negotiation. You can't bargain with someone who doesn't want to make a deal. Still, I tried.

When I had finished, she said, "I'll call you."

She walked back to her car. I clung to that promise like a sinking raft. If she'd smiled or kissed my cheek goodbye, I'd have believed her.

Rita pulled away, stopping more traffic, executed an elegant U-turn around the flagpole, and went by with both hands on the wheel, accelerating south. Next minute Main Street was empty, except for cars and trucks and people.

"You've been dumped, fella."

Saying it out loud made me feel a little better.

Of course, I'd been expecting something like this ever since her sex-as-religion remark. Even a thoroughly insensitive fool would guess something was wrong when the woman he loved had trouble sleeping nights he stayed over. Actually, knowing the score was a bit of a relief. It beat guessing.

The only reason my heart was still pounding was that I'd drunk too much coffee on too little sleep.

Scooter MacKay lumbered up, got a cup, joined me outside, and lit a smoke. "Heard you and Aunt Connie threw a heck of a party." He sounded miffed he hadn't been invited.

I was settling down nicely, thinking I might give Marian Boyce a call, or maybe invite Vicky for dinner tonight at the Brassée. Just casual, nothing to do with a destroyed ego, much less a broken heart. I felt fine.

"Scooter, could I bum a cigarette?"

"Huh?"

"A cigarette. Could you spare a cigarette?"

"You quit smoking in prep school."

"Give me a goddamned cigarette."

Scooter opened his Marlboros, raised one above its fellows for my convenience, and extended the box. His old-fashioned Zippo flamed.

"You know your hands are shaking?"

"Too much coffee— Jesus, these taste awful. How do you stand it?"

"Something wrong with your eye?"

"I got goddamned smoke in it."

"You okay?"

"Fine."

"Hey, where you going?"

"Find some bourbon."

"Hang on, I'll join you."

"It's okay."

"Where you going?"

"The Drover—no, Waterbury."

"*Waterbury?* I don't have time. I gotta work."

"Don't worry about it."

"Hey," he called after me. "Thought you weren't supposed to drink with that head."

He was right about that. The little bit of wine I'd had at Connie's last night had been more than enough. Bourbon would be foolhardy. So no bourbon. That wouldn't stop me from swinging by Waterbury on my way to New York. It was only forty or fifty miles out of the way.

Why not check out Ramos's Bar? Ask some questions. Ask who'd seen Little John Martello. Maybe I'd get lucky and run into some gangstas looking for a fight.

Despite the earnest attempts of civic groups to brighten up the Waterbury Green, nearby Ramos's was the only business left open on its block. Even that was debatable, as they had left their mesh security gates across the front window.

A heavyset lookout was leaning on the gate—a wise precaution at a gang hangout. I parked my Olds where I could see it from the window and told the lookout, "Anybody messes with my car I'll kick your ass."

Strangling his protest with a Leavenworth Look he'd remember, I shoved through the door into the sort of joint where only the bartender could afford to play the jukebox. It was a quiet, dim, sad, sorry notch below a "Friends in Low Places" country honkytonk like River End, where all but the poorest had pickup trucks, rudimentary skills with shovel and chainsaw, and mothers to go home to when their spouses threw them out.

Things got even quieter when I took a stool near the door and studied the room in the back bar mirror. Perhaps the dozen beer drinkers hard-eyeing me back saw a guy dumped by his girl, looking to ease the pain by punching somebody out. Or maybe they noticed my shortage of Spanish ancestors—though in fact I spotted two broad Sicilians as well as a blue-eyed bruiser who I'd have bet money was on leave from the Irish Republican Army, and a graying woman two stools down who had started life as a blonde. No, the real reason for quiet became apparent when the bartender nodded to a couple of thugs who wandered outside to look for my backup.

They thought I was a cop. I didn't really look like a cop. But I had the general build, and when I wore a sports jacket and open shirt, I did sort of look like a cop who was trying not to look like a cop. This came in handy, because a cop trying not to look like a cop was taken very seriously by a certain element.

I ordered a beer and slapped two fresh twenties on the Formica.

"This one's for the beer." I pushed it toward the bartender. "This one's for Little John Martello." I wasn't feeling subtle.

"You're in the wrong bar, mister."

"Does that mean Martello doesn't drink here? Or you don't like my face?"

The bartender was not looking for a fight—at least until he got a report on my backup. "This is Latin Popes. Martello is Knights."

"What is that supposed to mean?"

"It means," said the woman two stools down, "that if Little John Martello were to walk in here, someone would shoot him. As he knows that, he is unlikely to walk in."

I looked at her. She was large in a loose housedress, had a husky cigarette voice, wrinkling biceps, and—despite the wreckage of hard-lived years—the commanding demeanor of a Nightengale-Bamford School headmistress.

When you don't give a damn, you don't get distracted worrying what'll happen next. I said, "The state police gang file says he drinks here."

"It's out of date. Half the people in that file are in jail, dead, or switched sides. Little John joined the Knights."

"Who are the Knights?"

"Drugdealing, murdering, backstabbing terrorist thugs."

"I've heard the same said about the Popes."

Three gangsters rushed to defend their honor. I swung off the stool, intending to take out the left and the right before dealing with the big one in the middle, but the woman waved them off. They slunk back to their beers, muttering threats.

She said, "If you want to get killed, why not try skydiving?"

"Who are you?" I didn't want to talk to a woman, and I certainly didn't want to fight one.

"I'm president of the Latin Popes."

"You're joking."

"Who are you?"

"Ben Abbott from Newbury, Madame President. It's up north. Martello knows the way."

"How'd he find it?"

"That's what I want to know."

"How'd you find *your* way to Waterbury?"

"Used to come down to watch the Cincinnati Reds farm team."

She sneered. "People like you commute to Hartford and Stamford, split by five; New Haven for school or the theater; Bridgeport for the ferry. Does anybody in Newbury give a damn about the disaster in Waterbury?"

Maybe I *could* slug it out with a woman. "Listen, lady, Waterbury used to be called the Brass City. It was the Silicon Valley of its day, when clocks and locks and metal instruments carried the day. A friend of mine, Al Bell, owned a factory here. He told me a story that might help you understand what's going on: Once upon a time, early in World War Two, engineers from Rensselaer Polytechnic Institute sent their latest engineering breakthrough to a Waterbury wire factory. It was a length of wire so thin they delivered it with a microscope. Top that! The Waterbury boys drilled a hole through it."

"What's your point?"

"Along came plastic, and they were history. Point is, neighborhoods and cities are more than location, they're functions of time and *purpose* as well as place. Waterbury's time and purpose have gone."

"Splendid theory, Mr. Abbott. What about the people who live here?"

"They need a function or they better move." I was really getting harsh, though it didn't make me feel better.

She turned away, motioning the bartender for more rye.

Curious about this smart-talking oddball, I asked, "Where you from?"

"Grosse Pointe."

"Jesus Christ, Grosse Pointe set the standard for urban flight. And you're on *my* case for Newbury?"

"I didn't ask to be born there."

"Your grandfather made his money with his hands, right?"

"Clutch plates."

"Your dad with his brain."

"Ford division chief."

"You studied art history in college."

"English lit."

"While you were wallowing in Jane Austen, Japanese fathers got busy with their hands, built better cars, new materials, plastic instead of brass."

"So it's my fault?"

"No, I blame your father. Should have made you study engineering. How'd you go from English lit to street gangs?"

"Chicago. Days of Rage."

"Weathermen?" I guess my brows shot up at that—'Sixties history, live, two stools down.

"Surprised you know," she said.

"Studied it in prep school."

"Thanks for that reminder of my age."

"You've been breaking windows your whole life?"

"Somebody has to. As long as people like you use theories like yours to blame the Popes for looking after themselves."

"I don't blame groups. I blame Mr. Martello and friend who broke into my house looking after themselves."

"I don't have much good to say about Little John. But I'm curious what you think his options are. Do you think he chose to rob your house instead of taking a job at IBM? Do you imagine him saying to his buddy, Yo, Spider, whatch wanna do today, write some new software, or rob a house?"

"How would you feel if he and Spider robbed your place?"

"They already have. Let me tell you, Mr. Abbott, it doesn't feel that much different than the cops tossing the place. At least the burglars don't hate you."

I didn't see much point in calling up solidarity by telling her that I too knew what it felt like to have your home tossed.

"Do you own this bar?"

She looked at me as if I hadn't understood a word she had said.

"Are you serious? If they kick me off welfare, I'll be living in a box."

"Are you really president of the Popes?"

"Are you really paying for information?"

I slid her the twenty. She said, yes, she was president of the Waterbury Chapter.

"How'd you get the job?"

"Since the men are mostly in jail, we make them president of inside chapters and women head of outside chapters. In my particular case, I've had some experience organizing, so I rose to my level. Got any more money?"

I took out another twenty. "Where do I find Martello?"

"Are you going to arrest him?"

"I'm not a cop."

"Buy dope?"

I started to answer no, thought better of it, and said, "Maybe."

"Be very careful. The junk he sells can kill you."

"Where do I find him?"

"Haven't seen him in a week. Heard he got hurt and split to Bridgeport. He's got family there."

"Is there any way I can leave a message for him?"

"Give me money and I'll see he gets it."

"How about a hundred?"

"How about two hundred?"

Every instinct told me this was one negotiation I would lose. So I didn't bother and forked over two hundred dollars I couldn't afford, along with my business card. "Tell him to call me."

"Real estate agent? This for real?"

"What do you think?"

"I think if you're really looking for dope you're taking your life in your hands, and if you're some sort of cop you're in over your head. But if this whole thing is a hustle to set *me* up, you're going to be disappointed, again. I'll tell you what I've told every damned cop who's busted in here or tossed my apartment: The Popes are not a gang. We're a family. We fight to keep our kids in school, off dope, and out of jail."

"Good luck."

I stood up to go, passed her my change from the beer I hadn't touched, minus a couple of bucks for the bartender. "Can I ask you something?"

"Try."

"Is it worth it?"

"Ever hear of Joe Hill?"

"He was a labor organizer."

"When they hung him, his last words to a friend were, 'Well, Gurly, we fought the good fight.' I'd like to be able to say that when my turn comes."

I left Waterbury, west on I-84, thinking Connie Abbott might have liked her. But she made me uncomfortable, wondering what the hell I was doing with my life. I plugged in the car phone and called Ramos's Bar. "I don't know her name, but the lady I was sitting next to . . . Madame President? Listen, if you ever do end up living in a box? Call me." I figured if worse came to worst, I could somehow squeeze her into the barn with Alison and Mrs. Mealy.

She told me she had no plans to retire.

My sleepless night was dragging me down, again. Yawning through Danbury, I almost rear-ended a truck. With time to spare before my dinner reservation, I pulled off on the shoulder just before the New York line and shut my eyes.

A trooper woke me, rapping his flashlight on the window. Sleeping wasn't allowed. Still spoiling for trouble, I told him it was pull over or run into a bridge abutment. He made me breathe on his hand to check my breath. Here, at last, a guy I could fight. But when I passed, he gave me polite directions to the next rest stop.

New York. Downtown, on a warm summer night.

I found Brassée casting friendly light on an oddly angled Tribeca corner, and a few blocks south a parking garage brightly lit and freshly painted to appear safe to nervous out-of-towners like Reg Hopkins. The attendant didn't recognize his picture.

Walking up to the restaurant, I suddenly recognized a vestige of

my past. Brassée was a 'Nineties reincarnation of an 'Eighties min-
imalist nouvelle cuisinery that I and my fellow financial wizards
would occasionally hit for a quick plate of hundred-dollar monkfish
and snowpeas. I couldn't recall the original place's name; what lin-
gered was a vague memory of feeling ripped off, but being far too
rich—and way too busy—to mind very much.

Gone were the monochrome paintings that had hung on infinitely
more interesting peach walls, gone the steel-and-laminate chairs er-
gonomically designed to discourage slow eaters, gone the cacophony
of self-congratulation echoing like jackhammers between hardwood
floor and plaster ceiling. The new place was romantically candlelit,
quieter, lusher, darker, sexier, and happier—as if the proprietors of
a bistro and a bordello had fallen in love, long after either thought
such a thing was still possible, and had celebrated their good fortune
by going into business together.

I noticed three things as I waited for the maitre d' to deal with
those ahead of me. Brassée was a late scene, my nine-thirty dinner
reservation nowhere near the tail of the evening. The twenties I had
brought for information should have been fifties, although I had to
admit it didn't look like a place Reg had scored heroin. And, while
the well-dressed, well-heeled crowd was a high-octane Manhattan
mix of Wall Street suits, downtown art and movie entrepreneurs,
Seventh Avenue fashion shakers, and uptown ad execs, I was one of
the very few straight guys in the restaurant, and the only one without
a date.

# 20

Reg?

The maitre d', a first-class professional who greeted customers politely *before* checking his reservations book, managed to be efficient, friendly, and flatteringly flirtatious all in the same breath. He made people feel welcome and attractive—provided, of course, they had dressed to the top of whatever fashion they conformed to, and had a reservation. If an aging Paul Stuart blazer and Burberry trousers were a trifle bumpkinous, at least I had had the wit to book ahead.

Reg, gay?

"Mr. Abbott, for two. It will be just a teensy wait." Then, glancing over my shoulder, "Your companion?"

*Reg, gay?* No way.

Flummoxed by the unexpected, the unimaginable, the impossible—and with Rita still churning my brain—I blurted, "I may have been stood up."

Well, that sounded just wonderful, and he smiled. "Maybe you'll get lucky at the bar."

Maybe I should have turned around and walked out the door. But even a frothing-at-the-mouth homophobe—which I was not— would have stayed a week to find out how, of all the three or four or ten thousand restaurants in Manhattan, his old friend, the elk-shooting, fish-hooking founder of Hopkins's Septic, had discovered this mostly gay one the night he died.

I accepted the maitre d's promise of a table soon and let him direct me toward the bar—a fine affair of French-polished walnut, and a welcome change from last decade's zinc and stainless steel. I reminded myself that I had no proof, yet, that Reg had actually dined at Brassée. *Then,* I wanted to know what the hell he was doing here? And with whom?

I discovered at the bar that Brassée was not a singles scene. Couples and foursomes were waiting for tables. In fact, I was the only guy who looked like he was cruising. Wonderful.

The bartender noticed and hurried over.

I ordered club soda. When he brought it, I laid three twenties on the bar. "Could I trouble you for a fifty?"

"What about the other ten?"

"I was hoping it would cover the club soda."

"Barely," he commiserated in a pleasant way and scampered off to fetch my fifty. I guessed that he was a kid recently off the bus from Nebraska—a country boy come to shine in New York. That was a good break. I could talk to a country boy. (Heck, son, I'm from Newbury? We got pigs and horses just like you.)

"I'm looking for someone," I said.

He smoothed his cowlick, a mite warily.

"Saturday around eight o'clock, three weeks ago. Were you on?"

"I think so. Yes. I started a month ago, a week before that."

"Welcome to New York."

He actually said, "Thank you." He was so nice I wanted to take him home and give him to my mother. (Here you go, Mom. A son you can be proud of.) He had, however, been in town long enough to notice I had left the fifty on the bar, and he paid attention when I said, "A man named Reg Hopkins. He would have had a reservation for eight or eight-thirty."

"What does he look like?"

I showed him the photograph from the *Clarion.* Scooter had

dredged it up from his morgue, a shot several years old, commemorating Reg's Rotary Club presidency.

"Nice," said the man next to me.

Having crashed somebody else's scene, the least I could do was be polite. The trick here was to be polite without adding to the confusion. I smiled. The man next to me looked confused, and the nice bartender—despite a hungry eye on my fifty—admitted he had never seen Reg and suggested I ask the maitre d', who had the reservation book. Except, as the maitre d' was hustling his buns all over the dining room, I had to continue confusing people at the bar until he had finally settled the nine-thirty seating.

When he had, it was nearly ten o'clock. I cornered him as he sank wearily behind his desk, complaining, "It's the standing that kills you."

"This man," I said, extending the newspaper photo with the fifty-dollar bill, "my friend Reg. Was he in here three Saturdays ago?"

"Oh, hon, if I got in the middle of these things I wouldn't have a friend in town." Still, he glanced at the picture. "Well, no wonder you got stood up."

"Beg pardon?"

"Tit for tat. *You* stood him up. Tonight he stands you up. Fortunately, I have a couple at the bar who will kill for your table. Maybe next time you two will get your acts together."

"Reg came here?"

The maitre d' sighed and returned the picture, minus my fifty. "I shouldn't tell you this, but he looked a lot more disappointed than you do. Do you ever ask yourself why you're putting him through this?"

"How long did he wait?"

"He gave you forty-five minutes—twenty more than you'd get from me."

"Was he high?"

"No, he wasn't high. He was sad. . . . Life is shorter than ever, hon. Don't waste it. Give a little, get along— If he comes by, want me to tell him where you'll be?"

"Tell him I went straight home."

There'd been a shift change at the garage, and the new attendant remembered Reg fondly. "Man says he's staying overnight."

"All night?"

"I go, 'You sure?' He goes, 'I sure hope so.' That being the case, I take it up in the back. Bunch more all-nighters come in, I take them up and in the back. Then your man comes back in less than one hour and wants his Blazer. I go, 'You kidding? It's buried.' He goes, 'You an undertaker?' "

I laughed. That was Reg.

The attendant was not so easily amused. "Oldest joke in the parking game. I go, 'Sorry, mister. You said all night. It'll take me an *hour* to move all them cars in front of yours.' Know what he does?"

"What?"

"The man gets *tears* in his eyes. I'm thinking, What is this, like an actor, gonna cry to make me feel sorry for him? But he whips out his wallet—you know how some folks carry an emergency hundred?"

I nodded. I'd given both of mine to the president of the Latin Popes.

"*Hundred* dollars. The man goes, 'I wanna go home. This is yours if I'm outta this damned place in five minutes.' "

"What happened?"

"What *happened?* I'm tossing cars like poker chips. He comes up with me and helps out—real smooth—does exactly what I tell him. 'Tween the two of us, Blazer's down here in ten minutes. Not five, but he gives me the money anyway. Even pays separate for the ticket—so I got the whole hundred. You tell me how many people woulda done *that*."

I drove straight home.

I think the parking story threw me harder than the fact that Reg had been stood up by a dinner date in a mostly gay restaurant. It was so like him. The way the man told the story, the ten minutes' camaraderie would stay with him longer than the money.

I felt a grim triumph in finally filling in Reg's missing hours: After he had freed his car, he had just enough time, stepping on it, to get back to Newbury and swing by Dr. Mead's for ice cream.

As for Reg's date at Brassée, I could think of no way I'd ever find out who he was meeting. The Brassée had been the only New York number listed on his entire long-distance bill. Whether the guy he was meeting had called Reg, or had a local number that wouldn't show up on the bill, I couldn't guess.

Why did I assume it was a man and not a woman? Ninety-five percent of the Brassée's patrons had been men; and the maitre d' who recalled him had assumed Reg was gay. (I was not unaware he had made similar assumptions about me too, but I chalked that up to context.) Also, I recalled the expression of distaste wrinkling Janey's lips when I had asked whether Reg was dating. Janey knew.

I tried to imagine the sheer loneliness Reg would have endured in his marriage. And how desolate he must have felt among his friends. We certainly had been no help.

Beyond sympathy and a vague sense of guilt, however, I wasn't sure how I felt. Reg and I had known each other since we were four feet tall. How many years had he carried his secret? How long had he lived like a spy in his own town? What would I have done if he told me?

I made the flagpole a little after eleven, just about the time he had. The town was quiet. I debated swinging down Church Hill in hopes of persuading Dr. Mead to draw me a pistachio cone—I was starving—but it had been a hell of a long day, much of it in the car, and I felt too punchy to make a decision. The car rolled to a stop in the deserted intersection. Then, gazing blearily up Main Street, I noticed an unmarked state police cruiser parked in front of my house.

Major Case Squad Detective Sergeant Bender was sitting on my front step, swatting mosquitoes. He stood up, dodged moths circling the light, ignored my hand, and extended an envelope.

"What's this?"

"Warrant to search your house, your car, and your person."

"For what?"

"Your guns."

"What the hell for?"

Bender did an excellent job of looking simultaneously world-weary and alert. And for a little guy, he had a remarkable ability to look dangerous, as if any second he would spring straight at the throat, like a mink or a weasel.

"I don't really believe that you were stupid enough to ask for Little John Martello in Waterbury, leave your business card, then drive down to Bridgeport to shoot the whacked-out bastard. But I'll sleep better after I check your guns."

"Somebody shot Martello?" I echoed stupidly.

*Wait a minute.* Somebody shot Little John the *day* after I informed the Jacuzzi Eight I knew Reg had died at their party?

"I'll start with your person," said Sergeant Bender.

I hardly heard him. *One* day after I asked them who knew John Martello, the gangsta was dead?

"Spread 'em!"

I heard that—like wooden clubs banging iron bars—and turned angrily on Bender: "Unless you want to start reading me my rights while I call my lawyer, why don't we start with my alibi?"

"Where were you?"

"Not within twenty miles of Bridgeport."

"Where were you?"

"I drove from Waterbury—I'm sure you can tell me what time I left—to New York City and back here."

"Bridgeport happens to be between Waterbury and New York."

"Not if you take I-84. Bridgeport's on 95. I can prove I spent a half hour in a Manhattan restaurant, and I have a parking receipt for my car."

"Can you prove you took 84?"

"You can. One of your road cops caught me sleeping on the shoulder, just east of the New York line."

"Got his badge number?"

"Yeah, right."

Sergeant Bender wrote down the time and asked to see the parking receipt. He wanted to keep it. I demanded he write me a receipt for it.

"Oh, yeah, and I made a phone call from 84. Ask Lynx Mobil. It was to the lady in Ramos's Bar, the one who probably turned me in."

"Told you I didn't think you were that stupid. Well, at least it saves me having to root through your house, though I will have a look in your car. And maybe a peek under your jacket."

I looked around, confirmed the street was empty, and said, "Be my guest."

Bender patted the places I might have a gun and then searched my Olds from trunk to engine with a mini-Maglite. "What the hell is this?"

"The motor."

"From what, a locomotive?" He played the light lovingly over it and finally closed the hood. "You're clean."

"Could have saved yourself the drive to Newbury."

"I remembered you were stupid enough to lie to me about not spotting Martello in the gang file."

"Is he dead?"

"Extremely. One shot to the head, close range."

"Suicide?"

"The back of his head."

"I hear he sold bad dope, and he quit his gang, which I gather was frowned upon."

"Especially when you then start up your own gang."

"Close range?" I asked. "I thought the Popes did drive-bys."

Bender shrugged. "Maybe they couldn't find a car to steal."

"Who was his buddy? The Spanish guy?"

He turned away. "What's the matter, couldn't find him in the file?"

I trailed him down the front walk. "The file is out of date. Do you know his name? He's 'Spider' on the street."

Bender paused with his door open, looked at the night sky peeping through the trees, and said, "You know what I wish? I wish this thing was a convertible. I'd really like to ride home with the top down."

I offered to lend him a can opener.

He told me that if I went looking for Spider, the entire Connecticut state police force would go out of the way to make my life miserable. He demonstrated this ability by writing me a citation for the expired emissions sticker he had noticed on my windshield.

"I'm not a polluter," I protested. "The car runs cleaner than a new one."

"Tough."

At last, someone I could fight with. "Screw you." I tore up the ticket and ground the pieces into the walk.

Bender wrote a second one for littering. "You got ten days to pay the fines or I'll get a bench warrant for your arrest."

I stomped into the house and telephoned Ramos's Bar. It was after midnight, but I bet few of the afternoon drinkers had strayed. "Ben Abbott, again," I told the bartender. "The lady at the bar I was talking to? Madame President?"

She came on, a little slurry of tongue. I said, "Since when do radicals rat to pigs?"

"You're not a Pope, Mr. Abbott. You've got no call on solidarity from me."

"Neither was Martello."

"Little John was a misguided thug. But compared to you, he's family."

"I didn't shoot him."

"That's between you and the police. Or would you rather I had passed your name to the Knights?"

"Remember the two hundred I gave you?"

"Do you need a receipt for your taxes?"

"Just do me a favor: Tell Spider I'm looking for him."

"So you can shoot him too?"

"Pass the word."

"Again, I recommend skydiving, Mr. Abbott."

"Tell him! When Spider gets in touch, I'll mail you another two hundred."

"Whatever you say. Only do *me* a favor and put it in your will so I'm sure to collect."

I banged down the phone. Plastic shattered and I was left with a handful of printed circuit boards and gaily colored wires. "Terrific."

I noticed the answering machine blinking and I lunged for it, thinking it was Rita. It wasn't, of course—only someone who wanted to sell a house and to whom I already owed a call.

I erased the message. I deep-sixed chunks of telephone.

I counted coincidences.

Little John Martello sold bad dope; the president of the Latin Popes had warned me herself. Bad dope had killed Reg. But when I questioned whether Reg was a doper, who broke into my house but Little John Martello? And friend Spider. Two Waterbury gangstas—whose sum total experience of rural Connecticut was a mugging on the Waterbury Green—had made a beeline for a town that was barely a blur on the map.

And now—the day after I told the Fisk Frolickers that I knew Reg had died at their party and asked about Little John Martello—Little John Martello was shot.

Lots of coincidences, but no connections. Spider, whoever he was, wasn't in the gang file, and Madame President would march cheerfully to the scaffold before naming him, so I could only hope that Little John's sidekick would respond to my message. Or stop by for another visit.

In case he did, I got the key to the iron safe, went down to the cellar, and unlimbered the Old Man's .38—a simple revolver even a child could handle—and locked it in my night table. I was hopeless with handguns, always had been. Dad had kept promising to teach me, but he never got around to it. My Chevalley uncles had made me competent with hunting weapons, but at the Academy, Navy instructors still discuss my sidearm exploits in the hushed tones traditionally reserved for capsizings, mid-Atlantic.

I showered, thinking to clear my head, but when I climbed into bed, my brain was still spinning. At least I was done picking fights over Rita. Not that I didn't mourn her. Nor, I supposed, would I stop dredging dimly recalled conversations I might somehow re-interpret for hope.

But my anger had shifted focus in the course of the endless day, from lost love to my murdered friend. I felt it settle in for the long haul. When it was almost tangible—cool, like stone in the dark—I acknowledged what I had suspected the instant Sergeant Bender told me Martello had been shot: Whoever had murdered Reg had en-joyed dinner at Aunt Connie's last night.

# 21

I woke up humble. I'd been so full of myself in Connie's library—so proud I had proved that eight people couldn't sustain a lie—that I'd been hustled.

With humility came insight: Maybe I wasn't the only one who'd been hustled.

What if the important lie—the real lie—was not that eight friends had dumped an accidental OD victim's body in the covered bridge? What if the real lie was that whoever had murdered Reg had tricked the innocent into conspiring in a cover-up?

What if by frightening and bullying them into helping get rid of the body, the killer or killers had made them unwitting accomplices? What if he had forced them unknowingly to be his alibi?

Why was Reg murdered? I didn't know.

How was Reg murdered? That was a question for a pro.

Doctor Steve Greenan didn't keep office hours anymore, but he still made house calls on his older patients and acted, of course, as an assistant county medical examiner. That part-time work brought in some money and provided, he confessed freely, the main excitement in his life. A tall man, stooped with age, he had delivered me and most of my friends. Aunt Connie, a generation his senior, still called him "Stevie" and thought he was "too handsome for his own good."

His twin brother, "Stonewall" Alfred, owned Greenan Oldsmobile, a small dealership up Route 7 where, since 1934, shrewd Yankee traders had discovered humility negotiating the price of a new car. I found Steve in the showroom, playing chess with his brother, who, between moves, was explaining to a customer that the reason he couldn't lower the price of a block-long, '73 gas-guzzling station wagon was that big comfortable cars were becoming quite rare.

"Mildred said I'd find you here. She said it's time to turn the compost heap."

"That's why I'm here. How's your head?"

Alfred devoured a pawn and said, "Looks like you been using it to straighten dents in a backhoe."

Steve walked me over to the window and examined my face in the light and probed my skull with his powerful fingers. "This hurt?"

"Sore."

"How about this?"

"Awh!"

"You'll live. What's up?"

"Steve? Can we take a little walk?"

The doctor looked at me curiously, called, "Back in a minute, Alf," and we walked outside and strolled the double line of used cars.

"I don't know if you can discuss this. Tell me if I'm out of line."

"I will."

"Is it possible that Reg died of something other than a heroin overdose?"

"Read the report. It's public record. Scooter's probably got a copy."

"I read it."

"In that case, you know the stuff he was snorting was powerful enough to kill a camp of lumberjacks."

"Could your boss have made a mistake?"

"Highly unlikely. It's a good office. The new toxicologist has got himself in place. Highly unlikely."

I was proceeding on thin ice. The fact was, a mistake *had* been made. I knew that Reg had not died in the bridge, he had been dumped there. So if Steve and the cops missed that, what else had they overlooked?

"Could the state cops have screwed up somehow?"

"How?"

"Missed a wound or something?"

"That was my job." Steve's mouth worked a little; it made him look older. "But anything I missed, I'd expect the M.E. would have found and reamed me out for it."

"Did he ream you out, Steve?"

"Nope."

"But I'm out of line."

"You're edging that way."

"I'm sorry. . . . Could Reg have died elsewhere? Could the body have been moved? I know I've read there are ways you tell, but I was wondering . . ."

Steve didn't bite.

"They taught me some basics at ONI. I seem to recall that fixed lividity sets in after four or five hours. After that you get no blanching. If I remember right, if a body were moved after that time, the 'livor' which settled down with gravity would not shift."

Steve still didn't bite.

I asked, straight out, "Is it possible to move a body and fool the M.E.?"

"Anything's possible."

"Would time be a factor? How long the person was dead before he was moved?"

Steve smiled. "If you're planning on moving a body, Ben, and want to fool the old doctor, let me recommend that you move it and dump it in the same position it died. And do it very quickly."

"Would an hour be quick enough?"

"Plenty, particularly if the old doctor was, shall we say, overly influenced by a preponderance of other evidence—like the dope on the victim matching the dope in the victim, et cetera, et cetera. . . ."

Steve threw his arm around my shoulders and walked me back toward the showroom. "You know, Dick Parmalee told me he's trying to get ahold of you. Left a couple of messages. Wants to sell his house."

"Christ, I forgot. Thanks for reminding me."

"I went up to give Vicky a hand with the phones. She thought you were coming, but you didn't show. Tim said you haven't been around."

"I got tied up."

"La France's running strong. Old 'Guns and Dogs' stirred up the Scudder Mountain crowd. He's got people signed up to vote with an X."

"Guns and Dogs" was Steve La France's father, Frank, famous for his proclamations at town meetings that this country needed more people who owned guns and dogs. Scudder Mountain was home to woodies and hardscrabble farmers and retirees in house trailers who had not forgiven President Eisenhower's radical liberalism. "Now he's working Frenchtown."

"I had to go to New York. I'm back now. I'll help. I've been busy as hell."

"I heard you been busy asking questions. All I can tell you, it's a damned shame, but Reg Hopkins died a classic hotload death. We've had fifty in the state since January. The only thing that distinguished Reg from the rest was the potency he inhaled. The heroin in his stash was the most powerful recorded so far—so pure it could have been cut twenty times."

"Are you saying it wasn't cut at all? Someone sold him pure heroin?"

"Oh, they tried to cut it with baking soda. But they were sloppy and he got damn near the full hit. It's not like cutting cocaine. And in the current market, heroin costs a lot less, so they're not making any effort to knock it down."

"Did you see his stash?"

"You're edging that line again."

"What was it in? Plastic bag?"

Steve laughed. "Where've you been? I thought you knew your way around. They don't sell their poison in a plastic bag. Comes in a printed wrapper with a goddamned brand name."

"What was the brand name?"

"Oh, this was really literate. Knight Out! Knight spelled with a *K*."

"Steve, I think it might be a good idea to do another autopsy."

Steve removed his arm and said coolly, "Why don't you ask a cop?"

# 22

"So how'd *you* get involved?" asked Marian Boyce.

The sergeant and I were sharing a rock in the middle of the river, which, like the stream under the covered bridge, was running low. Our perch was streaked with Grumman Green paint where canoes had bashed it last spring. She had her bare feet in the water and her skirt hitched some distance up her strong thighs. Her unmarked Crown Victoria sat on the riverbank, muttering radio talk from the Plainfield barracks. It sounded like a lonesome drunk.

"The widow didn't want to believe that her husband died from a drug overdose."

"This the same widow who was divorcing him?"

"Same widow." I had already unwrapped sandwiches from the Newbury General Store. Now I opened cans from a six-pack chilling in the river—Diet Pepsies, this being a working picnic.

"So the disbelieving widow hired a real estate agent." Marian chomped reflectively on a smoked turkey sandwich. "Makes sense. Why go to the police for free when you can pay a real estate agent good money to solve a mystery?"

"I tried to talk her out of it."

Marian gave me her road cop look—medium intensity—fine-focused to shrivel a speeder's laminated operator's license without injuring his hand. "I'll bet you did."

"The guy was also a good friend of mine."

"Emotionally involved too? That always clears the head."

"Give me a break."

"And now, stymied, unable to deliver, stressed out, you invite me on a picnic to pump me."

"I wouldn't put it that crudely."

"There's nothing crude about two people who like each other enjoying—providing they take precautions—enjoying— Oh! You thought I meant pump me for privileged police information. Silly Marian, what a jerk I am." A steel-edged smile suggested that there was only one jerk in the river and she wasn't it.

"What are the odds," she asked, "that someday you will invite me out for a meal *not* to pick my brain?"

"I thought you're seeing someone."

"I can still enjoy a meal out."

"What's he like?"

"Hassle-free."

"Sounds exciting."

"He's a nice quiet Pratt and Whitney sales engineer. He just got promoted. He's very handsome. He used to be a tennis pro."

"Does Jason like him?"

Jason was her six-year-old, and remarkably well-adjusted for a child who shuttled between Marian's condo in Plainfield and his dad's resident state trooper cottage in North Stonington on the far side of Connecticut. Weekly, trooper uncles handed him across the state in patrol stages. With a birthday on the horizon, there was talk of chipping in for his own riot gun.

"Seems to."

"The guy sounds great."

Marian shrugged. "Low maintenance—unlike certain people I know."

"I need help," I said. "I'm in over my head."

I saw the fire ignite in her eyes and knew too late I'd made a mistake. Brilliant. Like a con artist suddenly forced to hide *two* peas under three shells, I had to conceal First-Select-Mystery-Guest Vicky *and* my Jacuzzi-dipping, body-moving friends, while trying to bamboozle Sergeant Marian into guessing that the empty shell held the truth.

I dropped my sandwich, lunged for it, and fell in the river. Marian pulled me out, dried my face with a wad of paper napkins. The diversion hadn't worked. Thoroughly undistracted, she asked, "Have you broken the law?"

"No."

"You realize, I now assume you're lying?"

"Marian, you know I'm not a liar."

"Yeah, that's what's confusing me. . . . Start at the beginning."

"I already told you the beginning."

"What do you want from me?"

I was still rolling toward the fire, downhill, no brakes. "Let me make a suggestion that will help both of us."

"If I were meeting you for the first time, at this point I would draw my weapon."

"But you *do* know me."

Marian reached out and touched the back of my hand. I felt a sexual jolt and saw it crackle through her too. It was so intense I forgot that one reason she was such a successful detective was that she was brilliant at shifting gears—a woman qualified to play good-cop-bad-cop all by herself.

"Tell me what you want."

"I suggest you take a cold hard look at the autopsy on Reg Hopkins."

She nodded as indifferently as if I had remarked that I'd read in the paper there was a sale on table lamps at the Danbury Mall. "Why?"

"Get a court order to exhume his body and get the Plainfield M.E. to re-examine it for a closer look at what killed him."

"Wha'd you have in mind?"

Her apparent indifference was driving me over the top. Pose or not, it had the effect of making me talk louder, faster, and without restraint. "Find out if someone deliberately injected him with super-pure heroin."

"Injected?"

"With a *needle?* Tell the M.E. to look for marks."

Marian nodded and looked away, but not before I saw the fire leap like volcanoes.

"You like that." I wondered what I had unleashed. "Don't you?"

"Tell me where you got this idea."

Oh, boy. "Well, I can tell you every place he went the night he died, from when he left his office until a little after eleven o'clock."

Marian jumped up, skipped across the rocks, up the riverbank to her car, and came back with her notebook. "Tell me."

I did.

"And then?"

"I can also tell you that everyone who saw him says he was stone-cold sober."

"And then?"

"And shortly after two o'clock his Blazer was seen in the covered bridge."

"Who saw it?"

"Couple of guys trying to leave the reservation. They couldn't because it was blocking the bridge."

"I asked *who* saw it."

"They didn't realize the body was in it."

"Why not? The door was open, the courtesy lights must have been on."

I scampered off thin ice. "Apparently his battery had died. Also, it had tinted glass. Also, they'd been drinking."

Marian made a note I couldn't see and repeated, *"Who?"*

"I can't tell you."

"Can't or won't?"

"Won't. But I believe them. I know exactly what they were doing that night. I checked them out."

"Excellent, Ben. That's a great relief. The real estate agent corroborates the witnesses' stories and assures the Major Case Squad detective that the witnesses riding around the woods at two in the morning who saw the victim's car didn't see the victim, didn't share their dope with the victim, didn't kill the victim."

"My Great-aunt Connie says sarcasm is the language of the devil."

"My dad says amateurs are idiots."

I smiled. Touché. She didn't.

"It took me twelve years to make Major Case Squad. You've got some nerve jerking me around."

Bad cop, I could handle. "These guys aren't dopers. They didn't kill Reg Hopkins."

We traded cold glares. Had it gone on much longer, the river would have iced up. Marian broke first. Not that I was any tougher than she was. But she surmised, correctly, that even if she could find some excuse to lock me up, I could never rat.

"What happened between 'a little after eleven' and two o'clock?"

I knew, of course, Reg had died at the Fisks', but that wasn't the point. The point was to persuade Marian to exhume him to find how somebody had murdered him. "Only amateur guesses."

"Try me, Sherlock."

"Either he bought his dope, drove out to the bridge, snorted up, and died. Or—"

"Bought it where?"

"Almost three hours; he could have made it to Waterbury, and back. If he stepped on it."

"Or?"

"Or he met somebody who killed him."

Marian said, "Or someone simply sold him bad dope. Or shared it with him, panicked, and ran."

"Did you see any evidence of that in the Blazer?"

She squinted at me, as if looking through a dirty window.

I asked, "What if someone killed him and faked the death to look like a hotload OD? Hotloads have been in the news. Maybe whoever killed him was betting the police would jump to the obvious conclusion."

The expression on the face of the officer in charge of that investigation suggested no help if I fell in the river again.

"Let me ask you sometime," she said. "You've been so busy speculating—not to mention establishing the innocence of your witnesses—have you had any time to consider the killer's motive?"

"No."

"No guesses? No leaps of the imagination? No dazzling intuition?"

"None I can 'corroborate.' "

"No old standards, Ben? Spurned lover? Betrayed wife? Defrauded partner? Hmm?"

"Marian, you're having too much fun at my expense. I've brought you something potentially interesting, not to mention a possible boost to your career. I don't expect you to fling your clothes off in gratitude. But a simple thank you— What are you doing?"

"Unbuttoning my shirt, what does it look like?"

"I get the impression we're done talking."

"Would you help me with my bra?"

"Your gun's in the way."

"Do I have your attention now?"

"Full attention."

"Then answer this: What's the oldest cliché in criminal investigation?"

"Follow the money."

"There's your killer's motive."

"Great. Who's my killer?"

Marian sat up and shook off my hands. "Your client."

# 23

"No way. Absolutely ridiculous. That's the stupidest thing I ever heard."

"Excellent," said Marian, reattaching the only one of her bra hooks I'd managed to unfumble. "That means I can count on a clear field. You won't get in the way. And I won't have to share the credit when I arrest her."

"You're not serious."

"She's the one, dummy. Don't you get it?"

"No, I don't get it. Janey Hopkins had nothing against Reg."

"She was divorcing him."

"Yeah, but Reg wasn't fighting her."

"Connecticut's a shared-property state, Sherlock. House, cars, bank account, business, split fifty-fifty. Unless one party ODs. Then the surviving party gets it all."

"Yeah, but everything was mortgaged."

"All the more reason. If she can make the payments she doesn't have to sell. If they were splitting equity they'd have to sell everything."

"Yeah, but without Reg the business . . ." My voice trailed off.

"Yes?"

"She's decided to make a go of the septic business."

"Right!" Marian was flying—face flushed, eyes sparkling—flying a winner. She stopped buttoning her shirt, seized my wet head, pressed my face to her breasts for an instant. "Yes!"

"Wait a minute. Wait a minute. If you're right and Janey killed Reg so she could inherit everything instead of split fifty-fifty, how come she hired me to prove that he didn't OD on heroin?"

"Two possible answers to that very good question, Ben. One, she's greedy and wants the insurance—along with everything else—like Kathleen Turner in *Body Heat*."

"That's crazy."

"Kathleen got away with it."

"In a movie."

"In real life, what did Mrs. Hopkins have to lose, trying to spook the insurance company? The bastards might think twice about going to court against a young widow and two children. Maybe between you bumbling around and her smart lawyer, she'd force a settlement."

"Yeah, but what if I bumbled into proving she killed him?"

"She didn't hire a pro, Ben. She didn't go to the police. She hired a dumb amateur. All she was doing was blowing smoke."

"Yeah, but she's thrown in the towel."

"So it didn't work. What did it cost her? Couple of hundred bucks?"

"I cleared nine hundred. Minus expenses."

"You've got some nerve. Anyhow, it costs her nine hundred bucks to take a shot at the insurance *and*—and this is a big 'and'—by hiring you to clear Reg she throws off any suspicion."

"Even though I'm an amateur."

"She got her money's worth in that regard—I doubt there's anybody in Connecticut who hasn't heard you're asking questions about Reg Hopkins." With that final insult, Marian picked up her notebook and started hopping rocks toward shore.

"So when do you arrest her?"

She paused daintily, on one foot on a slippery rock, and I thought, If there is a God, she will fall in.

"I work a little more conservatively, Ben. I'm an orderly person. First I'll find out if he was indeed murdered. If he was, I'll gather evidence against my suspect—keeping an open mind on the subject of her possible innocence. *Then* I'll arrest her."

"Where you going now?"

"Get a shovel. Dig up your friend. If the M.E. finds evidence of homicide, I'll turn Newbury upside down and shake."

"How long is this going to take?"

Marian looked at her watch. "I hope I can get a court order this afternoon. Any luck, we'll have him on a slab by dark. Otherwise, first thing in the morning. I doubt I'll have any trouble persuading the M.E. that it's in his interest to get right to work."

"Could you wait ten days?"

"Of course not. Why?"

"We've got a special primary in ten days."

"So?"

"My friend Vicky's in a tough fight for renomination. Turning Newbury upside down won't make it any easier."

I didn't have to explain why to Marian. She had her own political ambitions and a carefully thought out agenda to pursue when she retired from the state police. (In fact, it was quite possible that she and Vicky might one day compete for high office.)

"That's a shame," she said.

"Yeah, but—" There was still a chance she would slip off the rocks.

"But what?"

I had been about to say, "Yeah, but I already know that somebody at the Fisk party killed Reg." But if I said that, I'd really bring hellfire down on Vicky. Because once Vicky learned the police were questioning the Fisks and their guests, she would feel honor-bound to step into a merciless spotlight.

"*What?*"

"Nothing."

"Thanks for lunch. And thanks for the tip." She stepped lightly ashore and scrambled up the bank, put on her shoes, called in on the radio, and fired up the Crown Victoria.

"Hey Ben?" She waved, grinning happily.

"Yeah?" I answered from the river, where I was wondering, Was she somehow right? Had Janey Hopkins put the use on me?

"I love your picnic spot. After this blows over, what do you say we put that rock to better use?"

"If you can stand it with an amateur."

"I'll close my eyes and pretend you're selling houses.— Oh, and by the way, fella . . ."

"Yeah?"

"If you want to stay friends, don't tell your client."

"Ex-client. She paid me off."

"And got her money's worth. Bye." The Crown Victoria tore up the dirt and disappeared in a dust cloud.

I stuffed wrappers and napkins into the bag, retrieved the Pepsies, and ran to my car. I had thought it would be smart to share certain select suspicions to get Marian to reopen the case and re-examine Reg's body. But my timing had proved as atrocious as my choice of confidante. Should have gone to Sergeant Bender, a choice I had rejected as too cautious. Too late. And now I had about two days to expose Reg's killer—or killers—before Marian raided Newbury like Attila the Hun in an expansive mood.

# 24

---

Who killed Reg Hopkins?

Beautiful Susan? Fragile Georgia? Sherry of the roving eye? Fiery Michelle? Dark Ted? Buttoned-down-corporate, trying-too-hard Rick? Big Bill Carter? Boss Duane, the most successful of the men and Reg's best friend?

Or Janey Hopkins—my client—Reg's about-to-be ex?

I figured I had to consider Janey, because she was Sergeant Marian's prime suspect, and Marian was a professional and probably smarter than I. I couldn't deny she'd hit upon a dandy motive. Janey *could* have opted for widowhood, with a one hundred percent inheritance, instead of the financial wreckage of a fifty percent divorce settlement. She *could* have slipped a hotload to Reg—who then had the bad manners to snort the poison in the Fisk kitchen. It *could* have happened that way.

I preferred *my* theory: that the guilty of the Jacuzzi gang had tricked the innocent into dumping Reg's body. Long on suspects and short on motive, I still believed I'd been hustled in Connie's library. And I had my doubts that Reg had just happened to end up at the Fisk party.

But time was running out if I was going to protect Vicky.

So I concluded, in the course of a long night, that I had to put full faith in what I thought I knew and all my energy in what I didn't know.

I made lists. Lists and more lists. I'd have liked to have run my lists past Connie's keen eye. But I was skating on legal ice too thin to risk involving her.

I listed what I didn't know, in what seemed a likely order of precedence: I didn't know the killer or killers; didn't know their motive; didn't know how they had forced the hotload on Reg— though that was Marian's bailiwick; didn't know if Reg was gay; and if he was gay, didn't know if being gay had anything to do with his murder.

Taking the bleak view, I didn't know much. On the bright side, I knew more than Ms. Major Case Squad. But she'd catch up fast, once she got a new autopsy. Still, I knew about the Fisk party and Marian didn't. Yet.

Under the gun, feeling the pressure, I did what many a stressed-out Newburian had done over the years: I went out to lunch at the Newbury Country Club, a pleasant duffer's course spread across an abandoned dairy farm. I wasn't a member, but my dad had been president, and I was greeted warmly by the manager.

"Georgia Bowland here yet?"

"Haven't seen her."

"Did she remember to make a lunch reservation?" I put enough weight on "remember" to hint that for reasons we both knew, Georgia could be on occasion forgetful.

Henry, good club manager that he was, consulted his book with an expression that covered responses ranging from "I wasn't aware Georgia was forgetful" to "Only yesterday the barmaids trundled her home in a wheelbarrow."

"Nooooo, I don't see it."

"Can you squeeze us in, Henry?"

"No problem."

"Tell her I'll be in the bar," I asked him, and headed that way feeling a little skeezy. I told myself I didn't have time to be nice. I'd struck out, essentially, with the guys, and I couldn't mine Michelle for any more information either. That left the other women: Sherry and Susan, and Georgia Bowland, the Jacuzzi gang's weak sister.

The clubhouse was simple, built after World War II when knotty pine had seemed a lively break with tradition. The dining room had a dance floor and a lot of windows that cast a cheerful light on the tables set for lunch, while the bar, reflecting a time when people took drinking seriously, was long, dark, and private. On a summer weekday like today, Grandma could enjoy her martini undisturbed by the little ones. Several grandmothers were doing just that, in the company of some grandpas. Everyone looked tanned and healthy and quite happily retired, and I couldn't help but think that, with God's blessing, here in thirty years would settle the innocent among my suspects.

I said hello to everybody, accepted a drink from Scooter's granddad, and joined in, while I watched for Georgia. Conversation swirled around the morning's eighteen on drought-baked fairways, exploits of grandchildren in the swimming pool, Vicky McLachlan's dwindling chances of renomination. The death of Reg Hopkins got me some looks. Marian was right, everyone knew I'd been asking questions. To my surprise, in this crowd, Reg gossip had developed more staying power than the Fisk party, which no one mentioned —possibly because they preferred fond memories of their own escapades.

I explained that my yellowing bruises looked worse than they were, received congratulations for putting up a good fight, and firm advice to lock my doors and get a gun.

"What happened to your dad's collection?"

"Locked in the safe." I explained about Alison and her friends. All agreed that guns and kids were a deadly mix, and the conversation drifted toward a weekend tournament that Duane Fisk was expected to dominate. That stirred memories of team play with Reg Hopkins, more sad shakes of gray heads, and a hasty retreat to the weather forecast and the vague possibility of rain.

Georgia wandered in, looking quite pretty and very stylish. She was no heart-stopping beauty like Rita Long, but she shared an eye for Henri Bendel clothes that announced New York Woman Lost in Hick Town. Her honey-colored hair had been cut shoulder-length by an expensive genius, her makeup was restrained, her jewelry a few quiet pieces. While there was truth in Aunt Connie's prediction that alcohol would wither her good looks, she looked, at one o'clock on a summer day, like she had a ways to go before that happened.

She also looked puzzled. "Henry said you were expecting me?"

"I must have confused him. I thought I saw your car in the lot. Thought you and Rick might want to have lunch."

"Rick's at work." And then, before I had to maneuver her any more, she said, "*We* can have lunch."

"Great. Drink first?"

"Ummm. Okay. Sure. Why not?" I signaled a bartender and walked Georgia away from the crowd, trailed by a grandfatherly chortle: "Hey, Ben caught a cutie. Wait'll I tell Rick."

Georgia proved a capital hand at clubhouse banter. "And I'll tell you-know-who about the new lifeguard."

This occasioned roars of laughter and a genuinely chagrined expression on the face of the chortler.

"You hit that nail on the head."

Georgia laughed. "I shouldn't have said it, but oh God, yesterday he was all over her. How are you, Ben? That was a neat party before it got so heavy."

"Ended well, that's the main thing. What would you like?"

"What are you having?"

"Well, I had a martini with Mr. MacKay. I could do another."

"Sounds good."

"Straight up?"

"Absolutely."

I ordered Burnett's martinis, dry, with olives.

The club's oversized cocktail glass boasted the capacity of a swimming hole. Etched into the side were a florid "NCC" and, below the rim, a fill line which the bartenders cheerfully submerged. I had emptied most of my first in a geranium pot, but from here on I was on my own.

"What are you doing here? You're not a member, are you?"

"My dad was. Cheers."

"Cheers. . . . Ummm. *My* dad used to say, 'That's like jumping into a cool pond.'"

We sipped our respective cool ponds for a while.

"How'd you end up flacking for Steve La France?"

"Michelle talked me into it."

"I guess PR for Steve means keeping his foot out of his mouth."

Georgia smiled. "He says what people want to hear. But he *is* a little ahead of the curve."

"Exactly like his old man. Frank La France used to haunt town meetings like the ghost of Andrew Jackson. 'What this country needs is more guns and dogs.' Drove my dad *nuts* on the school budgets. Of course, back then, people still believed their kids were getting their money's worth, so when old Guns and Dogs finally ran out of steam they'd vote the budget and everyone was basically content enough to re-elect my father."

"Steve's no Guns and Dogs. He's doing an excellent job of playing his one big advantage: The voters are terrified of taxes. He's a publicist's dream—a clear position on a single issue."

I nodded affably. We both understood that public relations demanded public loyalty to the client. We drank some more, comfortable with the world we shared beyond the town line.

"Dr. Greenan told me that Guns and Dogs is rounding up new voters."

Georgia shrugged.

"Small pond?" I commiserated.

"Beats no pond. I guess." She brightened. "I convinced him to challenge Vicky to a debate. It's win-win for Steve. She'll lose if she refuses. And lose worse if she accepts."

"Whatever happened to the 'Stomp for Steve' fundraiser?"

"We'll do that for the regular election, after he beats Vicky."

"Did you do political campaigns when you worked?"

"I was hired on at the end of the last Bush campaign."

"That must have been a grim one."

Georgia grew animated describing an atmosphere that resembled the last hours of the czar's entourage with the revolutionaries in hot pursuit. I ordered another round.

"Thanks. Cheers. They were so isolated. I got into huge fights with people who wouldn't tell them what was happening. PR works two ways: Sure you spew it out, but dammit Ben, you've got to *listen,* too. They were clinging to surveys that meant nothing. All you had to do was *look* at the crowds' faces. Or talk to anybody in a diner."

"But he drew crowds on that train tour, didn't he?"

"So did Lincoln's funeral. They didn't come to vote! They came to watch a sunset. Oh, Ben. The fights. And then later, the blaming. Shoot the innocent."

"Did you get shot?"

Georgia frowned at her glass. She picked it off the bar like a newfound object, swirled the clear gin. "By my husband."

"Beg pardon?"

"Rick shot me. He used the situation to convince me to quit working. I was kind of shaky—I mean, I knew I had really screwed up."

"What do you mean, 'screwed up'? It wasn't your fault Bush lost."

"If I had done my job right I would have convinced his people not to make certain mistakes— Don't look at me like a therapist; I *know* I have a warped sense of responsibility. Anyhow, I wasn't feeling great about myself and Rick really started pestering me about kids. Every night, 'Come on, Georgia. If we don't have kids now, we never will, da-dat, da-dat, da-dat.' You know the spiel, you probably hear it from Vicky."

I nodded. I certainly knew it from Vicky, who, though younger than Rick and Georgia, was growing terrified about never having babies.

"So I gave in and here we are. Rick and me and little Ian makes three. . . . I couldn't believe it when he wanted to move up here. We were down in Darien before. I could run into New York. We were near my mother, so I had help with the baby and there was some kind of a life—you know, our kind of a life, you know, Ben."

"Newbury's great for kids."

"Great for kids. Great for Dad. Great for Mom— Look at me, I get to go to the country club every day—thanks to my darling nanny. How did I get started on this? I'm sorry— What are you thinking?"

"I'm thinking either I should have something to eat or another drink." In truth, I was having second thoughts. Georgia was an interesting, articulate woman, a nice person, and wearing a large sign that read "Vulnerable."

"I'm easy," she said. But she peered into her empty glass and looked relieved when I ordered another round. Then she asked, "Why are you getting me drunk?"

# 25

---

"Let's have a burger at the bar."

"I guess. . . . Make mine tuna on toast. I'll be right back."

She swayed off to a ladies' room designated by a golfer in a skirt. I ordered our lunch. The bar had cleared out as everyone went off to the dining room, and we had the place to ourselves except for the bartender, who busied herself beyond earshot.

Georgia returned, bright-eyed and smiling. "Everyone's gone. Just us."

"And the bartender."

"Can't lose her."

Christ, I thought. She'd had a hit of coke in the stalls.

I had paid lip service to the concept that addiction was a disease. Certainly no one who had worked on the Street in the 'Eighties was a stranger to coke—and I had my own warm relationship with alcohol—but sitting in the club with Georgia, I felt it more personally than I had before. Reg floated into memory. Before he'd signed up with AA, he'd probably had lunches like this too, where tanking up wasn't quite enough.

"So why are you getting me drunk, Ben?"

"I'm getting drunk right along with you." Even with what I'd managed to spill.

"Is this some sort of seduction?"

"No."

"Feels like one."

"I've always preferred my seductions sober. And my seductees."

"Not me."

"In that case," I assured her, "we're both safe."

"Great. Let's be friends." She reached over and we shook hands, elaborately. "So why are you getting me drunk?"

"You tell me."

Back when I was around the stuff, for which I never developed much of a taste, I had noticed that the chief benefit of cocaine, for the users, was how marvelous it made their own voices sound, while simultaneously insulating their ears. Georgia was enjoying this effect, and she answered me at some length, whole paragraphs galloping forth like the hounds, horses, and riders of the Plainfield County Hunt on the tail of an aromatic fox.

Straight, she was a gifted talker, a weaver of full, rich sentences. Stoned, she surpassed herself. She began with a history of recent events: my leaving a message for her; our meeting in the bar; our choice of libation; our rate of consumption. Next came a treatise on refills, observations on my habit of eating the olives versus hers of stacking them to keep count.

She digressed to a learned discussion of full-flavored gins like Burnett's and Beefeaters, and digressed further to disparage vodka martinis, people who drank them, and the barbarous—her word— custom of substituting lemon twist for olives. A further digression introduced her father, who had introduced her to martinis. Daddy had been a man of many parts, which she endeavored to describe in detail.

I interrupted, remarking on the coincidence that Vicky McLachlan had made the acquaintance of alcohol in the exact same fashion, though in their case the old man's liquid of choice had been beer. Georgia appeared to listen attentively. She perked up her ears, nod-ded, smiled, but never stopped talking.

Lunch arrived. My hamburger grew cold, her tuna warm. At last,

she looked down at her plate, with the surprised expression of someone who hadn't noticed the arrival of a small elephant. "Oh, wow,
am I hungry."

We had still not answered the question of why I was trying to get
her drunk. I let her get halfway through her tuna sandwich. Then I
said, "Georgia, can I ask you something?"

"What?" The stuff had worn off. She looked beat.

"I don't want to upset you."

Now she looked frightened. "Oh, Ben, you're not starting that
again, are you?"

"I'm sorry."

"Oh, please don't. Please, Ben."

"I've got to ask you something."

She dropped her sandwich, wiped her mouth with her napkin,
and started to crumple it onto the bar.

"Please don't go."

"You're sneaky," she said. "That's what I don't like about you."

"Sorry."

"But you're gentle. And that I do like."

"I've gotten myself into a real mess here," I said. "Someone I care
about could get hurt and someone else I cared about is dead. So
I'm worried and I'm feeling guilty and I'm trying to work it out."

"Are you in therapy?"

"No. Now listen—"

"Maybe you should be."

"Later. Listen— Hey, please don't go."

"I'm just going to the ladies' room. I'll be back in a minute."

"Could you wait on the hit?"

She turned back, eyebrows rising, with a studied, "I beg your
pardon."

"Come on, Georgia, you can fool the country boys, but give me
a break."

"I'm afraid I don't understand."

"I'm asking you to answer my questions before you go into the
ladies' room to snort coke."

Her mouth trembled.

I said, "It's your business what you do to yourself, but coke at lunch is possibly, shall we say, moving toward a problem."

"You don't know what it's like."

"I don't presume to. But I would say this: You're spending too much time alone. You need some people—and I don't mean 'doing lunch' with Michelle's gang. They're not going to call you on sneaking off for a hit."

"Susan did," she whispered.

"Well, I'd expect her to. You're not going to fool a nurse. But I don't put her in Michelle's gang. She's too busy working. Sit down. Coffee? Dessert?"

"Both," she murmured.

I ordered, hoping cream pie might sop up the toxins. We waited in silence until it came.

"You're wrong," she said.

"About what?"

"Some of them do coke."

"I'm aware of that. But they don't sneak coke at lunch."

"Michelle's really into it. She's my connection when I can't get down to New York."

"You're kidding. You buy from her?"

"When I have to. What she makes on me probably keeps her and Duane supplied."

I hadn't put much thought into supply, but of course somebody had to sell it. "What about Bill and Sherry?"

"At a party."

"Susan and Ted?"

"No way."

"Rick?"

Her expression hardened. "Rick inhabits a 1958 time warp. He knows I drink too much. But if he caught me doing lines in the kitchen, he'd assume I was learning how to bake, which would make him very happy."

"Were they doing coke at the party?"

"Oh God, it was so lame. At one point, I thought, Hell must be a weekend with local yokels who think they're hip. Michelle laid lines *around* the Jacuzzi—it's round, you see, and the idea was to snort your way around in a circle. While you're in the water? Bill Carter kicked up waves and turned about two hundred dollars' worth of cocaine into library paste."

We both laughed.

"God, was Michelle pissed."

"How did Rick incorporate that into his time warp?"

"He was upstairs with Sherry— Oh, Ben, you should see yourself. Look in the mirror." She turned me toward the bottles and I saw my jaw slowly rise from the bar.

"I'm amazed. I mean, I heard all the dumb rumors, but I'm still amazed. Are you sure?"

"Sure enough for it to ruin *my* night."

"You mean—"

"I didn't go there to swap." She shuddered. "God, what a thought. Eeeyyaaach. Duane? Bill? Spare me. I may have my problems, but desperation to get laid is not among them."

"Ted?"

"*Ted?* Are you joking? Ted and Susan were joined surgically at their wedding. They're like Siamese twins. You couldn't get between them if you tried, and if you tried too hard, either one of them would cut your throat. Don't you find them a little scary?"

"No."

"I do. I mean I like them a lot. And I admire them enormously. I never met anyone who dealt better with defeat than those two. But I wouldn't want them mad at me. Silent Ted? Ooooooohhh. And Susan? How she seems to materialize, like something *looming* out of the fog. Don't you find that?"

"What time was that, when Rick was upstairs—if he was—with Sherry?"

"About eleven."

"Before Reg got there?"

"Before."

"How long were they up there?"

"Not long. Rick's somewhat of a rabbit."

Maybe the couple Vicky heard. Maybe not. "If you weren't swapping, who'd Bill go with?"

"Bill was too smashed on those stupid Tombstones. I doubt he noticed. Or didn't want to notice. Sherry likes men. They've got some sort of tacit arrangement."

"Do you *know* all this or are you guessing? I mean, you're kind of new in town, by comparison. But you seem to have a take on everybody. All the down and dirty."

Georgia smiled. "People forget you're there when you're drunk. Sometimes the girls'll have lunch and it's like Georgia doesn't exist."

"Did Reg get into the Jacuzzi?"

"No. He just hung out."

"Did he do any lines?"

Georgia laughed. "Nobody did any lines after Bill's walrus act."

"Did Michelle freak when Reg arrived?"

"No. She had a real thing with Reg."

" 'Thing'?"

"They were close." Georgia attempted to cross two fingers to demonstrate how close, but her fingers wouldn't obey. She kept trying.

"How close?"

"Friends. Buddies."

"Lovers?"

"I don't think so."

"But she told me how angry she was. Remember at Connie's, she yelled at Duane about how Reg was always wrecking their parties?"

"Close. Buddies. Friends. Pals."

"But not lovers."

Georgia shook her head. "It didn't feel that way. At least not to me."

"How was Duane about that?"

"That's why I don't think they were lovers. He sort of encouraged them, like he enjoyed their friendship. As you said yourself, these people have known each other a long time, Ben. Like you, since childhood."

"But I thought Michelle told Reg to leave."

"No. It didn't happen that way. Reg was just kind of mooning around and finally Michelle climbed out of the Jacuzzi and said, 'Come on, I'll make you some coffee.' She put on a robe and they went to the kitchen."

"Just the two of them?"

"I don't know."

"What do you mean? Oh, you mean Sherry and Rick might have joined them."

"Or Ted and Susan."

"Where were they?"

"I don't know. They kind of drifted away when the lines started. Susan's down on drugs. I thought nurses were really into drugs—thanks to an enviable availability—but not Susan."

"Ted and Susan seem a little out of place in that crowd, wouldn't you say? No swapping, no dope. What was left?"

"Booze. Susan must have had three Tombstones without even blinking. Ted matched her, glass for glass. And business," Georgia added as an afterthought.

"What do you mean?"

"They're trying to get back in the game— Gosh, you don't know *anything*, do you?"

I admitted I didn't, to keep her talking, though it was hardly a surprise that Ted and Susan would cultivate the Fisks and Carters to get back into building houses. "Did they talk about the Mount Pleasant project?"

"It was more like they listened. Duane and Bill were at them about zoning problems. I must admit my concentration wavered when they got into setbacks and grades."

"Were they asking Ted for something specific?" This was of double interest to me, as Ted was a zoning commissioner and ruled on variances. There wasn't much I could do about it, but it never hurt to know who was diddling whom in the name of progress.

"They kept saying, 'Why do we need four-acre lots when three is plenty?' "

"Three means they could build twelve more houses on their acreage."

"Sounds like money."

"About a million bucks. . . . Did Reg get into any of that?"

"He didn't seem to care. He looked so sad. I thought he would cry at any minute. When Michelle led him away he looked like a condemned prisoner."

"Leaving you with Duane and Bill in the Jacuzzi."

"Right."

"Then what happened?"

"Bill asked if he could borrow my bathing suit."

I had wondered, but had not asked, about costume. "And?"

"I was bombed enough to think that was the funniest thing I'd ever heard. I started laughing so hard I almost drowned. Big Bill came to the rescue, which he used for an excuse to put his hand on me. I tried to pull away, but he was really strong, and really bombed. I got scared. So I bit him."

She got very quiet and toyed with her empty glass. "You should never drink with guys."

"What happened?"

"Well, he jumped and let go. Then he turned to Duane and he said, 'Come on, Duane, give me a hand.'

"I was so scared I was suddenly sober. That party wing of theirs was all the way to hell and gone the far end of the house. And we were all alone, just me and them. And I thought, Oh God, even if I scream, who's going to notice?"

I said, "I'm surprised Bill would do that."

Georgia shrugged. "Daddy always said, 'Careful drinking with men.' " Her eyes filled with tears. "I can't tell you, Ben, you're a guy, you can't know, how scary it is. It was so horrible to be in that position, knowing that the only thing that could save me was Duane, and he's standing there with this look on his face. Bill circled so they had me between them. He said, 'Ready, Duane?' "

"I said, 'Come on, guys.' Bill laughed. 'Come on, Duane. She's so drunk she'll never remember—hell, we're so drunk, *we* won't remember. Ha. Ha. Ha.' Duane said, 'Screw you, Billy.' Just like that. 'Screw you, Billy.' Then my knight in shining armor climbed out and walked away."

"Where?"

"To the kitchen, I guess."

"Leaving you with Bill?"

"Bill said, 'I was kidding.' That was B.S. but I said, 'Okay.' We settled into the water—on opposite sides—and stared at each other like a pair of amoeba. Bill started sinking, sliding off the seat. The water covered his nostrils and he started coughing. Next minute Sherry walked in, looking pleased. She pounded his back. Then Rick slunk in, guilty as sin. Somebody poured more Tombstones and things settled down."

Georgia stood off her barstool and held the bar for support. "Right back." She took her bag and worked her way to the ladies' room. When she finally came back, she had washed her face and brightened her eyes.

"Well, *that's* better. Now where were we? Oh, yes."

And off we went, after the fox. Trampled by verbiage, I managed to isolate the following events: Susan and Ted returned to the party room and joined Georgia, Rick, Bill, and Sherry in the Jacuzzi. Duane came back from the kitchen and cranked up his overworked blenders for a new round of Tombstones. There was some desultory talk about how unhappy Reg seemed, and with Michelle still out of the room, considerable laughter about the cocaine Bill Carter had tidal-waved.

"Duane didn't mind?"

"Duane was laughing along with the rest of us—he couldn't have cared less, even though he'd paid for the stuff. He's much freer than Michelle, you know, more generous. Michelle's always worried about getting ripped off. I know Duane's supposed to be a hardheaded businessman and all, but he's really kind of a pussycat, compared to Michelle, though a lot of people don't understand that at first because all they see is a fat, beer-drinking slob bossing people around."

"Could be confusing," I agreed, but Georgia's ear for irony was chemically blocked and she kept talking.

Michelle came back from the kitchen, without Reg, and climbed into the Jacuzzi between Duane and "invisible" Georgia.

"Where's Reg?" asked Duane.

"In the kitchen."

"How's he doing?"

"He's flying," said Michelle.

"On what?"

"*I* don't know. I went to the bathroom, and when I came back he was stoned out of his gourd. At least he's starting to cheer up. I told him to come join us."

"Think I should check him out?"

Michelle, Georgia said, had answered, "Bring him back in here if he's mellowed out."

At that point Susan said, "I told him to come back and he said he would."

"Wait a minute," I interrupted Georgia. "Susan had been in the kitchen with Reg?"

"Apparently."

"And Ted?"

"Surgically attached. In fact—now I remember—Ted said he'd go get him. But Duane hopped out first and said he'd do it."

"Did he?"

"He was gone a long time—or at least it seemed long—I don't know. I was feeling no pain, except when Rick got in beside me and tried to touch me. Yeeccch. I swam over to Susan and closed my eyes."

Warm water had swirled. Tombstones were drained. Conversation drifted, wandered on currents and counterflows. Suddenly, Duane burst into the party room, yelling for Susan.

"Come quick! Come quick! Something's wrong with Reg."

# 26

"Duane was so wired his eyes were bulging," Georgia contined. "Susan didn't get it at first and he started screaming, 'You're a nurse. You're a nurse. Do something!'

"She jumped out of the water and ran, dripping, slipping, *ran* through the house. Ted scrambled after her. Then Michelle, and Bill and Sherry. Next thing I knew I was alone in the Jacuzzi with my horrible husband.

"Rick said, 'Do you think we should?' I said, 'Don't talk to me, you slime,' or something along those lines. He asked, 'What's wrong, darling?' I said the traditional, 'I think you know what's wrong.' And after a while he got out and lunked off to the kitchen."

"Leaving you alone in the Jacuzzi? Everyone else had gone?"

"Alone at last. God, was I glad they'd all gone. The water felt like silk and the night air was blowing through the screens. I turned off the jets so I could hear the bugs singing. And I lowered the lights so I could even see stars. And up in the mirror there was this beautiful girl sprawled in the water like a nymph. It was me. I looked so beautiful. Except my hair was all wet and plastered around my face. Am I crazy, Ben?"

"Didn't you wonder what was going on in the kitchen?"

"I didn't care. I thought, Hell, they're not coming back. So I took off my bathing suit and spread out naked, admiring myself with naked admiration. Heaven. Then I began to wonder—I kind of began to remember why they'd gone to the kitchen. Something about Reg. And Duane yelling for Susan. Wait a minute. That broke the spell. I jumped out, dried off, put on my clothes, and went out there.

"What a scene. I'll never forget it. They had Reg on his back on the floor. Susan was hunched over him, shining a light in his eyes. Duane was sobbing, 'Please, Susan. Please save him.'

"Susan was so tender. She turned out the light and pulled Duane to her like a baby. 'He's gone, Duane. I'm sorry.'

"Michelle looked like wax—frozen, white, catatonic. Bill and Sherry were holding each other. Rick looked like his boss had fired him. My heart went out to him. I know him so well. . . .'"

"What about Ted?"

"Ted stood there like Gregory Peck in *On the Beach*: 'Sorry, Australians, we've had a little trouble in the Northern Hemisphere.'"

Georgia's giggle was a prelude to tears. Soon she was mopping her eyes with cocktail napkins and soldiering on in a broken voice. "Poor Reg. The poor man. Ben, I'd just seen him a little while ago in the party room and, and, and *now* he looked like plastic furniture. His skin was blue. Huge, empty eyes staring at the ceiling.

"I mean, I didn't know him that well—we socialized a bit before Janey left him—but he was *nice*. Like you, he was gentle. And smart. And did something with his life—not one of these beer-drinking couch potatoes. Interested in stuff. Suddenly dead. *D-E-A-D* gone. And nobody cared. Except Duane."

"But you just said they were upset."

"They were *stunned*. Shocked. But they didn't *care*. Duane cared. Fat, beer-drinking Duane cried like a baby. He made me cry. I stood there trying to mourn Reg, but I was really crying for Duane. I kept waiting for Michelle to comfort him, but first she was catatonic and then, when she snapped out of it, boy did she go into action.

"'What are we going to do?' she asked.

"Nobody answered. What the hell *were* we going to do?

"Michelle said, 'We have to do something, Duane. What are we going to do?' Duane stopped crying. Bill Carter said, 'Boy are we in trouble.'

"Well, that got everybody's attention. Like you said at your Aunt Connie's, Ben, there was a sudden realization that we had a terrible problem on our hands."

"What did you think?" I interrupted her.

"Me? I knew we were going to get caught. I knew that the second I saw him lying there. I could see Court TV: Pan Main Street, flagpole, General Store; closeup Fisks' Jacuzzi; wide angle four prosperous couples in handcuffs. State's attorney: 'And you, Ms. Georgia Bowland, what did you do to your friend who died?' I knew it was all over."

"But Michelle didn't."

"She kept screaming, 'What are we going to do? What are we going to do?' "

"Whose idea was it to move the body?"

"I don't know. Not mine."

"Come on, Georgia. You were there. Somebody must have taken charge."

"I was ten percent there. I was bombed. My husband had just betrayed me with goddamned Sherry Carter. I was scared. And I was so sad for Duane."

"Georgia, you are an incredibly intelligent woman. You must have noticed when things started moving."

"Well, I didn't. All of a sudden things were moving. The guys picked him up and sat him on the chair."

"Why?"

"I don't know why."

"Who told them to sit Reg on the chair?"

"Does it matter? He was flopping around like a doll. It was grotesque. Rick couldn't bear to touch him. Duane and Bill did it."

"It matters. Who told them to pick Reg up?"

"I don't know. I was blanking out. Ohmigod."

"What?"

"I just remembered: Duane and Bill were wearing gloves."

"Gloves?"

"Garden gloves. I just realized that. Makes sense. Fingerprints."

"So they knew what they were going to do. Somebody got it started. Who?"

"I don't know. I just now remembered the gloves. They must have got them in the mudroom. Except they were clean. Oh, yeah, I remember thinking, Good move, clean gloves. If they were dirty they'd leave marks. Amazing how much I blocked out."

"But you didn't block out who got them started."

"Yes, I did."

"The person who got them started was someone you like a lot. Liked more than the others. Admired. You know who I mean."

Georgia started crying. "Don't make me do this, Ben."

"I'm not making you do anything. You know who told them to pick the body up."

She stood up, reeling, and pushed away from me when I reached to help her. "No!"

"Relax," I said. "I know who it was. There was only one person who knew what to do. Sitting the body on the chair was a crucial, vital decision. Without doing that you would have been caught. The medical examiner would have seen right away you had moved the body."

"The nurse," Georgia whispered.

"Of course, Susan," I said. "She was the only one qualified to know that the body had to be moved quickly—in the position you intended to dump it. And, being a nurse, she was also the one with her head on straight at such a horrible moment."

"Hey, it doesn't mean anything, except she thought fast."

I agreed, to comfort Georgia. Fact was, Susan had thought fast. And smart. But I had to wonder: Had the nurse planned ahead? I held Georgia's hand a minute. "Everything we talked about is between you and me. I really appreciate your help."

She took a deep breath. "It was kind of like your dinner party—fun, till it got heavy."

I found Sherry Carter in a construction trailer next to a renovation Bill was performing on an old sawmill that had been converted into a house in the 1930s. I'd sold it to the new people, a New York doctor-lawyer couple with an impressive art collection to house and considerably more money than sense. Their total expenditure when Bill got done would total out at about twice the property market value—in case I needed another reminder that love defied reason.

Sherry was poking keys on a computer. Her desk was neat, her In box empty, her Out box full. On the wall was a telephone and a list of suppliers and subcontractors. Atop their numbers was scrawled the trailer's phone number. She was wearing jeans, a blue workshirt, and, from what I could see as she folded her hands behind her head and turned to me with a smile, no bra.

"Well, hi there, Ben. You just missed Bill. He went to the lumberyard. Coke?" She bent over an under-the-counter refrigerator and brought out a pair of cold Diet Pepsies. "Cheers."

"Cheers."

"You look like you had a liquid lunch."

"Stopped by the Club. Had a few with Scooter's granddad."

"Under-the-table time."

"I held my own." In fact, my mouth tasted of stale gin and my eyes ached.

Sherry winked. "And now you've come to play with someone your age?"

"When's Bill coming back?"

"Couple of hours. Anything I can do for you?"

"Maybe something I can do for you."

"Oh really? Something fun?"

"Something a little embarrassing, actually."

"For you or me?"

"Embarrassing for me to say, and embarrassing for you if what I heard is true."

"What are you talking about?"

"Listen, I don't go looking for gossip. And I sure as hell don't like getting between people. But just as a friend, I've got to tell you—before Bill hears it somewhere—that I picked up some talk about you and Rick Bowland."

I had no idea how she would react to this little ploy. It never occurred to me she would laugh. Much less a huge laugh, with her big eyes wide, and her lovely teeth gleaming and her head thrown back and her whole, long, lanky frame stretching out, then doubling up, dissolving in giggles as she tried to catch her breath.

"Where did you hear that?"

"I gather it's not true."

"Not true? Rick *Bowland?* Ben?" She cracked up again. Unfolded and threw her arms around me. "I hope you told whoever said that, Don't be ridiculous. Did you?"

"I didn't want to dignify it with a denial."

"Rick Bowland's a skinny tightass. I go for big bears like Bill. And medium bears like you."

# 27

I guess I should have been grateful I'd come this far in life before I'd been called a medium bear, but it rankled.

"What's the matter?" she asked, arms draped over my shoulders. "Tell Sherry."

"I don't want to be a medium bear."

"Well, you're not a big bear. And you're certainly not a little bear. So—"

"I don't want to be a bear at all. It sounds fat."

"I didn't mean fat. I meant cuddly. Hold-on-able." She demonstrated.

"Sherry, there's carpenters over there."

"Ohmigod." She slithered past me and locked the door. "Now, where were we?"

"Where did anybody get the idea that you and Rick were hooked up?"

"Did Georgia tell you that?"

"My lips are sealed."

"Oh God, I've got to talk to her. I thought something was bugging her. You know the party—well of course you know the party, *the* party—Georgia gave me this look, like, You've been screwing my husband, bitch. I was so drunk I didn't really pick up on it, and then everything hit the fan."

"What made her think you were?"

"I went outside for air. I couldn't breathe. Those stupid drinks Duane was shoving down us. Tombstones. Sweetened Drano was more like it. I sat under a tree and kind of mellowed out. But after a while the mosquitoes started, so I headed in. I fell over Rick; he was passed out on the lawn. If I didn't wake him up the mosquitoes would suck him dry. So I nudged him with my toe, but he was really out.

"I knelt down and shook his bony little shoulders. He came out of it all groggy, kind of focusing on me like I'm spinning in circles. I'm going, 'Hey, Rick. Wake up, hon, before the mosquitoes eat you.' He goes, 'Hit the snooze alarm,' and I realize Rick's thinking I'm Georgia telling him to haul his tail to IBM.

" 'Rick. Wake up. Come inside, we'll jump in the Jacuzzi.' Suddenly he's awake. Totally aware. He knows he's in the grass. He knows I'm not Georgia. And he thinks I'm trying to jump his bones. I said, 'Oh, no. No, no, no.' Rick goes, 'You're overdressed'—must have heard it in a movie—I'm wearing a bikini made of kite string. He grabbed, and pulled, and ripped. My tits fall out. He goes, 'Oh God,' like it's supposed to be a compliment."

Sherry laughed. "I hit him so hard I thought I knocked him out. You should have seen it, Ben. It was great. I tied my string and went inside. I thought, Wow, I decked a guy!"

I must have been gaping a little, because she explained, "Keep in mind, the drinking?"

"Did anybody notice?"

"Well, it certainly sounds like Georgia noticed. Damn. I like her. I don't want her to think I want her stupid husband."

"Did she say anything?"

"No. But after I got in the water, in came Rick, looking weirded out. I guess Georgia thought he looked guilty. Thanks for telling me, Ben. I've got to clear this up with her."

"Would you keep my name out of it?"

"Absolutely. I'll just tell her what happened, minus the grab. Can't blame Rick for being drunk as I was."

"Did he go upstairs?"

"I don't know."

"Do you think Ted and Susan made the same assumption as Georgia?"

"No. They didn't see us come in."

"Didn't Bill wonder?"

"Bill?"

"Your husband."

"Bill doesn't have a jealous bone in his body. I mean, if he walked in right now and saw me doing this! To you."

"Sherry!"

"He might be pissed."

"Hands off."

"Or this! But he thinks I'm only kidding around."

"If you don't stop doing *that,* I'm going to start taking you seriously."

"I'm sorry; I'm teasing. I have a thing about you bears. But you're no fun. You never follow through."

"And end up punched out like Rick Bowland?"

"Okay," she said, with a businesslike glance at her watch. "Let's get serious. Bill's gone two hours."

I reached for the door.

"Chicken?" She smiled.

"Call me sometime when you've got a week." It seemed a safe bet she'd never get a full week free, which, while it would be marvelous, was not something I wanted to do to my friend Bill.

"I might," she said.

"In the meantime, can I ask you one more thing?"

She crossed her arms and smiled indulgently. "Sure, Ben. What's up?"

"Didn't anybody want to call 911?"

"Oh, Ben. You're still doing that. What's the matter? You feeling guilty for your friend?"

"Sure."

Sherry looked at the locked door. "Now, listen. This goes no further than you. If you repeat it, I'll say you're lying."

"Why?"

"Because nothing will bring him back."

"Who called 911?"

"Bill tried."

"Tried?"

"They stopped him."

"Who stopped him?"

"Ted."

"What do you mean, 'stopped him'?"

"Susan was doing CPR. I said to Bill, 'Shouldn't we call an ambulance?' Bill grabbed the phone. Ted leaned over and said something to Susan. She shook her head. Ted grabbed the phone and said, 'Wait.'

" 'What do you mean, Wait?' Duane comes over. 'What's going on?' Bill said, 'I want to call an ambulance. Ted says wait!' Duane was really confused. The next second Susan called, 'He's gone.' And it was over. It wouldn't have made any difference."

"How long did she work on him before you said to call an ambulance?"

"Ben, I've worried about that over and over. And you know what I think happened? I think I saw her being a nurse, being in charge, being the expert, doing her job; and I thought, Okay, she knows what's best. I'm just a spectator. Which I was. I was just watching an accident. Like you pull over on the side of the road, but you don't get in the ambulance crew's way. Susan was the ambulance crew."

"I guess so."

"It has to be so, Ben. Could have been any one of us. We've been friends for so long, through so much. . . . Do you remember how we worked in the 'Eighties, throwing up houses like there was no tomorrow—But you weren't here—Let me tell you, Ben, we had fun. We were so young. We were still in our twenties. Ted had the big boat and we all had plenty of money. It was fun and work and fun and work and fun. Who knew, growing up here, we'd make ten times what our parents ever did?

"Then everybody got mangled in the recession. But we survived. Sure, some people disappeared, but we brought in Rick and Georgia and they're full of life. And you came home. It's getting good again, except for poor Reg. Christ, I don't know. It makes you feel old, sometimes. But we've *survived*. And we've got new things cooking. And if you'll sell that turkey over on Mine Hill Road, life'll be good. Is that too much to ask?"

"Suppose not."

"Ben, do you believe I didn't screw Rick Bowland?"

"If you say so."

"Would you care if I did?"

"I'd figure it was none of my business. . . . Although I would wonder if you did it in the upstairs guest room."

"I never went upstairs. Would it make you more or less inclined to sleep with me if I screwed Rick?"

"None of your business."

I went home. No messages. I telephoned Ramos's Bar. The bartender recognized my voice and passed the phone when I asked, "May I speak with the president, please?"

Before I could ask about Spider, she said, "The troopers tapped this phone, again."

I hung up before they could trace me.

My basil hadn't recovered, so I boiled some mushroom tortellini, drenched it in oil and garlic, and ate it. The night had turned hot. A dense mugginess had arrived from the south, shoving out the cool, dry air the Canadian high had blessed us with.

The porch was thick. I gathered my lists and retreated to my library. Deep in the oldest part of the house, the stone chimney exudes a coolness on the worst day. I spread out on the reading table and crossed off Bill and Sherry.

I was down to Duane and Michelle and Ted and Susan as my only suspects who'd been with Reg in the kitchen. I felt I was closing in. Except for one problem. Motive.

Pondering that imponderable, I turned again to Reg's telephone bill and studied it closely. Twice I dialed numbers that intrigued me. Neither was answered by the dinner date who'd stood him up at Brassée.

The library was the quietest room in the house, insulated from the street sounds. I thought I heard a door. I listened. A board creaked in the hall.

"In here, Spider."

# 28

---

"Mind your step," I cautioned, indicating the warped saddle where he might trip and break his neck just when I needed him.

Spider was the size I remembered from our last meeting, wide and square. He looked a little shorter now that he wasn't standing over me kicking. But the .44 Ruger Redhawk he had tucked against his hip probably made him feel taller. I recognized the gun because Reg and Duane had bought them for their elk hunts—a powerful, big-bore "stopper" in the event they blundered into an angry grizzly. "Five shots for the bear," Reg used to say. "The sixth for me."

"I see you got my message."

"You crazy, man?" I remembered his voice too, the quick-burst delivery in the melting-pot accent of a Brooklyn street corner.

"Who killed Little John?"

"You."

"Get off it. Why the hell would I send word for you if I killed your buddy?"

"Tryin' to kill me too."

"Spider, you're holding the gun."

"Believe I'm holdin' the gun."

"If you're here for revenge, you got the wrong guy. I'm as confused as you are. What do you say we trade notes?"

"Say what?"

"I want to know who shot him. That's why I sent for you."

"Why?"

"Was it a gang thing?"

"No way."

"What do you mean, 'No way'?—Come in, come in. Sit down. Take the wing chair."

Puzzlement clouded Spider's face. He rubbed a knuckle on his tears tattoo.

I pointed. "That's a wing chair."

He eased into it, the gun tracking me like a radar-guided cannon.

"What do you mean, 'No way'? The Popes would have banged him first chance they got."

"Popes wouldn'ta got so close. 'Sides, Popes woulda pulled a drive-by. Little John bought a head shot." (Exactly the point I had argued with Sergeant Bender.)

"Someone he trusted?"

"Only guy he trusted was me. And I didn't do it."

"Why would he trust me? Think, Spider. Who else did he trust?"

Spider thought long and hard. Slowly, like a rainy dawn, his face brightened. "Shit!"

"What?"

"The rich bitch," he said with sudden conviction.

"What rich bitch?"

"She shot Little John. It weren't you and it weren't the Popes, the rich bitch did him."

"Who?"

"Little John's woman."

"What's her name?"

Spider shrugged.

This was a woman I wanted to meet. "Listen, Spider, so you don't waste the trip, maybe I can slip you a couple of bucks to fill me in on the rich bitch."

Spider got a crafty look in his eyes that I didn't particularly like.

Street guys are like hungry lions. If they can't catch a wildebeest, woe to the wart hog they stumble upon.

"Gimme the watch."

"Watch?" I echoed blankly.

"Hell with your coupla bucks, gimme the watch."

"What watch?"

He waved the Ruger. "Other night you said you had a fifteen-thousand-dollar watch."

"Come on, I'm not giving you my watch."

"I'm takin' your watch." He jumped up. "Let's go, man. Where is it?"

"I was trying to distract you. There was no watch."

Spider cocked the revolver. "There better be a watch."

"Okay. There's a watch. In the attic. You want me to run up and get it?"

He backed through the door, beckoning with the gun. I obeyed and led him down the hall to the front of the house and up the stairs. I showed him the narrow door next to the guest bathroom that opened on the attic stairs, opened it on his orders, turned on the light, and headed up into the heat trapped under the roof.

Spider trailed. Once he got too close and I could have kicked his gun hand. But I might have missed. We stood on the dusty boards. I pointed to a long row of zippered clothes-storage bags hanging from a pipe nailed across the rafters.

"In there, in a suit."

The attic contained things my grandparents had no use for, like wooden golf clubs and tennis racquets, and relics of my own past, mothballed in the unlikely event a change in career ever coincided with a return to 'Eighties fashion. In the even more unlikely event the military ever needed me again, I still had my uniforms.

I reached for the Wall Street bag.

"Hold it!" He slammed the heavy gun hard against my shoulder. It hurt a lot. He raised it high, threatening to hit me again, savoring the power it gave him. At that point we both realized that when he found the watch, he would celebrate a successful evening by pistol-whipping bone fragments out of my skull.

I'd made a mistake luring him here in the first place. Out of his world too long, I'd forgotten that their biggest high was the thrill of total control. Ultimately my watch would be a souvenir of that wonderful time he'd killed a guy in his attic. Until he fenced it.

Eyes and gun on me, Spider felt for the zipper and unzipped the bag.

"Dark blue suit," I said. "Right-hand pocket."

Spider fumbled around. He had to look away to see blue. I got one of my hands out of sight and worked open the uniform bag and felt inside.

"I don't see no watch. What are— Wait. Wait. What do we have here?" He drew it out by the strap and raised it lovingly to the light. "Whoa." He held it to his ear.

"Move it around, it's self-winding. Yeah, that's right, just shake it a little."

Spider spun the watch. When he saw the second hand moving, he actually smiled, a smile that faded when he heard the *slaaaannnt* of steel.

He whirled, still holding the watch, swinging the big Ruger to bear. What he saw made him laugh. I had whipped my dress saber from its scabbard and had assumed a guard posture that must have looked very silly to a man with a gun.

As I've mentioned, had the small-arms instructors had their way, I'd never have graduated Annapolis. Fortunately, the fencing master put in a kind word. Not that I was his star pupil—I never would have made the team if mono hadn't felled several upperclassmen— but he was proud of the jump lunge we'd developed to compensate for my abysmal defense. My teammates had dubbed it the *hari kari parry,* as it was often as deadly to me as to my opponent, but it sure covered ground.

Spider was still laughing when I skewered his wrist.

He wanted to pull the trigger. But his fingers were opening even as he fought to keep the heavy gun from falling. It thunked to the floor at the same instant he felt the pain. He screamed, yanked his arm. Blood flew. The blade emerged, red.

Yelling, he stumbled around, holding his wrist, reaching for the gun.

I advanced, pointing the tip at his eye. He backed away.

"What you do that for?" he screamed.

"A kick in the head. Busted-up face. And torn ear. You got a problem with that?"

"A sword?" he moaned. Next he would complain, "No fair."

I picked up his gun, made sure I at least looked like I knew how to shoot it, and backed away. "Okay, Spider. Who shot Little John?"

"Fuck you."

"Spider. I count six shots in this thing. I'll use six to kill you."

He looked up with contempt. "You don't have the balls."

I raked him with a Leavenworth Look. It lacked impact. He had me. There was no way I could shoot him unless he threatened me and he knew it. I felt like an honest cop faced with a career criminal flaunting his civil rights. What are you going to do but book him and see him in court?

As he looked to steal another advantage, his eye lighted on my watch, which lay on the floor where he'd dropped it when I cut him. He raised a dirty Adidas high, dared me to shoot, and stomped down hard. The point he was attempting to make about my inability to shoot him was valid—the survival genie didn't really care what time it was. But why Spider assumed I wouldn't use the saber was beyond me.

"*Ahhh!*" He fell backward, hit the floor with a crash that shook the house, and grabbed his calf. I retrieved my watch. The little moon face flashed a grateful smile.

"On your belly, Spider. Roll over." I waved the gun and prodded him with the blade. "Hands behind your back. Close your eyes. *Close 'em.*" I grabbed a wire coathanger, untwisted it, and knelt with a knee in the small of his back. It wasn't easy wrapping his wrists while holding the gun, but I managed.

"On your feet."

He stood up, a trifle less cocky, favoring his wounded leg. Two cuts in quick succession had left him white-faced. And the wire was an unpleasant touch.

"Down the stairs. Slowly. When you reach the hall keep moving."

"Where we going?"

"For a ride."

"Where?"

"Where'd you park your car, Spider?"

"Up yours, man."

I accepted that as a reminder that a skewered wrist and a punctured calf weren't enough to take a Waterbury Latin Knight out of action. "I ask because if it's on the street, the state trooper'll check it out."

"The lot by that Yankee thing."

"Good move."

"That's where we parked last time."

"Excellent. Okay, let's get something straight. If you try anything I will shoot you. It's my town. All I have to say is that a Waterbury lowlife broke into my house again. They'll give me a civic award. *Capish?*"

He *capished* enough to shut up.

I wrapped a wad of paper towels around his wrist.

I was worried about Alison and her mother, but the lights were out in the barn. I walked him to the Olds, standing close with the gun in his side. I put him in the passenger seat, got in, backed out of the drive, and headed north on Main and up Route 7. The night closed in around the car and the trees swallowed the headlights.

"Where the hell we going?"

"The woods."

"What?"

"Deep woods."

I drove slowly for miles and turned off on Crabtree. Spider looked back at the last house lights, fading behind us. The road turned to dirt. I slowed down, switched off the AC, and opened the windows. The air felt like warm water, and sounded like katydids and crickets had declared war on each other. Spider didn't like it. He looked as unhappy as a Newbury kid like Pete Stock in a Waterbury alley.

"How far we going?" Spider peered intently into the dim tunnel of light the headlights projected.

The headlights picked up an intersection. I stopped, hesitated, then turned onto a rutted track that had been a lumber road. The Olds bucked, scraping its bottom.

"We're going to get stuck out here," Spider warned me.

"Not me," I said, the gun in my left hand, across my lap, pointed at him. I assumed that by now he had worked his wrists loose. The road forked. I chose one at random, followed it for a mile, and stopped.

"What's this?"

Huge moths circled in the headlights. I shut the engine, pocketed the key.

"Hey."

The lights-on warning went *Bong, bong, bong.*

I shut the lights. Dark descended like a blanket.

*"Hey!"*

I stepped quickly from the car. Spider turned to me, eyes big in the courtesy light until I shut the door.

"Where you goin'?"

I said nothing, just leaned against a tree and let my eyes adjust. Soon I could see him huddled in the front seat, craning his head to see out.

"Hey!" he called. The tree and I were one.

Bugs warred. An owl barked. Something screamed an astonished last breath.

"Where'd you go?"

I slipped quietly behind the car and alongside his window.

"Talk to me, Spider. Who's the rich bitch?"

# 29
---

"Mother! I thought you split."

"I'm going to split. With my car. I'm going to leave you here, Spider. All night."

"Oh, yeah. You do that, man. Somebody'll come along."

"Anyone who comes along this road, you don't want to meet. Or any *thing*."

"What do ya mean?"

"Bears."

"Shit man, you're joking."

"Going to talk to me?"

"Up yours."

I opened the door.

"Hey, come on."

"*Out!*"

"Hey, man. Just, like—what you wanna know?"

"Who's the rich bitch?"

"I don't know."

"You said the rich bitch shot Little John. Who is she?"

"I don't know, man."

"Get out!"

"No. No, I never met her. Little John kept her to hisself."

"You never saw her face?"

"Never saw her anything, man."

"Never heard her name?"

"He never said it."

"You're going to have to do better, Spider. Or I'm out of here. Start at the beginning: How did Little John know her?"

"I don't know. He kept her for hisself."

"You already said that."

"Truth, man. He had a great thing going. Sex for dope. She'd do anything he wanted for it."

"I thought you said she was rich."

"Kicks, man. She had money. She had it all her way. Made him wear a condom? Believe that? Little John wearing a condom. He said he'd shoot me if I told."

"But he told you."

"We hung together. He only told me once. He was high."

"He must have told you more than that when he was high. Was she good-looking?"

"A real piece."

"What color hair?"

"Little John don't say."

"But really beautiful?"

"A piece, man. Drove a big Benz."

"Mercedes Benz?" That I hadn't expected. Michelle had her Audi, Susan a dying Colt, and Janey had something Japanese. Maybe Greg Riggs, Esquire, drove a Mercedes. "What color?"

"I don't know. Jesus, who cares?"

"Your ride home cares."

"Ask me something I know," he blustered back unconvincingly. He *had* freed his hands, but only to hunch over, gripping his wounded calf, which seemed to trouble him more than his wrist. "Come on, man. Let's get outta here."

"What kind of dope did she buy?"

"Coke. H. Whatever he had."

"Did she buy a lot?"

"Hey, Little John wasn't heavy duty, if you know what I mean."

"What do you mean?"

"He sold whatever shit he could get his hands on. We ran a bunch of little dealers. No big deal. Assholes smokin' up their own stuff, gettin' arrested, gettin' shot for steppin' on it too hard. When you're only two guys, you don't have enough muscle to build a clientele. We'd take a street and the Popes would kick our ass. You can't sell dope on the run, you know. You gotta have turf you own. You know?"

"Tough business."

"Toughest. One time we took over a house? Got four or five families holdin' and sellin' for us? Popes torched it. We open up across the street, cops blew us off."

"So the rich bitch was a pretty good deal? Nice, steady customer?"

"Yeah, but Little John's *givin'* it to her. I say, 'Little John, you want free sex, hit the crackheads.' John goes, 'It ain't the same, man.' "

I treated Spider to some hard-won wisdom. "You know what they say: If you want to go partners, you better pick a partner who has the same goals as you."

"Righteous, man. Righteous. You both gotta want the same thing. One day we score pure H. This shit would fly you to the moon. I go, 'We're in, Little John. Step on this ten times and we're still selling the best dope in the neighborhood.' John goes, '*Yes.*' He says he'll cut it. Sends me out to round up our best salesmen. I get back, and instead of two hundred hits, he's only got a hundred. I go, 'You didn't step on it enough. There's only a hundred.' John goes, 'I stepped it plenty.' You know what he did?"

"Beats me."

"Kept back *half.* Never cut it. Says it's for a special customer. Guess who?"

"The rich bitch."

"He's givin her *pure!* For what? A lay? Enough stuff there for a hundred lays. You know what he says? 'It ain't the same.' "

I asked him, "What tag were you selling, Knight Out?"

"Yeah, that was us. Knight Out. How'd you know?"

"Buddy of mine was partial to it."

"Can we go home? My leg's hurtin' like a bitch." It was too dark to see his hands, but he seemed to be massaging his leg.

"Let me ask you something, Spider."

"What?"

"How'd you and Little John happen to break into my house?"

"I don't know."

"Spider. You broke into my house and nearly killed me. Then you shot at a state trooper. 'I don't know' implies you suddenly woke up in the midst of a terrible dream."

"I don't. It was Little John's score. He said he had something. I said, 'Cool.'"

It suddenly occurred to me that while I was lulling Spider into a conversation I hoped would produce information, he was lulling me into a fatal mistake. Spider wasn't afraid of the dark anymore. I heard it in his voice. I'd forgotten the coathanger.

I started to draw back. He whipped his arm out the window. I saw, too late, that he had used the time he'd been chatting so affably about the business problems of the dope trade to fashion a shank.

An ordinary street fighter would have raked the broken wire across my gun hand. Only a stone killer would have tried to drive it through my heart. That, coupled with the fact that I was already drawing back, saved my life. The thing scraped my left biceps, tearing skin like a carpenter's saw. I swung the gun blindly. The long barrel crunched his nose.

Spider dropped the wire shank and clamped both hands to his face, gasping with pain. I took a deep breath, thanked God I was able, and tried to swallow down the adrenaline. When I stopped shaking, I cocked the Ruger. The metal click was so loud the bugs fell silent. It wasn't hard to sound deadly.

"No more games, Spider. You don't play nice. Why'd you break into my house?"

"You—"

"Don't tell me I broke your nose. I know I broke your nose and you know why. Answer me."

"Little John said he knew about this house in this hick town." His voice was nasal, and muffled by his hands.

"Newbury."

"Yeah, Newbury."

"How'd you find it?"

"He had a map."

"Where'd he get the map?"

"From a gas station."

"And what was in the house?"

"Stuff. Anything we wanted."

"You mean, just walk in and take it?"

"Said the guy was there alone. No locks. All we had to do was bounce him and then we could take anything we wanted."

" 'Bounce' is like a beat down?"

"Same."

"Were you supposed to kill me?"

Spider looked up over his fingers. There was just enough light to see a glint in his eye. "You're alive, aren't you?"

"So the word was *don't* kill me."

"Biggest mistake we ever made."

I said, "Wait a minute. I seem to recall that *you* stopped Little John from shooting me."

"Little John had a temper."

"What did you care?"

"The deal was a thousand bucks to bounce you. Nothing if we killed you."

That was interesting. Obviously, I was glad to be alive. Grateful, even, to whomever had sicced these bozos on me, for working up an incentive system to keep them in line.

"Where was the thousand bucks coming from?"

"Little John didn't say."

"But you guessed."

"It was easy. Who the hell did John know with a thousand bucks?"

"I don't want to put words in your mouth."

"The rich bitch."

"Thank you, Spider."

"Let's go, man. My whole face hurts."

"Two more questions."

He groaned.

"First: I spent two days in the hospital with two concussions and had a face for a week that frightened children. You've got stab wounds you better get disinfected and one broken nose. Are we about even?"

"I'll make you a deal," he said. "I won't come to your goddamned town if you don't come to mine."

"No deal. I'll stay out of your neighborhood. But you don't own Waterbury."

"Okay. Okay. Let's go."

"Second question."

"What?"

None of my suspects owned a Mercedes Benz. I said, "Is it possible that Little John might have exaggerated about the rich bitch?"

"How you mean?"

"Maybe she wasn't that beautiful."

"Maybe."

"Or that rich."

"Rich enough."

"Maybe didn't drive a Benz? Maybe a Toyota?"

"Maybe."

"Or wasn't that good a lay?"

Spider laughed at my naivete. That made him yell in pain as the laugh rattled his nose. He gasped, caught his breath, and explained to the Newbury hick, "Listen. If Little John wanted a bad lay, he coulda stayed in the neighborhood."

I drove Spider to his car in the Yankee Drover parking lot, advised him again to get his wounds looked at, and watched him leave town. I went home, showered, and poured hydrogen peroxide on my arm. It stung like fire. But nothing like it would sting Spider when he poured it into those punctures. Consoled by that thought, I slapped on some Band-Aids and a long-sleeved shirt.

I rolled the cuffs for relief from the heat and took a walk on the old streets of the town, where the streetlights were smothered by maple leaves and tree roots had heaved the sidewalks. I stopped at Ted and Susan's cottage at midnight.

Their lights were still on. I arranged an apologetic expression and knocked on the screen. Ted came, flipped on the front light, and let me in. "You okay, Ben? It's kind of late."

"I saw the light."

"Oh, we're up. Just having a nightcap on the porch."

"I don't want to intrude." Actually I very much wanted to intrude.

"Come on, come on." He led me through the little house, calling, "Ben's here, hon."

"Hi, Ben. Come on out. Get a drink."

Ted poured me a beer and led me to the porch. Susan was dressed in summer pajamas. That dandy old word "fetching" came to mind. "I'm sorry. I saw the light."

"Don't worry. School's closed and I've a week off. It's fun to stay up late."

The little screen porch was crowded, with wicker furniture from bigger houses. It overlooked a tiny backyard that Susan had transformed into a flower garden. She'd even found room to plant an herb maze, and the scent of lavender drifted through the screen.

When I complimented her on the garden, she complained it was a struggle in the shade of the neighbors' trees—a perennial in-town problem they'd never suffered in their former homes.

Ted said that Connie had invited Susan to tea. He talked about the Mount Pleasant project, subtly feeling me out on the subject of

challenging the four-acre zoning requirement. I listened politely, re-
fusing to be led, while I reviewed in my mind what I had learned
that afternoon.

Neither Sherry, nor Georgia, nor Rick, nor Bill had been in the
kitchen before Reg died. Rick and Sherry were out on the lawn—
despite Georgia's belief that they had gone upstairs. Later they had
rejoined Georgia and Bill in the Jacuzzi, after each of the men
had groped the other's wife, unsuccessfully.

Michelle had taken Reg into the kitchen for coffee. Duane had
joined them after declining to partake of a rape among friends with
Bill and Georgia.

I had two questions: Were Ted and Susan in the kitchen with
Reg? And who had Vicky overheard screwing in the guest room?
Ted and Michelle? Or Reg and Michelle? Or Reg and Susan? (It
seemed a safe bet that whoever was upstairs had not killed Reg.
Unless, of course, Reg was the lucky guy upstairs. In which case, I
longed more than ever to know who had stood him up at Brassée.)

"Duane," said Ted, "suggested that prominent real estate brokers
speaking in favor of three-acre zoning might carry some weight with
the board. Do you think Fred Gleason would be interested?"

"I hope not."

"You can't stop progress, Ben. There's pressure to build. It comes
from people."

"We've got one two-lane highway from the south. That holds off
the people pressure. The pressure you're talking about comes from
developers."

"How about real estate agents? They stand to profit too."

"Speaking for myself—and, I think, Fred—I'll take my profits
from quality, not quantity. Besides, if you think we have school
budget problems now? Wait 'til you launch a housing boom."

"New houses pay taxes."

"Never as much as it costs to educate their children."

Ted shrugged. "Fact is, if Steve wins, he'll push to rewrite zoning.
So it'll be out of our hands. Right?"

"Terrific."

"I agree with Ben," Susan said quietly. "I like it the way it is."

Ted smiled, and I saw the wise, fatherly Gregory Peck quality that Georgia had alluded to—the leader, who knew best, the man above, apart, and ultimately in control. "Enough politics. How've you been, Ben? That was a good party before you snookered us."

"I'm glad you enjoyed yourselves. . . . Speaking of which . . ."

"What?"

"I'm not sure how to put this."

"Try straight," said Susan, "for a change."

"Did you see Reg in the kitchen before he overdosed?"

Susan looked at Ted. "No," they chorused. "Except," Ted added, "for a few seconds, when we passed through."

"Then you must have been the couple upstairs in the guest room."

Anybody can lie. Some do it well. Some botch it, shuffling feet or staring far more intently than a truthsayer would. But no one—not even the greatest actor in the world, not even Gregory Peck—could blush on cue.

Susan turned red as a rose, covered her mouth with her hands, and looked beseechingly at Ted. Ted attempted to look stern, or outraged, but he couldn't conceal a smirk of manly pride.

"What about it?"

"All I wanted to know. I'm outta here."

"Did they listen at the door?" Susan wailed.

"No. Nobody knows it was you."

"Except you. I just want you to know, I didn't want to go to that damn party in the first place. Boil in a Jacuzzi while Bill Carter drools at my bathing suit. Then Michelle opens her drugstore. Who needs it?"

"We needed it," said Ted. "We needed to be there."

"Excuse me," Susan jumped up and ran from the porch.

"Where you going?"

She didn't answer, but in a moment we heard water running in the kitchen and then the clatter of china.

"You want to go—"

Ted said, "No. Let her be."

"I'm sorry."

"She's very . . ." He shopped for words and came up with ". . . private."

We sat not speaking while Susan banged dishes. Finally I said, "I presumed it wasn't news that you and Susan sleep together."

He smiled. "Oh, we do." He shook his head. "I swear, after everything else went to hell, we got better. We used to be too busy working all day, and the books and the phone at night. We became like business partners. Now we've got a little time on our hands, we're back to high school."

"Congratulations."

"Yeah, it's like I'm having an affair with my own wife."

"You must be the first married couple in a hundred years to grope each other at a party."

Ted laughed. "What happened was, the rest of them started doing lines. That's not our scene. Susan wanted to go home. I didn't want to leave 'cause I know that if Duane gets that Mount Pleasant project going, he's going to need a major construction partner."

"In addition to the barn job?"

"Oh, sure. That's just one house. Chance for me to play contractor on the weekends."

"But what about Bill Carter? Wouldn't he be up for the partnership?"

"Well, that's why I didn't want to leave the party. Bill was cozied up with Duane. Let me tell you, he was drooling more for Duane's borrowing power than he was for Susan's bathing suit."

"Sounds to me like he's got his priorities skewed."

Ted smiled. "Somebody once told me sex and money are the same thing. Point is, Bill's tapped out at the banks and Duane's not. If *I* walked in for a loan, they'd hit the alarm, but they'll give Duane a blank check."

Ted formed a fist and gently pounded the arm of his chair. "Duane's got that *base* with Newbury Pre-cast. The banks look at him and say, This guy's real."

"Mainly they say, We'll take a piece of Newbury Pre-cast for collateral."

"You think they're still that tight? Even for Duane?" Ted looked disappointed. I figured he hadn't been paying much attention lately, as if sick of news that would keep him out of the business.

"The banks are back to making money the old-fashioned way: borrow from the Fed at three percent; lend it at seven, for real collateral like a finished house, a thriving business. Next time we get clobbered by a downturn, they won't lose. Duane will— Who's he with, Peebles?" Peebles Bank, a 1982 creation founded, rumor had it, by four drunken sailors, had avoided a Federal takeover by the hairs of its chinny-chin-chin.

"No. I hear he got Newbury Savings."

"If that's true, I guarantee you Newbury Savings has Duane's balls in the back of their vault under a huge sack of quarters."

Ted shrugged. "That's his problem. My problem is to convince Duane that I'd make a better partner than Bill."

"Maybe there's room for both."

"There's only so many ways you can cut the Mount Pleasant pie."

"Unless you guys slip through a three-acre variance."

Ted looked grim.

I asked, "What did Reg bring to the pie?"

"Reg brought Reg."

"I don't follow."

"Duane would never cut a deal without Reg."

"Why was that?"

"I don't know. But he never did."

Thinking back, I couldn't recall a Duane project that Reg hadn't been part of. "Did Reg bring money?"

"Not that I know of. But with Reg, Duane knew he had no worries about septic and drainage."

That made sense. A hillside project meant culverts for the roads and driveways; curtain drains above every house, all tied into storm drains; and septic fields that wouldn't bubble up in the neighbors' barbecue.

"So you and Susan took a walk?"

"We got as far as the kitchen. I found us some beer in the fridge. We'd had it with those damned Tombstones. Susan was wearing a terrycloth robe and it kind of fell open and I said, 'Wonder where those stairs go?' So we went upstairs."

I laughed. "You lucky bastard."

Susan walked in, calmer. "Who's a lucky bastard?"

"Your husband."

"Were you listening at the door?"

"No. I left the cookout at seven."

"Wish we had. Damnit, I ended up playing morgue attendant because they didn't call me soon enough."

"Could you have saved Reg?" I asked.

"If I'd gotten to him while he was still conscious, I would have walked him around and tried to keep him awake 'til the ambulance got there."

"No," Ted said firmly. "That's not true. You read the report— we got a copy from a friend, Ben. Once that stuff hit Reg, he was gone."

"I could have tried. Jesus. I thought when I started working at the daycare I was done with bodies. Ben, I really hope this is the last conversation we have on the subject."

"Same here," said Ted.

I didn't have the heart to tell them that unless I got a lot smarter by tomorrow, their next conversation on the subject would be in the glacial presence of Sergeant Marian. So I thanked them for the beer and hurried home to a fitful sleep, and dreams of Spider sticking coathangers in my eye.

# 30

I woke up worrying: Was I a sucker for a lovely couple? Had Susan Barrett blushed with embarrassment? Or flushed with anger?

Maybe Vicky had a clue. I showered off the muggy night and walked to the General Store for breakfast. On the way, I lost my appetite. Every lightpole wore a poster:

DEBATE DEBATE DEBATE
THE SCHOOL BUDGET OR YOUR BUDGET

BELIEVABLE STEVE
VS
SLICKY VICKY

TOWN HALL
8 O'CLOCK TONIGHT

Slicky Vicky? It appeared that Georgia Bowland had sobered up sufficiently to recall a Bush trick or two. That Bush had lost was no consolation. He hadn't lost by much.

I bought a large container of coffee, tea for Vicky, and some fresh-baked shortbread that benefited the ambulance fund drive. Vicky was already at her desk. If Believable Steve's posters were intended to rattle her, his people had miscalculated badly. Pope Alexander, when informed that Emperor Frederick wished to come in out of the snow, could not have looked more implacable.

"I have a strange question for you," I said, presenting tea and shortbread.

"No, I have a question for *you:* You've been no goddamned help at all in this campaign. But right now I need your brain."

"Now?"

*"Now."*

"It's yours." I perched in a deep window that overlooked Main Street and glanced at the clock. "Shoot."

"I'm finally getting a sense of what's happening with Steve. You've been around Newbury politics your whole life. Answer me yes or no: This whole challenge and campaign is entirely about the school budget. Right?"

"Yes. Yes. And yes. It's about money. Which is to say taxes, which is to say the school budget."

"And Steve is smart enough to concentrate on it. I've made a bad mistake running on my record."

"Your excellent record."

"History," she retorted. "Whatever good I've done is over, done and forgotten. If I'm going to beat that scum—did you see those posters?"

"I noticed something or other on a lightpole."

"Very funny. I'm going to beat him on his own subject. 'Slicky Vicky?' Gloves are off, Ben. I'm going to tear his heart out."

"By eight o'clock tonight? Let me lay a quick thought on you: Who's against the budget?"

"The weekenders. The Scudder Mountain crowd. A lot of people in Frenchtown. And a lot of retirees—not all, thank God for grandchildren."

"Who's for it?"

"The people with kids."

"There's still more of them."

"But even the people with kids are worried about taxes. What's your suggestion?"

I told Vicky about my prep school conversation with Steve and his beer customers. "Somehow, we've got to paint a picture of what it would be like if the schools shut down for a few months."

"That's not an option."

"But it's a nasty picture."

"I'll think about it. Now what's your 'strange question'?"

I leaned back in the window and watched Main Street. "It's *very* strange. I want you to give me the first thought that comes to your mind."

"The first thought that comes to my mind is that a politician who loses her party's nomination is totally incapable of earning a living."

"I haven't asked my question, yet."

"Ask. Quickly."

"Go back to the Fisks' guest bathroom. You're asleep on the rug—"

"Passed out."

"Passed out on the rug. Something wakes you. Noise. Someone's right outside in the guest room. You hurry to the door."

"I crawl to the door."

"You crawl to the door and lock it. You hear two people. They're talking about Duane's Tombstones. But they're not there for the conversation and soon they get it on. Right?"

"Right." Vicky looked at her watch.

"Here's the strange question. Do you hear a man and a woman? Or two men? Or two women?"

"Two *men?*"

"*Or* two women?"

"*What* are you talking about?"

"I'm asking you what you heard. Not what you *assumed* you should have heard, but what you actually heard."

"A man and a woman. Like I told you before."

"Are you sure? Are you sure you weren't just assuming that two people who snuck off to screw had to be a man and a woman?"

"Positive."

"You heard a man's voice. And a woman's voice."

"Yes."

"Reg and Michelle?"

"No."

"Ted and Susan?"

"Maybe."

"You're not sure."

"I'm sure it wasn't Reg and Michelle."

"Thank you." I started to swing my feet to the floor. "Oh, Christ."

"What is it?"

"Nothing," I lied.

A beige unmarked Crown Victoria glided past Town Hall and pulled into Trooper Moody's driveway. Marian Boyce climbed out, wearing road cop mirrored sunglasses, and looked up and down Main Street like Darth Vader scouting targets for the Death Star.

I bought more shortbread and coffee and hurried that offering down Church Hill Road to the offices of Hopkins Septic.

Janey was at her desk—resolute in blue jeans and a red Hopkins Septic T-shirt—issuing orders to young Pete Stock, who was wearing a brand new Hopkins Septic cap. I congratulated him on his new job and his release from the Plainfield County jail.

"Freddy Butler says I should sue the state cops for false arrest."

"You might want to get a second opinion from Tim Hall."

"Tim doesn't think it's such a good idea. What do you think, Ben?"

"Did they slap you around?"

"No."

"Lock you up with hardasses?"

"No. They gave me my own cell. You should have seen some of those guys."

"I can imagine. Did they apologize when they let you go?"

"Not really. But I got my truck back."

"Well, I'll tell you, Pete. State cops make better friends than enemies. Besides, Mrs. Hopkins'll keep you hopping; you won't have time for a lawsuit."

Janey handed him a clipboard and pointed out the window at a truck. Pete left. She said, "Thank you. That's all I'd need, angry troopers pulling my trucks over."

"Brought you morning coffee."

"What's up?"

"Could I possibly have a peek at some more phone bills?"

"What for?"

"Could I tell you later?"

"No. Tell me now."

"When's the last time Reg and Duane went elk hunting?"

"Last November."

"Could I see the bill for last October and November?"

"No."

"Janey? Please?"

Her square jaw set hard. "They're none of your business. I hired you. I paid you. The job's done."

"I'm afraid I have to insist."

"Insist?" She stood up, recapped the coffee she had just opened, and shoved it at me. "Get out. What right do you have to 'insist'? Get out!"

"The right of the ripped off."

"The what?"

"You ripped me off, Janey. You watched me stumble around Newbury wasting my time and your money while you pretended you didn't know the most important fact of all."

She grabbed the telephone. "I'm calling Trooper Moody if you don't leave."

"Too late, Janey. Remember when you first hired me? What did I tell you?"

She weighed the receiver in her hand, then gently cradled it. "I don't remember," she said dully. "Something about you'd find out what I didn't tell you."

"Actually, I think I said I'd find it first thing. That turned out to be a gross exaggeration of my talents. It's taken me a lot longer. Now I'm asking you to please give me that phone bill so I can confirm it."

"I don't know what you're talking about."

I pulled my copy of Reg's last month's phone bill from my shirt pocket and uncurled it on the desk. "What are these Long Island calls? 516 code is Long Island."

Janey glanced at them. "Reg and Duane canceled their fishing trip. I guess Reg had to change reservations or something."

"I thought they fished from Montauk. This says Fire Island."

Janey shrugged. "It's on the ocean. Right?"

"That's what I thought, at first. The exchange is 597. That's eastern Fire Island. Know anybody out there?"

"It's the fishing boat."

"And in November they went elk hunting. Show me November."

Janey bit her lips. But neither of us was surprised that she opened her records without any more argument, tugging a tax box from a closet and riffling through rubberbanded envelopes. I scanned the long-distance sheets.

"Got a phone book?"

Moving like a sleepwalker, she brought out a phone book. I turned to the area-code map. Montana code was 406. I thought I knew 305, and sure enough, it was south Florida. She watched, stony-eyed, while I dialed 305-555-1212 and inquired about the exchange.

"Funny. Before they went elk hunting, Reg made calls to Florida. But none to Montana. How'd he make reservations?"

"Eight-hundred numbers don't show up on the bill."

My single experience elk hunting had involved riding a surly horse through a four-day blizzard in the company of a taciturn mountain man who swore when it was over that he'd seen plenty elk last time. So I doubted Big Country hunting guides maintained 800 numbers. Perhaps the outfitters who supplied tents and horses? 1-800-STIRRUP? I didn't think so.

"Janey. Everyone who saw Reg that last night said he was either crying or on the verge of tears. Why do you suppose that was?"

"The divorce was tearing him up."

"You separated six months ago."

"Delayed reaction."

"I'm sorry, Janey. I'm very sorry. I found out what you weren't telling me."

"What?"

"Reg was heartbroken. But he wasn't heartbroken over you. Was he?"

She shook her head.

"Who was it?"

Her mouth curled like a leaf again, the way it had when I asked if Reg was dating. "You're so smart, you tell me who."

"But you know. Don't you?"

She sat frozen, neither confirming nor denying.

I said, "He was heartbroken as he could be only at the end of a long, long love affair. Years and years."

"You don't understand."

"I understand now why Greg Riggs told you to drop it. How long did you stay with Reg after you knew?"

". . . It seemed forever. . . . But it was only a couple of years. Once I gave up on him, I got involved with Greg. It was like I had to. I had to prove that I was still . . ." She shook her head, too shamed to say it out loud. "Reg kept promising to break it off. I kept hoping. He was still a good father. But finally—I guess after he joined AA—I had to admit it was hopeless. He loved somebody else." She made a fist and pounded it softly on her desk. "I think I only really got that the other day: forget the details; what hurt most was that he loved someone more than me. . . . I feel so stupid."

"Love first, smart later."

She didn't smile, but she did say, "Yeah, right."

I got up to leave.

"Does Greg drive a Mercedes?"

"Jeep Cherokee— Where are you going?"

"You know where I'm going. Why don't you go home and grab ahold of Greg? You've paid your dues."

I'd certainly paid mine. The price of trusting clients. Jesus, was I an idiot. On the other hand, what joy to eliminate Sergeant Marian's favorite suspect.

And speaking of that devilette, whom did I meet in the Hopkins parking lot, making a leggy exit from her car? I saluted. "Hello, Sergeant."

"I told you not to rat to your client."

"I didn't. But I have a tip for you."

"Mail it in."

"You won't like it."

"Try me."

"The re-autopsy? The second post mortem?"

"What about it?" she asked impatiently, and I knew the medical examiner had already told her the bad news.

"No foul play. No needle marks. Nothing new. Inhaled pure H. Hotload, like the M.E. said the first time."

Marian took off her sunglasses. Her eyes were gray as icebergs in the Roaring 'Forties. "If I find who leaked, I'll put you both inside."

"I'll take that as confirmation, thank you. So what brings you to Newbury?"

"Because this thing stinks, anyway." She shouldered me aside and shoved through Janey's door.

I ran to the Smoke Shop, the nearest pay phone, begged change from Eddie Singleton, and dialed Hopkins Septic. When Janey answered, I said, "Stall that woman. She knows nothing. If she leans on you, call Greg."

Janey said, "Don't flush till we pump you out."

I spent another quarter on a call to Newbury Pre-cast.

"Duane? Ben. How are you?"

"Hot as hell. How you doing, buddy?"

"I'm hot too. We got to talk about some stuff. It occurs to me I'm the last guy in Newbury who hasn't chilled out in your Jacuzzi. How about beers and business?"

"Five o'clock?"

"Hey, you're the boss. Can't you get out of there early?"

"Three."

"Told you you're the boss. See you at three. Will Michelle be there?"

"If it's business, we'll both be there."

"It's business."

"We'll be there."

# 31

The more money Newbury Pre-cast generated, the deeper the banks extended his lines of credit, Duane still drank Budweiser beer. Working man's Bud was the key to his success—a blunt warning to their employees not to be misled by the French Colonial, the Audi, and the deluxe truck. The Fisks remained down and dirty—on top over every detail.

A can of the brew and a bunched towel sat within easy reach on the Jacuzzi's granite surround. "Fridge under the bar," he called from the bubbling water. "Beck's for wimps, Bud for men. If you want to shower, it's thataway."

I rinsed off in a marble shower, put on my bathing suit, and re-entered the party room, which rumor had not done justice. It was big, with a handsome octagonal timbered dome. The sun streamed through skylights. Sliding glass and screens looked into the woods. The carpet was as deep as Marie Butler had reported, but for some reason, none of the gossips had reported that the Jacuzzi was not the standard molded plastic, but hand-built of granite. The masonry alone must have cost forty thousand, with another one-fifty for the room.

I grabbed a Beck's and stepped into the water. Duane watched, submerged like a hippo to his eyes and nose. "What happened to your arm?"

"Scratched it on a coathanger."

"How come you never get fat? You son of a bitch, I never saw anybody eat like you, but you never get fat."

"God's reward for good behavior."

"He caught up with me. I'm turning into Two-ton Tony."

"Where's Michelle?"

"Lunch at the club. The girls're prepping Steve for the great debate. Jesus, poor Vicky. I thought Steve was a joke, but the guy turns up a winner."

"Just what the town needs, a discount Ribbentrop."

"Who?"

"Champagne salesman the Nazis appointed Foreign Minister."

"Steve's no Nazi."

"That's a relief."

"So what's up?"

"When's Michelle coming?"

"Any minute."

I had plenty of material to stall with. I told Duane I'd been thinking about Mount Pleasant and my New York customers: times were changing; people were so busy, we might have a shot at second-home buyers if we offered some sort of maintenance contract in the deal.

"Lawn mowing and snow plowing."

"Sure."

"And maybe a handyman, someone they can leave the keys with who'll check pipes in the winter, turn on the outside water in the spring."

"How about gardeners?" Duane suggested. "Fertilizer and all that crap."

We bounced it around awhile, with rising enthusiasm, both realizing we'd hit on something we could sell.

"Now, what about the stone retaining walls? It's part of the package. Quality and quality care."

"Christ, don't hit Michelle with that right off. Let me break it to her gentle."

"Break what to me gentle?" Michelle called, gliding across the carpet on bare feet.

"Didn't hear you come in, hon."

"Hey, Ben."

"How'd Steve prep?"

"He's going to kick ass." Michelle dropped her terry robe on the surround, revealing a one-piece black maillot that suited her round figure. "Break what to me gently?" she reiterated, stepping into the Jacuzzi, descending the underwater steps. Waist deep, she moved to the bench across from Duane and me and sunk to her chin. "Oh. Nice. God, it's awful out. Duane, you want to close the windows and turn on the AC?"

"Not if it means standing up."

"We were talking about Mount Pleasant."

Duane said, "Ben's got a great idea how to get his New Yorkers. Tell her, Ben."

I repeated the essence of our conversation. Michelle liked it. She wondered aloud whether they should form a maintenance crew or contract it. I suggested contracting the Meadows Brothers for the grounds work. Duane thought Pete Stock would make a good handyman.

"No, Janey's hired him."

"I guess she's back in gear."

"Are you going to use her?"

"Sure," Michelle answered, "if she gets things moving. We'd rather work with people we know."

"I was just over there. She looked pretty good."

"What were you doing there?"

"Going through her telephone bills."

"What are you, a bookkeeper on the side? God, you could go through my bills, save me the trouble."

"I'd like that."

"Beg pardon?"

"I said, I wouldn't mind checking your phone bills—your long-distance bills—but I don't really have to. I got it all at Janey's."

"Am I missing something?" asked Duane.

"Got what all?" asked Michelle.

I said, "Though, actually, I wouldn't mind checking yours for Waterbury calls. Maybe even Bridgeport."

Duane stirred. The hippo awake—contemplating a tasty canoe. "What in hell are you talking about?"

"Waterbury and Bridgeport are only a side issue. Though a big side issue. Aren't they, Michelle? Kind of a heavy-duty version of that scary note you sent Janey."

"I don't know what you're talking about," she said. But although she looked angry and her eyes were snapping, she did not tell me to leave. I debated dropping Little John Martello on her but decided to keep him in reserve. If I was right, her supplier would dance in her brain without any help from me.

"Let me tell you a story about a friend of mine."

"No," said Duane. "What's this about phone bills?"

"Oh, just some calls to Long Island and Florida."

The hippo hunkered down, very quietly.

I wasn't sure which Fisk, if either, I wanted on my side, so I didn't know who to be nice to. I moved to a neutral corner. "This story happened the night you gave that great cookout. My friend drove by, saw everybody scarfing down your great lamb, would have liked some, but he was feeling kind of low—for good reason—and besides, he had a date in New York. A special date. The first time you go out after you got your heart mangled— You wouldn't know. You're married and all, but let me tell you, when you're not, it happens. Take my word for it.

"So my friend drove to New York. I'm not sure, I think it might have been a blind date—you know, set up by some pal. Or maybe someone he'd gotten to know recently. Could have been through the personals— Anyhow, they were meeting at a terrific, romantic restaurant. The kind of scene you just don't see up here—a New York scene, where if things go right, you walk around the city afterwards thanking God there's such a town.

"Unfortunately, that's not what happened. He got stood up. Somebody lost their nerve. Or somebody set him up as a cruel joke—someone who had a reason to set him up for a fall that night, hurt him, unsettle him so bad he'd let an old friend talk him into 'just one.'

"He spent an awful hour alone in a restaurant and finally fled home, home to Newbury. Swung by Dr. Mead's and gobbled down some ice cream. That didn't help. He still felt like dying—lonely and rejected—all that awful stuff that hurts double when you're already suffering. You guys are right to be married. Who needs it?"

Michelle returned a thin smile. "When Steve wins, you'll have a woman with time on her hands."

"At any rate, he knew the party would still be going here—*everybody* in town knew. So he came over here to see his oldest and dearest friends."

"Didn't we go through this at your aunt's?" Duane growled.

"No. We stepped around it. So Reg, my friend, arrives—crashes, some would say. And finds you guys in the Jacuzzi. You invited him to hop in the water. But he kind of mooned around instead and was generally a drag. Wouldn't take a drink. Maybe he'd do lines, but the coke was all wet, thanks to big Bill making waves. So finally, Michelle, you took pity, and took him out to the kitchen for a cup of coffee. And dessert."

Michelle glanced at Duane. Duane's shoulders broke the surface in a shrug. I still didn't know which one to cultivate. I'd been hoping one would ask me what I meant by "dessert" but neither did me the favor.

"After a while, you spelled each other. Michelle left him in the kitchen, and Duane, you went to keep him company."

"And the next thing I knew he was dead," said Duane. "Like you said at your aunt's. We had a body on our hands. We had to get rid of it."

"You sure did. . . ."

"Jesus Christ. We've been through this fifteen times. We had a party. Innocent people—"

"The party. The party bothered me."

"What about it?"

"Way, way in the back of my mind—since before Reg died—I wondered why you didn't cancel."

"Why should we cancel?"

"The word got around that the hot couples in town were going to have a weekend swap. Most people would have canceled. Remember? Everybody was calling you up—they wanted to get laid too—but you just bulled ahead."

"Screw them," yelled Michelle. "I'll do what I want in my house. We weren't breaking any laws—except a little coke. No way I'd cancel for a bunch of gossips."

"Besides, you needed a party."

"*Needed* a party?"

"It worked. Reg came."

"What's that supposed to mean?"

"Reg came. So did your innocent guests. Rick and Georgia. Bill and Sherry. Ted and Susan. All good friends in a pinch. All vulnerable."

"What do you mean, 'vulnerable'?"

"You didn't invite anyone like me."

"You?"

"No one with nothing to lose. If I'd been there, I'd have said, Call the cops. Everybody knows I'm a screwup. But your guests still had reputations—plenty to lose."

"What is the point of all this?" Duane yelled. "Reg killed himself."

"No he didn't."

"Oh, hell," said Michelle. "Have it your way. Call it suicide. Or call it a goddamned accident if that makes you happy."

"I'll call it murder."

# 32

"And it doesn't make me happy, 'cause I can't figure out which of you did it. Or if you both did it."

"*Neither* of us did it. Jesus Christ, Ben. You're out of your friggin' mind." This from Duane, looking baffled and indignant.

"Why would we kill Reg?" demanded Michelle, even more indignant. She glanced at her robe. I had already resolved to get there first if she moved toward it. Duane took a sip of beer and left his hand near his bunched towel. A big enough bunch to hide a grizzly-stopping Ruger?

No sweat. Unless, of course, they both moved.

"The phone calls," I said.

"Huh?"

"We were talking earlier about phone calls to Long Island and Florida."

"What calls?" Michelle demanded. "When?"

"Reg's calls. Every year, right before he and Duane went elk hunting and fishing. You know, calls to reserve rooms and stuff."

"I don't know what the hell you're talking about."

"But Duane does." I turned to him and said, "Don't you?"

Duane looked sullen. Then he sighed and the folds of his face dissolved like a gelatin mold too long in the sun. "Yeah. I know."

He looked at me, and for a second I thought I saw relief in his eyes.

"You want to tell her or should I?"

Duane closed his eyes. "She knows."

"Knows what, goddamnit?" Michelle demanded.

"Every winter," I said, "when Duane and Reg said they were shooting elk in Montana, they were really in Key West. Every summer, when they claimed to be terrorizing swordfish off Montauk, they were on Fire Island. The Pines or Cherry Grove—the bills aren't specific."

"The Pines," Duane whispered. "We rented the same house every year."

"Don't tell him that!" Michelle screamed.

"He knows, for Christ sake."

"Ben, you don't understand."

"What don't I understand? That twice a year these guys stole a chance to be themselves?"

Michelle took a deep breath, covered her mouth, then formed fists which she pressed to her chin. "That doesn't mean he killed Reg."

"How long were you—how long were you and Reg—together, Duane?"

"Since high school."

"When'd you break up?"

"After Janey left him."

"Why?"

"Reg was a leech," said Michelle.

"He was not!" Duane shouted.

"So why'd you break up?"

"Duane finally came to his senses," said Michelle.

"Since when do lovers have senses?"

"Good question," muttered Duane.

I took Duane's angry mutter as the best opening they'd give me and plowed through it. "Sounds to me like Michelle talked you into breaking up, Duane."

Duane ignored me, eyes shut tight, his mouth a weary line. I turned to Michelle. "Did you talk him into dumping Reg?"

Michelle glowered. "Duane saw we had too much to lose."

"You mean if he divorced you to join Reg?"

"Duane saw it was time to grow up."

"Is that why you put up with the arrangement all these years? To protect your bank account?"

"Screw you, Ben. Duane saw it was time to grow up."

"I asked Janey why she stuck it out. She said she loved Reg."

"The dummy only found out two years ago," Michelle shot back.

"Did you stick it out for love?"

"Of course. And our family."

"And your business."

Michelle looked at her robe. "Everything we've worked for."

I said, "Is that why you killed him? So you wouldn't have to break up the business, like Reg and Janey?"

"Michelle didn't kill him," said Duane.

"You two had an arrangement that worked for years. Until Reg and Janey broke up. You saw the price they paid, losing the house, screwing up the business."

"Michelle didn't kill him."

"That means you did, Duane."

"Why would I kill him? I loved him, Ben. Nobody killed him. He snorted up garbage. That killed him."

"You did a heck of a job of fooling the cops. Not a mark on the body. Fooled Susan. They all thought what you wanted them to think: Reg snorted up an overdose."

"He did."

"That's right. He did. A real close friend—maybe a pal, maybe a lover—induced him to snort along with him or her. You lured him to the party. You set him up for a lonely night. I'd bet money you snookered him into a blind date to stand him up. Then, when he was really hurting, you offered him a hit to feel better. He *did* snort up garbage. Question is, where'd he get it?"

"Beats me."

"Waterbury?"

I looked at Michelle, but Duane answered, "I don't know. I don't do that stuff. We'll have a toot of coke if Michelle picks some up at the club. Jesus, Ben, do you see me driving my truck down to Waterbury to score heroin? Give me a break."

"I don't see Reg driving down there in his Blazer, either. Of course, plenty of middle-class people do, don't they? Come the weekend, you'll see lines of Benzes, BMWs, Audis. Waterbury kids must grow up thinking German cars are all the rich folk drive."

"I didn't kill him and Michelle didn't kill him. The poor bastard did it to himself."

"Did you see him snort it up?"

"No. He'd had a hit before I got there."

"With Michelle."

"No," said Michelle. "Not when I was there."

"People at the party said you came back, Michelle, and told Duane that Reg had mellowed out."

"That's right, hon," said Duane. "You did."

His eyes popped open.

"Ben, what the hell are you saying?"

"I'm saying she killed Reg so you wouldn't wreck yourselves financially in a divorce."

"How?" he asked, as if he hadn't heard a word since he admitted aloud they were lovers.

"She set him up for a fall with a phony date. Set up the party she knew he'd crash when he was really down. Set him up to snort heroin pure enough to kill a horse."

Duane looked shocked to the marrow. The blood rushed from his face. His lips turned white. "Jesus Christ, Michelle. You didn't— Oh Christ. *Oh, no.*"

"Hon," Michelle said gently. "Don't listen to Ben. Listen to me. I've backed you all these years. Why would I hurt Reg? He was part of our life—part of my life too, in some weird way. Why would I kill him?"

"Oh yeah? If he was part of our life, how come I had to break up with him when Janey left? You want to tell me that?"

"I was afraid you'd leave me, like he left Janey."

"I promised you I wouldn't."

"You promised for twelve years you'd leave *him* and you never did. How could I believe you?"

"Is Ben right?"

Michelle reached for her robe.

I yanked it into the water and held her off with one hand while I found the gun with the other. It was a little automatic, quite small, though big enough for John Martello.

Duane's jaw dropped open when he saw the gun.

Michelle screamed, clawing, splashing, throwing her weight at the gun.

"Get her off me," I said.

Duane pushed her across the Jacuzzi. For a long moment they stared at each other like strangers in the same cell. Duane seemed overwhelmed by the enormity of what she'd done. Rage and grief wrestled on his face. Grief won. Fat tears filled his eyes. Michelle moved to comfort him; he shook her off.

"If I did it," she said carefully, "I would have done it for us. Don't you know that, Hon? You want to end up like Janey, scrambling, broke?"

"You hated him."

"He hated *me*. Because I was stronger than him. I had the upper hand and he knew it. He hated me for keeping you."

"He did not. He liked you."

"Okay, we were friends, sort of. We talked and hacked around. But he was just sucking up to me so he could be around you."

"He trusted you. Before AA you always gave him stuff."

"He cried on my fucking shoulder," Michelle retorted.

Cold, bitter anger hardened Duane's features. "You hated him because I loved him."

Color darkened Michelle's face, and suddenly all the betrayals and broken promises exploded like a bomb. "Hey, you think I needed you for *love?* I didn't need you, you son of a bitch. I made my own life. Ask Ben. Hey, know-it-all! Ben! Tell him!"

I supposed she meant her walks on the wild side of Waterbury.

"Tell him!" she screamed.

"Last I heard, Little John was in the morgue."

"Fuck you. Fuck both of you. Get out of my house, Duane. You too, Ben. You can't prove anything."

Happy to leave such details to Sergeant Marian, I took Michelle's gun and checked that Duane's towel didn't cover a Ruger. Then I dripped a long, wet trail through the party room, the foyer, the living room, and into the kitchen, where I telephoned the number on Marian's card. The trooper who answered said she was in the field. "Beep her. It's urgent."

I left the Fisks' number and waited by the phone. Marian called back in two minutes.

"This better not be some invitation to pump me at dinner."

"I'm faced with a dilemma," I told her. "I have two choices."

"Choose the one you don't want. Do the right thing for once."

"It's an amateur's dilemma. I need a police officer to make an arrest. I think the professional word is 'collar.' Anyhow, I've got a 'collar' for somebody. Do I give it to Trooper Moody, whom I dislike? Or to you, who has been extraordinarily insulting of late?"

"To me. What collar?"

"Call me a sucker for a pretty face."

"Are you *looking* for ways to piss me off?"

"Are you looking for Reg Hopkins's killer? 'Cause if you are, the collar is yours. Hop in your car, drive down Church Hill Road, and get onto River Road. About four miles out you'll see an expensive, ugly French Colonial. My car's in the drive. We'll be in the party room."

"Who?"

"Me and the killer. And the killer's spouse."

"I'll be right there. Don't leave them alone."

I ran back to the party room.

Duane was standing waist-deep in the middle of the Jacuzzi, sipping Bud. His face was red and he was breathing hard.

"Call the cops."

"I already did. Where's Michelle?"

"She killed him," he said, his voice shaking with emotion.

He pointed down at the water as I stepped closer. Michelle was thrashing on the bottom of the Jacuzzi. Through the bubbles I could see her arms and legs darting like panicked fish. Duane held her down with a foot on her throat.

*"Let her up!"*

I jumped in to shove him off her. But he hunkered down low and used his weight and the water to shrug me off his slippery back. I crashed against the stone and pushed back through the water and hit him hard, twice. His heavy body seemed to swallow the punches.

I went for his face, yelling, *"Let her up!"*

He threw his hands up and backed off. "It's okay, Ben. It's over."

I heaved Michelle off the bottom. I laid her on the granite surround, tilted her head to drain the water, and felt in her mouth to clear her throat. Her head lolled grotesquely. I put my mouth to hers and tried to breathe air into her lungs.

"Too late," Duane said. "I put all my weight on her. Crushed her neck." He stuck his foot out of the water. In her fight to live, she had scratched bloody claw marks.

"Oh, Jesus, *Duane.*" He was right. There was nothing left. I tried to close her staring eyes.

Duane threw a towel over her.

For a while neither of us spoke. Duane smoothed the folds of the towel, spreading it evenly over Michelle. Then, in a collected, settled voice, he said, "It's better this way, Ben. No one has to know."

"Janey knows."

"She'll never tell. . . . *You* know. . . ."

Marian's siren carried far in the thick heat.

"I lied, before," he said. "It wasn't high school. It happened in eighth grade. 'Still crazy after all these years?' Still *lying* after all these years. We went swimming one day— Scared the *hell* out of ourselves. . . . Ben, we fought it every step of the way. We were so ashamed. Remember, I went into the Service? Didn't work. Then we married Michelle and Janey. Kids. They were a plus. But *nothing* worked. Kept breaking up, hooking up again."

"Did you ever think of coming out?"

"Yeah. We talked about it. Everybody was doing it. But we . . . Reg and me, we just weren't built that way. . . . What do you say, Ben? Give us a break?" He glanced at me, then down at the water. "Hell, you're staring at me like I'm sick or something. You don't even know what I'm talking about."

"Oh, I think I do."

He looked up, begging me to honor the long years of childhood. "I won't tell."

"Thank you. Thanks, old buddy." He seized my hand and shook it hard.

I squeezed back, sadly aware that I'd done him and Reg a big favor, allowing all of Newbury to assume that Duane Fisk was just a regular guy who'd killed his wife.

# 33

---

Tim Hall and Georgia Bowland had rallied their warring Newbury Democrats, and by a quarter to eight you couldn't *buy* a seat in the Leslie auditorium. Weekenders packed the front rows. The Scudder Mountain crowd held the balcony. The Frenchtown contingent huddled in back. Vicky's supporters, and a legion of fencesitters, occupied the middle.

The air conditioning had failed, and through the doors thrown open to the breeze we could see Republicans peering in, licking their chops.

Scooter MacKay moderated. He introduced Vicky and Steve, who took opposing lecterns. Vicky's famous chestnut curls danced in the lights. Steve stood gaunt and stern as Abe Lincoln. The rules called for each to deliver a five-minute opening statement.

Steve went first, savaging the mill rate, which he claimed had driven property taxes to a height where decent people were losing their homes. The Scudder Mountain crowd shook the balcony with volcanic roars and stomps.

Vicky offered a calm recitation of the town's recovery from fiscal disaster. She credited her tight-ship administration and the salutary effects of the gradually upturning economy. Education, she reminded her audience, was still the primary business of the town.

Then it was question time, with Scooter booming questions submitted by the audience. "A farmer on Morris Mountain asks: 'Keep it simple. In one sentence, how are you going to stop taxes from driving us off the land?' "

Steve La France pounced like a wolfhound: "*Cut* the mill rate. *Lower* property taxes. *Balance* the budget."

"But if we cut taxes," Vicky retorted, "we'll have to close our schools."

Steve said staunchly, "Maybe I'm just a frugal Yankee born in Newbury, but I know that the real 'primary' business of Newbury is to balance the budget. *Then* we'll worry about schools."

"Excuse me, Steve," Vicky asked, after Scooter had gaveled Scudder Mountain into remission. "But wouldn't such Yankee frugality mean closing our public schools?"

"Temporarily, if need be."

"How temporary, Steve? A month or two? A year?"

"Steve! Steve! Steve!" erupted somewhere.

Vicky asked, "What would we do with our teachers?"

Before Steve could answer, old Frank La France howled, "Let them fend for themselves," closing a trap his more astute son might still have backed out of.

Georgia Bowland covered her face. I imagined my father smiling in his grave.

Steve sounded reasonable. " I think my dad means that after we balance the budget, we'll start over with a new, stronger school."

"Are you advocating we close our schools and let parents teach their children at home?"

Aware at last that he was teetering above a pitful of tigers, Steve clutched at a pillar of conservatism. "A lot of parents I know would be glad of the chance to control what goes into their kids' heads."

"Glad too to have their children home all day? Every day?"

Sixty percent of the townsfolk in the auditorium turned pale. Somebody laughed.

Tim and I retreated, when the shouting had died down, to Vicky's office to discuss capitalizing upon this pleasant turn of events. We'd gotten lucky. We certainly hadn't won the renomination, not by a long shot, but the La France blunders had to slow the challenger's momentum. The trick now would be to gain our own.

Scooter MacKay lumbered in, notepad high, pencil flying, wondering how Steve's attack of hoof-in-mouth would affect the voting. Tim predicted a heavy turnout of "an appalled citizenry determined to defend their children's right to a quality education."

I said, "Scooter, if it's okay with Tim, how about you change 'an appalled citizenry' to 'loyal Democrats'?"

A telephone rang. Tim snatched it off Vicky's desk. "First Selectman's office—Now and Forever!"

Scooter nudged me. "Where in hell did Steve get that stupid idea to close the schools?"

"Beats me."

Tim passed the telephone. "For you."

"Who is it?"

"Sounds like your friend in the Castle."

My gut clenched and my heart soared. "Hi, there."

"I'm off to Hong Kong, for a while."

"Business?" Long Technical Systems owned a flash chip factory out there.

"Sort of. But I'm here tonight."

"Ummh." All the conversations I'd cooked in my head boiled down to "ummh," in a pinch.

"How does a humongous tin of caviar and a magnum of Dom sound?"

I thought that caviar, champagne, and Rita sounded absolutely terrific, but before I could say so, Vicky burst in, flushed with the scent of victory.

"What a break! Tim, order pizza. Ben—I need your brain."

"What's all that yelling?" Rita asked.

"The good guys won."

Vicky laughed, alight with the joy of a perfect night and filled with hope for tomorrow. "Come on, Ben. We've got work to do."

"Come on over," said Rita.

I wished Aunt Connie hadn't taught me right from wrong.